**Dom turned his head, successfully hiding the smile struggling to emerge.**

He didn't know why, but he hadn't expected to overhear the ribald curse that had flowed so effortlessly from Viola. "That's good to know because then that would definitely negate us becoming friends."

Viola narrowed her eyes, reminding him of a cat ready to attack. "Do you always test your friends?"

"Most times I do."

"Why, Dom?"

"Because I have trust issues." The admission had come out unbidden. And if he were completely forthcoming with Viola, then he would've said his distrust was with women. It didn't matter whether they were platonic or intimate, he'd made it a practice to keep them at a distance.

"Bad breakup with a girlfriend?"

"No," he said truthfully. "It was a marriage that ended with irreconcilable differences."

She blinked slowly. "Well, you're not the only one with trust issues."

Dear Reader,

Welcome back to Bainbridge House, where the restoration of the French-inspired château is still ongoing and will be for the next year or two. During that time all, or almost all, of Conrad Williamson's heirs will convert their father's ancestral estate into a hotel and wedding venue.

Viola Williamson, a professionally trained chef, is reluctant to join her brothers until she is passed over—once again—at the Michelin-star restaurant where she has worked for several years, and it is then she decides it's time she supervise her own kitchen. However, what she doesn't anticipate is becoming friends with the abandoned estate's enigmatic caretaker, Dominic Shaw, unaware that the lives of her adoptive father and Dominic's are inexorably entwined over many generations.

Dom has trust issues, but there is something about Viola's free-spirited personality he finds irresistible despite their trading barbs during their first encounter. Declaring a truce, they decide friendship is better than verbally sparring with each other, but at no time can he forget that Viola is heiress to an estate worth millions and his role is to maintain her family's property.

What begins as friendship evolves into friends with benefits. As Viola plans the reception dinner for her brother's and best friend's Christmas wedding at the château, an encounter with another family member the night before the event shatters her fairy-tale world. She then fears losing the only man she has ever loved at the most festive time of the year.

I hope you will enjoy *Christmas at the Château* as Viola and Dom overcome obstacles to find their own happily-ever-after.

Happy reading!

*Rochelle Alers*

# Christmas at the Château

ROCHELLE ALERS

Recycling programs for this product may not exist in your area.

ISBN-13: 978-1-335-40825-9

Christmas at the Château



This edition published by arrangement with Harlequin Books S.A.

For questions and comments about the quality of this book, please contact us at CustomerService@Harlequin.com.

Harlequin Enterprises ULC
22 Adelaide St. West, 40th Floor
Toronto, Ontario M5H 4E3, Canada
www.Harlequin.com

**Printed in U.S.A.**

Since 1988, nationally bestselling author **Rochelle Alers** has written more than eighty books and short stories. She has earned numerous honors, including the Zora Neale Hurston Award, the Vivian Stephens Award for Excellence in Romance Writing and a Career Achievement Award from *RT Book Reviews*. She is a member of Zeta Phi Beta Sorority, Inc., Iota Theta Zeta Chapter. A full-time writer, she lives in a charming hamlet on Long Island. Rochelle can be contacted through her website, www.rochellealers.org.

**Books by Rochelle Alers**

**Harlequin Special Edition**

***Bainbridge House***

*A New Foundation*

***Wickham Falls Weddings***

*Home to Wickham Falls*
*Her Wickham Falls SEAL*
*The Sheriff of Wickham Falls*
*Dealmaker, Heartbreaker*
*This Time for Keeps*
*Second-Chance Sweet Shop*

***American Heroes***

*Claiming the Captain's Baby*
*Twins for the Soldier*

Visit the Author Profile page
at Harlequin.com for more titles.

## *Chapter One*

Viola Williamson shifted on the cushioned rocker and closed her eyes. *I can't believe I'm a Jersey girl once again*, she mused.

It wasn't that there was anything wrong with living in the Garden State, but after growing up in Belleville with four older brothers, Viola had attended culinary school in Hyde Park, New York, and after graduating had moved to the West Village where she'd become a city girl in every sense of the word. There were times when she even found herself wearing all black year-round.

Turning on her heel, she left the balcony and closed the sliding screened-in doors behind her. Walking to the bedside table where she'd left her cell phone, she tapped a number. It rang twice before there was a break in the connection, and she smiled when she heard her best friend's voice.

"I thought you'd still be asleep."

"That's not happening anymore, Sonja."

When she'd worked at The Cellar, she usually slept in late because most days she didn't get home until well after midnight, and then it would take a while for her to wind down from the nonstop frenetic activity in the restaurant's kitchen. She'd shower and then get into bed to watch a recap of the day's news and, on occasion, a movie she'd missed. It would be close to dawn before she would be able to fall asleep.

"Taylor reminded me last night that your mother was leaving for her cruise today."

"The car service picked her up a few minutes ago. I know this is going to sound crazy, but now that I've moved in with her, I really like hanging out with my mother."

Sonja's sultry laugh came through the earpiece. "It's the same whenever I spend time with my mother. Even though we're mother and daughter, it's different because we've come to relate to each other as adults and whenever we have discussions, nothing is off-limits or even taboo. I told my mother that Taylor is the only man that—"

"Don't say it!" Viola interrupted, laughing. "I truly don't need to know what goes on between you and my brother in your bedroom."

Sonja also laughed. "Get your mind out of the gutter, Viola Williamson. That's where I draw the line because I have no intention of talking about my sex life with my mother. I wanted to say that Taylor is the only man that I'd want to father my children."

Viola ran her fingers through her curly hair. "Well, that can become a possibility in the future." She'd recommended architectural historian Sonja Rios-Martin to her brother to assist him on the Bainbridge House restoration project. No one had been more surprised than Viola when Sonja admitted that she and Taylor were living together and had planned to marry at the mansion the following Christmas.

"That's going to be sooner than later because Taylor and I have decided to marry this Christmas now that your mother is going to be stateside at the end of the year."

Viola curbed the urge to do a happy dance. "When did you two decide this?"

"Last night. Your mother gave us her cruise itinerary and even though she's going to be away for Thanksgiving, she plans to return to the States for six weeks beginning the first week in December. I told Taylor that I've always wanted a Christmas wedding and that if he can restore the smaller ballroom, the first-floor kitchen and a few of the second-story bedroom suites for out-of-town guests, then there's no reason why we can't have it at the château. But, before we make any more plans, I'd like to ask if you would stand as my maid of honor."

Viola paused, unable to speak because she was still attempting to process Sonja talking about marrying her brother at the end of the year. It was now mid-September and that meant they had three months to plan a wedding and reception. "Of course," she said once she recovered her voice. "I'm honored that you've asked me to be your maid of honor."

A beat passed before Sonja said, "I'd also like to ask another favor. I—"

"I know what you want to ask," Viola said, cutting her off. "You want me to prepare the food for your reception."

"How did you know?"

She heard laughter in her future sister-in-law's query. "Because how would it look if you hired another caterer to prepare the food when your fiancé's sister is a chef?"

"That thought would've never crossed my mind. I know you're ready to supervise your own kitchen and what better way to advertise your mad skills than at your brother's wedding."

Viola felt a shiver of excitement wash over her as she thought about preparing a wedding banquet at the French-inspired château. Sonja talking about holding the ceremony in one of the ballrooms and putting up out-of-town guests in the second-story bedroom suites meant those areas would have to be completely restored before the wedding. And that also included the smaller of the two kitchens.

"We have to get together to figure out what you want to serve. But before that, I need to go to Bainbridge House to really check out the kitchen to ascertain what appliances need to be replaced or updated."

The first time she'd visited the abandoned house was Easter Sunday when Elise had taken everyone to the property. Her mother had called the on-site caretaker to inform him she was coming and that he should open the gates protecting the estate from trespassers. Viola realized she'd been as awestruck as her brothers when they'd all stared at the structure that had reminded her of Disney's Magic Kingdom.

"Why don't you come now? You do remember how to get here?"

Viola scrunched up her nose. "Very funny, Sonja. Of course I remember. I'll text you before I get there so you can have the caretaker open the gates."

"That won't be necessary. The gates are opened around seven in the morning and aren't closed until five or six, because of the number of workers coming and going. When you get here, just ask anyone where the library is."

Viola ended the call and walked over to the closet to change out of her shorts and flip-flops and into jeans and well-worn Dr. Martens. Picking up a wide-tooth comb, she pulled it through her mussed curls before leaving the bedroom and heading for the staircase. She caught a glimpse of her reflection in the entryway mirror as she scooped up a set of keys for the condo and the fob for her mother's late-model Subaru. Her hair was longer than she usually wore it, but she decided to wait to visit a salon until later in the month.

Twenty-five minutes after leaving Sparta, Viola drove along the private road leading to Bainbridge House. The massive iron gates were open to the path bordered on both sides with towering age-old trees. She was awed by the panorama unfolding before her eyes. It was as if she'd stepped back in time when landed gentry lived on luxurious estates while competing with one another to host the most sought-after social events of the season. Viola still did not understand why her father had never mentioned the property. It wasn't until after his death that they'd been privy to the historic estate that bore his ancestor's family name.

She'd grown up with her four brothers in a 5000-square-foot farmhouse built on four acres with an in-ground pool and tennis and basketball courts, yet there was no way she could fathom living in a French-inspired 86,000-square-foot château with more than one hundred rooms. The nineteenth-century estate, listed on the National Register of Historic Places, was set on more than three-hundred-fifty acres with guesthouses, barns, a bridle path, vineyard, orchard, stables, formal gardens and a nine-hole golf course. Sonja had uncovered facts that the Gilded Age Bainbridge family had used the castle as their summer home to host lavish parties for heads of state, Hollywood stars, and occasionally, European royalty. Although the château had been abandoned years before a trust had been established to cover property taxes and salaries for generations of resident caretakers.

Viola noticed the number of vans and pickups lining the circular driveway and several dumpsters positioned on either side of the house. She maneuvered around to the rear to find a space where she could park without blocking other vehicles, and that was when she recognized Taylor's gray Infiniti SUV and pulled in next to it. Cutting off the engine, she slipped the Subaru's fob into her crossbody and walked around to the entrance of the magnificent structure.

Opening the door, she encountered a cacophony of sounds and activity from workers hammering, drilling and shouting over the upbeat music coming from a boom box. Builder board—temporary floor protection—was taped to the floor and the steps of twin circular staircases, concealing the original marble flooring in the entrance and great room. Yards of plastic covered furniture lined up against walls with fading and peeling wallpaper. She glanced up at the ceiling with capped wires that had once held a massive crystal chandelier.

She waited until someone noticed her. "Can you please direct me to the library?" she shouted to a stocky man in coveralls. He stared at her at the same time he ran a hand over his bushy gray beard. "I'm Taylor Williamson's sister."

The last time she'd come to the château she had taken a quick view of the kitchens. She hadn't lingered any appreciable length of time because workers had been involved with putting up scaffolding inside and around the building.

He nodded. "Come with me."

Viola followed the man down a wide hallway, also covered with floor protection, passing a room where several men were installing new windows. Taylor had mentioned it would take at least two years before the entire estate would be restored. Once she'd informed her brother that she was willing to become the executive chef for the future hotel and wedding venue, she'd decided not to live in the château. She planned to move into one of the guesthouses because she didn't want to live and work under the same roof.

"This is the library, miss."

"Thank you."

Viola knocked lightly on the ornately carved oak door and within seconds it opened. Sonja reached for her hand, pulled her inside and quickly shut it. She barely had time to examine the large room with its wall-to-wall, floor-to-ceiling built-in shelves packed tightly with leather-bound books.

"I'll never get used to all the noise whenever the door is open," Sonja explained.

Viola smiled at her friend. Falling in love and living with Taylor seemed to agree with the architectural historian. And it appeared as if she had put on weight. Her face had filled out and Viola wondered if her brother and his fiancée had moved up their wedding date because Sonja was pregnant. She stared at the ring on Sonja's left hand; a ring that had been passed down through generations of her father's side of the family. Sonja told her she'd had the ring appraised and the two-carat, flawless Asscher-cut diamond flanked by half-carat sapphires was priceless. She'd also had many other precious estate jewel items appraised and insured for more than eighteen million dollars.

"You look different, Sonja. What aren't you telling me?"

It wasn't her longer curly hair or the summer sun that had darkened her nut-brown complexion. Sonja lowered large brown eyes. "I wanted to wait and tell you in person."

Viola blinked once. "Tell me what?"

"That I'm pregnant, but it appears as if nothing escapes you."

Viola curbed the urge to scream. "When? How?"

Sonja rolled her eyes at her. "You have to know how. It was when your mother moved into her condo and Taylor and I began living together. I'd planned to take a contraceptive, but I kept putting off making an appointment with my gynecologist. Meanwhile we were relying on condoms for birth control, but then one night things got out of control and yours truly missed her period… When I finally took a home pregnancy test, I knew for certain that I was carrying Taylor's baby. I have an appointment to see my gynecologist this coming Friday."

Throwing her arms around Sonja's shoulders, Viola hugged her. "I'm going to be an auntie," she said in singsong. Easing back, she met Sonja's eyes. "Does my mother know?"

Sonja nodded. "Yes. I waited until she was at the airport to FaceTime her. And you know what she said?" Viola shook her head. "She said if I'd told her earlier she would've canceled her cruise to help me plan the wedding. And that's when I told her that's why I decided to wait."

"So that's what you meant when you told your mother that Taylor was the only man with whom you wanted children."

Sonja smiled and nodded. "Yup. I really wanted to wait at least a year after we were married before starting a family, but apparently, that wasn't in the stars. I'm going to be thirty-five in November and my biological clock will begin ticking, so it's better now than later."

"Who else have you told?" Viola asked Sonja.

"Just you, your mother and my parents."

"How did Taylor react when you told him?"

"He started dancing."

"You're kidding?"

"I wish," Sonja said as she struggled not to laugh. "He did a few Bruno Mars moves before he attempted a split and fell over laughing so hard, he couldn't get up for at least a couple of minutes."

Viola clapped a hand over her mouth to stem her own laughter from exploding from the back of her throat. "That's hilarious. Taylor only knows how to slow dance. But let me warn you that my mother is going to knit a complete layette for you with hats, booties, sweaters, blankets, and maybe even a stuffed dog or teddy bear.

Momma still spends all her free time knitting. She never had to buy hats, gloves, scarves, sweaters or even mittens for any of us when we were younger. She claims knitting is therapeutic for her."

Sonja smiled. "I suppose it would be when raising five children."

Viola closed her eyes for several seconds. "I had the best childhood any kid could ever wish for. If or when I ever have children, I pray I would be half the mother Momma is."

She'd been truthful when disclosing to her friend that Elise Williamson was the perfect mother. Unable to have children of her own, Elise had fostered four boys and one girl, homeschooling everyone, and then legally adopting all of them.

Resting a hand against her flat belly, Sonja nodded. "It's too early to think about what kind of mother I'll become. But whether I have a son or daughter, I want them to know they're loved and protected."

Her brother's fiancée lowered her head as tears filled her eyes. During the time she'd come to know Sonja Rios-Martin, Viola had never witnessed her become emotional. Even when she'd revealed details of her first marriage, it was as if she'd rehearsed everything she'd wanted to say to visibly conceal the horror she'd experienced with a much older, controlling husband. Now she'd been given a second chance with a man who loved her unconditionally.

"There's no doubt you and Taylor will be incredible parents. And whenever my niece or nephew comes to visit Auntie Viola, she's going to spoil the hell out of them."

Sonja blinked back tears. "I don't mind as long as they turn out like *Bébé's Kids*."

Viola smiled as she recalled the animated film about a man seeking to impress his new girlfriend and agreeing to look after her children, who turn out to be uncontrollably rambunctious. Pulling out a chair opposite Sonja, she sat. "How are you feeling?"

"Tired and a little queasy at times, and occasionally out of sorts, which I attribute to hormonal changes. I've also been reading about alternatives to morning sickness, so I try to have a few unsalted crackers on hand."

Viola shifted her attention to the table covered almost entirely with monogrammed silver table settings. Sonja had mentioned she'd spent countless hours cataloging sets of china, crystal and silver pieces. And that was another reason why Viola had deliberately stayed away from the estate: she didn't want to interfere with Sonja's recording of the items the Bainbridges had amassed during their lifetimes. Plus, Taylor had also revealed that there were a few projects underway, with contract workers arriving and leaving in different shifts that also added to the restorative goings-on.

"I hope you're not going to overdo it when you should be resting."

A hint of a smile tilted the corners of Sonja's mouth. "I go to bed a lot earlier than I used to. No more sitting up nights watching movies on Netflix."

Viola gave her a sheepish grin. "I have to confess that I binged *Bridgerton* a couple of weeks ago, watching all the episodes in one sitting. Then I waited a few days and watched it again, but only two episodes at a time."

Sonja rested a hand on her throat. "I also watched it twice. When I saw the reenactment of the balls, all I could think about was what Bainbridge House would've looked like when Charles Bainbridge and his wife hosted formal affairs with enormous banquets for their guests."

Viola gasped. "That's a fabulous idea for a Regency-themed wedding."

"Bite your tongue, Vi." Sonja scrunched up her nose. "The only thing that will resemble a Regency ball will be my empire gown because, by that time, I probably will have lost my waistline. And besides, it's going to be small and intimate. I doubt if we're going to invite more than thirty guests."

"That is a small wedding. Have you set a date?" Viola asked.

"Not yet, but I did tell Taylor that we have to give folks enough time to reply since it will be during the one of the busiest holiday seasons of the year. I'd like a Christmas Eve ceremony, but that may not be possible when people make plans to spend that time with their families."

Viola nodded. "You're right. What about the week before?"

Sonja stilled, appearing to be deep in thought. "That is a possibility." Reaching for her cell phone, she scrolled through the calendar. "This year, Christmas falls on a Saturday, so we can have out-of-town guests come in either late Thursday or early Friday to settle in and relax before the ceremony."

A jolt of excitement eddied through Viola. "I can prepare an evening buffet dinner for those coming in on Thursday and a buffet brunch for Friday. What you have to decide before creating the wedding menu is if you want a buffet or sit-down dinner."

Sonja pulled her lower lip between her teeth. "Will a sit-down be too much for you?"

"No," Viola replied while at the same time shaking her head. "If you're only having thirty guests, then that's not a problem. Of course, I'll hire enough waitstaff to make certain everything runs smoothly."

"You're definitely who I need to make certain everything runs smoothly."

"Have you thought about hiring a wedding planner?" Viola questioned.

"Yes, even though my mother has offered to help me plan everything. I told her I just want her to come and enjoy herself. It's the same with your mother."

"Planning a wedding is certain to keep everyone involved busy."

Sonja paused. "My mother never said it, but I know she felt slighted when I didn't give her the chance to be mother of the bride when I married Hugh. And when I told her about the baby and Taylor, and that I plan to marry this Christmas, she asked me if I was going to have a wedding with family and friends in attendance. That's when it hit me that I'd not only cheated her out of seeing her only daughter get married, I'd neglected to tell her about Hugh until after we'd exchanged vows."

"Now you'll give her the opportunity to witness her daughter having a traditional wedding ceremony."

Sonja gave Viola a steady stare. "You're right about that." She paused again. "Now that you've agreed to become the executive chef for Bainbridge House, you and I will have to put our heads together to create a menu for the reception."

Viola had predicted it would be close to two years before she would actively supervise the hotel's kitchens, but once she'd become responsible for her brother's wedding reception, she could exhibit her training and experience to potential guests even before the hotel officially opened for business.

"If you're estimating thirty guests, then that's very doable. And to be safe, I'll probably prepare enough for fifty."

Sonja exhaled an audible breath. "That's one thing I can now cross off my do-list."

Viola wanted to tell her friend that, as the maid of honor, she would help any way she could. And then there were the mothers of the bride and groom who were certain to assist to make the occasion special and memorable even if Sonja decided not to hire a wedding planner.

"What time of day do you plan on holding the ceremony?" Viola asked.

"That's something else I've really not thought about," Sonja admitted. "I do know I want a sit-down dinner followed with music and dancing, but I'm not certain whether I want formal or semiformal. What do you suggest?"

"I prefer semiformal." For Viola, that was a no-brainer. Men would have the option of wearing business suits rather than tuxedos and women could wear either cocktail dresses or floor-length gowns.

Sonja smiled. "I was hoping you would say that. What I don't want is a stuffy affair where people hold back having a good time. It will be the Christmas season and I want everything to be fun *and* festive."

"Do you have a color scheme for the decorations?"

"Red and green."

"Have you thought about a Christmas tartan?"

Sonja shook her head.

"My father's middle name is Bainbridge and it's

Gaelic for 'bridge over bright waters.' Although my brothers and I don't share Bainbridge DNA, it would be nice to honor Daddy's Scottish ancestry."

Sonja flashed a brilliant smile. "That's a wonderful idea. I'm familiar with a number of red-and-green tartans that would be perfect for boutonnieres, corsages and bouquets."

Viola was certain Sonja's day would be a special one as she stared at the ornately carved handles of the forks and spoons. "How many sets and serving pieces have you cataloged?"

"Too many to remember. There was one with place settings for one hundred."

"Who buys that many forks, spoons and knives?"

Sonja snorted. "Folks with an extensive social guest list who do a lot of entertaining. It appears that your father's ancestors were party animals. I've found receipts from various stationers for engraved invitations with gatherings ranging from fifty to more than one hundred guests at any given time. Smaller soirees were held in the ballroom with a maximum capacity of ninety, while the larger ballroom can hold more than one-fifty."

Viola's slowly shook her head. "That's comparable to a state banquet at Buckingham Palace."

Sonja's eyebrows lifted slightly. "Well, those were your father's people, and it looks as if the Bainbridges wanted to imitate European royalty even if they weren't."

"And they can now," Viola drawled, smiling. "Even though we are Bainbridges through adoption, there's no reason why the modern Bainbridges can't compete with those from the Gilded Age. And the first test will be your wedding."

Sonja held up both hands. "I don't want a spectacle, Vi."

"Thirty to fifty guests isn't a spectacle. One hundred and fifty or more is. Christmas is the most festive holiday of the year, and the food and the red, green and white color scheme can become the backdrop for the inaugural twenty-first-century wedding celebration at Bainbridge House."

Sonja's demeanor changed as a wide smile parted her lips. "We can have a huge live tree decorated with thousands of tiny white lights in the great room and the ballroom can be filled with red, white and green poinsettia plants." She pressed her palms together. "Oh my gosh, you've really got me thinking about what I'd like. I've toured enough historical homes during the Christmas season to have Bainbridge House appear as if we've gone back in time to the early twentieth century. I'd like the decorations to be ornate without being ostentatious."

"Everything is going to be perfect for your special day."

"I'm hoping it will," Sonja said. "Once we decide on a date, I'm going to ask my father to contact my brother so he can request a leave from the marines to attend the wedding. It's been a while since he, his wife and kids have come east for a visit. My mother complains that she doesn't get to see her grandchildren enough."

"At least your mother has grandchildren," Viola remarked. "I've overheard my mother tell her friends who are grandmothers that she doubts if she will ever reach that status before she turns eighty. I did remind her that my brother Patrick is engaged, even though he and his fiancée haven't set a wedding date." She didn't want to tell Sonja that Elise wasn't particularly fond of her future daughter-in-law.

"Well, Taylor and I will make her a grandmother either late May or early June. I told my mother that I want my parents' and your mother's name on the invitation."

"What did she say?"

"She loved the idea that your family will become her family."

Viola's gaze shifted to the leather-bound books tightly stacked on shelves. There were also ladders suspended on rails for easier access to the upper shelves.

"If you need my help with anything, and I mean anything, you know I'm just a text away. The last time I was here, Taylor took me to see one kitchen and I jotted down some notes, but I need to see it again, so I know what I'll be working with."

Picking up her cell phone, Sonja tapped an icon. "I'm going to contact someone to see if he's available to take you around." She waited for a response and then nodded. "He's on his way."

Three minutes later, there came a knock on the door. When it opened, a tall, slender man with a raven-black, lightly gray-streaked man bun and large dark green eyes in a deeply tanned face stared at Viola. Graying hair aside, his face was unlined. She estimated he was no older than her thirtysomething brothers.

Sonja stood, Viola rising with her. "Viola, this is Dominic Shaw. Dom, Viola Williamson, Taylor's sister and my best friend. She's the chef who will supervise the kitchens once the hotel is up and running. If you're not busy, I'd like you to take her to see the kitchens."

Galvanized into action, Viola took a step and extended her hand. "It's nice meeting you, Dominic."

He grasped her outstretched fingers, his larger hand closing over hers. "Same here. And it's Dom."

She recoiled as if struck across the face while easing her fingers from his firm grip. Why did she feel as if he'd chastised her because she'd called him by the wrong name? "If that's what you want, then Dom it is."

His eyes bored into her like shards of chipped green glass. "It is what I want. Come with me and I'll take you to the kitchens."

He turned on his heel, expecting Viola to follow. *Rude. Uncouth. Ill-mannered.* The derogatory adjectives flooded her mind when she really wanted to tell the man exactly what she thought of him. She shifted her gaze to Sonja, lifted her shoulders while shaking her head, then walked out of the library to find Dom standing a short distance away, waiting for her.

"Let's go," she ordered, hoping he would recognize she could hold her own when it came to men believing they could intimidate her. After all, she'd grown up with four older brothers.

She wanted to ask him who or what had set him off, but held her tongue. His less than affable mood was not her concern. Becoming the executive chef for Bainbridge House was.

## *Chapter Two*

Dom cursed under his breath; ugly raw expletives for coming at Viola Williamson like a rabid animal. When Sonja had sent a text asking if he would show Taylor's sister the kitchens, he hadn't known what to expect when he met her. But it hadn't been her eyes, which had reminded him of his ex-wife. Kaitlyn had gold-green eyes that changed color depending upon her moods. He could not have predicted that the carefree young woman with a quick laugh he'd dated and eventually married would turn into an unhappy, complaining wife he'd been unable to please regardless of what he said or did for her.

It had been more than five years since their separation and eventual divorce, yet Dom still found it hard to forget her duplicity despite everything he'd done within reason to make her happy. He'd dated occasionally after his divorce, but found himself ending a relationship whenever a woman talked about marriage. For Dominic Shaw, once was enough.

He slowed, waiting for Viola to walk beside him, while noticing the differences in their height. The top of her curly head came to his shoulder, yet there was another thing he noticed about her. She smelled wonderful. He gave her a sidelong glance. It was obvious by the set of her shoulders she was upset, and he didn't blame her.

"I'm sorry I barked at you back there."

Viola continued to stare straight ahead as they made their way down a narrow hallway. "Save it," she snapped.

Dom stopped and caught her upper arm, turning her around to face him. With them only inches apart, he stared at her, transfixed. Taylor Williamson's sister was beyond beautiful, even without a hint of makeup. Her gold-brown skin was flawless. But it was her large hazel eyes framed by long, black lashes that were mesmerizing. His eyes moved slowly over the short, delicate nose and still lower to her mouth, which women gave their plastic surgeons thousands to achieve. He focused on her throat rather than allow his gaze to shift to her chest.

"I'm serious, Viola. I am sorry for being rude. I had something else on my mind and I shouldn't have taken it out on you," he half lied. He couldn't tell her that "something" was his ex-wife—a woman who had made him countless promises only to break them as soon as they passed her lying lips.

Viola's shoulders slumped as if the tension had left her body. "Okay. I accept your apology this time." A hint of a smile played at the corners of her mouth. "But don't make it a habit."

Dom smiled, realizing he'd just dodged a bullet. Several months back, he'd had a verbal confrontation with Taylor about Sonja, and their association had become awkward and could have escalated into a permanent breach if Sonja hadn't explained to Taylor why he'd seen her hugging Dom. The altercation had been a tense one, but over time they'd come to respect each other, and Dom enjoyed working with Taylor. He shuddered to think how Taylor would react if he believed he'd offended his sister.

He extended his right hand. "Friends?"

A beat passed before she took his hand. "Yes, friends."

Dom was certain she heard his exhalation as he dropped her hand. "There's a kitchen here on the first floor. It's a lot smaller than the one downstairs because it was used only when the extended Bainbridge family ate together. However, whenever they entertained guests, the larger one on the lower level was utilized. There's also a pastry kitchen where the cooks prepared all the baked goods for the house."

Viola had begun to ask herself what she had done or not done to elicit such rancor from a man she'd never met before. But now that he'd apologized, she was willing to accept it. Despite not having much luck with men she'd dated, the same could not be said when it came to her relationships with her coworkers. She had managed to get along with everyone because they were a team. If one faltered, then the others picked him or her up. She'd also promised herself that whenever she supervised her own kitchen, she would never yell or denigrate anyone. She'd been on that receiving end more times than she could count until she'd learned to tune it out because she deemed it wasn't personal. Viola didn't fool herself into believing she did not have a lot more to learn, but she was ready to compete with anyone willing to test her. She was a talented chef, and had graduated at the top of her class at the Culinary Institute of America. She'd also made subsequent trips to major cities in Europe to hone and vary her cooking repertoire.

"How come you don't get lost in this place?" she asked Dom as they turned down yet another hallway.

"I used to when I was a boy, but after living here for years, I'm familiar with every nook and corner in this house."

She gave him a sidelong glance. "You grew up here?" There was a hint of surprise in her query.

He nodded. "Yes. I grew up on the property as the caretaker's son."

"And now you're the caretaker?"

He nodded again. "That's what the irrevocable trust states."

When her mother had revealed to Viola and her brothers that her late husband had left her the property and that she would be passing it on to her five children, Viola hadn't felt the need to delve into the terms and conditions concerning Bainbridge House because she'd had no intention of joining her brothers in the venture to restore the property and open it as a hotel and wedding venue. Six months ago, her sole focus had been to eventually own and manage her own restaurant independent of her family members.

Now that she was involved with the restoration of

Bainbridge House, Viola wanted and needed to know everything about the history of the property. Sonja had hinted she'd uncovered documents that allowed her insight into the lives of deceased Bainbridge family members, but wanted to wait until she'd completed her research before compiling her final report.

Dom had mentioned an irrevocable trust, which Viola surmised meant his role was subject to the financial budgets and projections her accountant brother Patrick now controlled.

Dom stopped at a set of café doors and held open the one on the right. "It's all yours."

Viola walked past him into a large space with gray-slate flooring and three brick-lined walls. A series of French doors spanned the fourth, offering views of a forested area.

"Gas or electric?"

Dom moved over to where she stood at the massive six-burner stove. "It's gas. However, it was turned off years ago after the last Bainbridge passed away."

"So, you're telling me nothing in here has been used in more than fifty years?"

"That's what I've been told."

Viola peered up at Dom and met his eyes. She did not think of him as handsome in the traditional sense, but attractive. His strong features afforded him a masculine sensuality she could not ignore.

"How much do you know about my father's people?" Not only was she curious about the people who had called Bainbridge House home, but also Dom's connection to them.

A thick black eyebrow lifted slightly. "A lot more than most outsiders."

Viola went completely still. Had he known Conrad and Elise's children were adopted? Did he consider them outsiders because they did not share DNA with Conrad Bainbridge Williamson?

"How well did you know *my* father?"

Dom shoved his hands into the front pockets of his jeans. "Well enough."

"That's not telling me much, Dom."

"What if I tell you that we spoke to each other a couple of times a month, Viola? But that was before he retired. After that, it would be six weeks or even longer before he'd contact me again. His excuse was that he was busy golfing."

She bit back a smile. When Dom had called her by her name, he'd made it sound like the instrument. She wanted to tell him it was pronounced *vie* and not *vee* but held her tongue. And she knew Dom was being truthful about her father's golfing. He'd discovered his love for the sport after he'd sold his investment company and joined the ranks of other retirees. He'd become a member of the nearby country club where he'd spent hours learning and playing the game.

"That means you were rather acquainted with each other."

Dom smiled for the first time, the expression softening his features and exhibiting a mouth filled with straight white teeth. "We were rather acquainted because, after all, I was and still am responsible for looking after his estate."

"Do you like being a caretaker?"

There was a pregnant pause before Dom said, "I like being caretaker here at Bainbridge House. I'm my own boss and I can come and go, as the Brits say, by my leave. I also grew up on the property."

"How well do you know my mother?" She'd asked yet another question.

His expression changed, becoming impassive. "I've never met your mother in person. The first time I heard from her was when she called Easter Sunday to ask if I would open the gate because she wanted to tour the property. Not wanting to intrude, I stayed in my home until she left."

Viola was unaware that she'd covered her mouth with her hand. "Are you telling me you didn't know my father had passed away?" she asked through outspread fingers.

Dom nodded. "I didn't know your father had passed, but when I received an email informing me of his memorial service, I was in Arizona visiting with my father. By the time I was able to book a flight, it was over."

"Everything was done very quickly. Dad left instructions for Mom that he wanted to be cremated and that he would come back to haunt her if she had a funeral service with folks staring at him in a casket. However, two days later, she decided to host a memorial service for his business associates and former employees."

There were a few more questions Viola wanted to ask Dom, but she also needed answers from her mother. Taylor had revealed their mother had hinted about property that had belonged to her husband, yet she had waited until all the Williamson siblings were together for the first time following Conrad's memorial service to tell them about the restoration project.

Viola was also aware that her father had been reluctant to talk about his childhood. Losing his parents in a boating accident and being raised by an unmarried aunt who had never wanted children had been traumatic for him. She recalled the time when she'd overheard her father tell her mother he had no plans to sell something and that he did not want to discuss it. It wasn't until their Easter Sunday family discussion regarding Bainbridge House that Viola had realized Conrad had been referring to the property. Elise had been more forthcoming when she'd admitted a developer had approached her about buying the property to put up condos, but she'd rejected his offer because her late husband had wanted her to keep it in the family.

Viola had also found it odd that Conrad had wanted his children to live at Bainbridge House when he'd opted not to raise them there.

"I know I don't have to tell you, but your father was an extraordinary man," Dom said quietly.

Viola's eyelids fluttered as she attempted to blink back the tears filling her eyes. Dom's statement was attuned to what she'd felt for the man who had raised her. Although she hadn't advertised it to others, she could not have selected better parents than Conrad and Elise Williamson. Not only did she miss her father, she missed hearing his voice and the bear hugs he gave her even as an adult. He'd declared her his princess and, at times, she truly felt as if she were.

She managed to bring her fragile emotions under control when she said, "He was the best." Viola touched her fingertip to the corner of one eye. "Even though Taylor says he intends to restore the house to its original specifications, that can't happen with the kitchens."

"You really intend to update them?"

"Yes. I'll need modern appliances if I'm going to prepare hundreds of meals for hotel and wedding guests.

Maybe back in the day whisking by hand was the norm, but nothing beats a commercial mixer, blender and food processor. I'll also need double ovens, sinks, dishwashers, microwaves and prep tables. And there's the issue of refrigeration. I'll need at least two commercial refrigerators and a walk-in freezer." Viola opened a large closet and smiled. Shelves were filled with copper pots and pans. She preferred cooking with copper cookware. Since it heated up evenly, she was able to cook food precisely. However, she intended to examine each piece carefully and, if necessary, have them lined with stainless steel to prevent copper from leeching into the food.

"This kitchen is more updated than the one on the lower level," Dom stated.

"Even if it is, it still isn't adequate for what I'll need to operate efficiently." After she inventoried the other kitchens on the lower level, Viola planned to research the appliances and supplies she needed to outfit all three kitchens. When she'd spoken to Patrick to inform him she was joining the venture, he'd encouraged her to submit her financial plan to him so he could disburse the funds she needed to operate as restaurant manager.

Dom was also right about the downstairs kitchen. Despite being much larger, it was equipped as if it had been stuck in the late nineteenth-century, with its three fireplaces and massive eight-burner stove. She'd viewed enough episodes of *Downton Abbey* to discern how the cook and her assistants had performed their duties. The pastry kitchen was even more archaic with only a wood-burning stove and oven.

"What do you think?"

Viola turned to find Dom leaning against a wall, arms crossed over his chest. "It's perfect if I were filming a period piece, but this is the twenty-first century and there's nothing here that I would be able to use to prepare meals for a half dozen folks." She focused her attention on a closet and opened the door to find more copper pots and pans for cooking and baking. Once she inventoried them, Viola doubted whether she would have to purchase many more pieces to outfit all the kitchens. "I must admit that it's very clean."

"That's because Taylor had every inch of this house cleaned from the turrets to the storerooms. It took a maintenance company with dozens of workers weeks to accomplish that."

She closed the closet doors. "What is it you do as the caretaker?"

"I maintain the property. All three-hundred-fifty-plus acres of it. And that includes mowing, weeding, pruning trees, inspecting all the buildings for leaks and rodent infestation. I've set up rotating schedules to open windows in every structure to air out the rooms year-round to stave off the build-up of mold and musky odors. I also inspect all pipes during the winter months to prevent bursting and flooding. Is there anything else you'd like to know about my duties?"

Viola recoiled again. There he was coming at her again as if she'd offended him. "There's no need for you to be condescending, Dom."

His eyebrows lifted slightly. "Was I?"

"Yes, you were," she snapped. "I didn't ask what you did as the caretaker as a put-down."

"Don't you mean as a servant?"

Viola threw up her hands at the same time she mumbled an expletive. The man was insufferable. They couldn't carry on a decent conversation without him taking digs at her. Had he taken perverse pleasure in seeing how far he could push her before she completely lost her temper?

"I am not your boss, so there's no way I could ever consider you a servant."

Dom turned his head, successfully hiding the smile struggling to emerge. He didn't know why, but he hadn't expected to overhear the ribald curse that had flowed so effortlessly from Viola. "That's good to know because that would definitely negate us becoming friends."

Viola narrowed her eyes, reminding him of a cat ready to attack. "Do you always test your friends?"

"Most times I do."

"Why, Dom?"

"Because I have trust issues." The admission had come out unbidden. But if he were completely forthcoming with Viola, then he would've said his distrust was with women. It didn't matter whether they were platonic or intimate, he'd made it a practice to keep their relationships at a distance.

"Bad breakup with a girlfriend?"

"No," he said truthfully. "It was a marriage that ended with irreconcilable differences."

She blinked slowly. "Well, you're not the only one with trust issues. And mine are not with an ex-husband but with the men I've dated. They say one thing and do something entirely different."

This time Dom did smile. She'd just given him the opening he'd needed to discover more about her. "Are you saying you're not currently involved with anyone?"

"That's exactly what I'm saying. I'm not involved and don't want to become involved. Right now, my sole focus is getting these kitchens renovated so that I can be ready once the hotel opens for business."

It appeared as if they were on the same page when it came to relationships. Neither wanted one. And for him, it would make her presence on the property a win-win. Although he'd found Viola attractive, just knowing she didn't want anything more than friendship would make it easy for Dom to relate to her as a friend.

"Do you have an idea as to what you want to offer your guests?" he asked, deftly changing the topic of conversation.

"That all depends on the clientele. If it's a wedding, then that would be at the discretion of the bride and groom. However, for guests coming for a business conference, the food would be different from what would be served at a wedding reception. Then there are folks that may just want to stop by to hang out at the lounge for drinks and to watch sports. For them, I would have a special bar menu."

"It sounds as if you have everything planned out in advance."

Viola flashed a dreamy smile. "I would have to. I can't afford to wait until we're ready to open for business to begin creating menus without taste testing every item beforehand."

Dom grinned from ear to ear. "I wouldn't mind becoming one of your taste testers."

She laughed. "I'll definitely keep that in mind."

Dom sobered. "When do you intend to come back here again?"

Viola also sobered. "Why?"

He met her eyes, seeing curiosity and something else he couldn't discern. "I'd like to take you on a tour of the entire property." She paused as if mulling over his offer. Dom knew there were sections of the estate she would probably find intriguing.

"I'm open, but only when it is convenient for you."

"How about this weekend? That's when the workers are off." Taylor had given the workers Fridays off during the months of July and August to spend more time with their families. After Labor Day, they'd resume their normal Monday through Friday schedule.

"Okay. What time should I come?"

"Any time after sunrise. I happen to be an early riser."

Viola scrunched up her pert nose. "I was just the opposite when I worked at a restaurant. I normally wouldn't get home until after midnight and, most times, I'd be so wound up that it would take me a while before I would be able to settle down enough to sleep."

"Have you thought about how it's not going to be much different once the hotel opens?"

"The difference will be ownership, Dom. If I'm going to stand on my feet for hours cooking over a hot stove, then why not for myself and not for someone else with an inflated ego because they'd been awarded a Michelin star?"

With wide eyes, Dom stared at Viola. "You worked at a Michelin-starred restaurant?"

"Yes," she replied, smiling. "I gave them more than two years of my life without any advancement. I kept waiting to be promoted from line cook to sous chef, but after being passed over three times, I knew I couldn't stay on. Meanwhile, when Taylor asked me if I'd come and supervise the kitchen, I kept putting him off because I told him, and myself, that I needed more experience."

"So being passed over once again was the last straw."

Viola nodded. "It was probably what I needed to stop procrastinating and join my brothers in this family venture. Even though it's going to be a while before the grand opening, it will give me time to purchase the appliances and equipment I'll need to operate a functional commercial kitchen. To create menus for breakfast, lunch, dinner and banquets, and eventually, to begin interviewing and hiring to staff the kitchen."

"I told you before, I'm willing to become your chief taste tester."

A smile crinkled her brilliant jewel-like eyes. "I'm definitely going to take you up on that. In fact, I'm going to enlist my brothers, too. However, I want to warn you that all my brothers have learned to cook quite well, so they would be perfect taste testers for me."

Dom stared at Viola under lowered lids. He wanted to remind her that only one of her brothers was on the estate. Taylor had mentioned his other brothers had commitments they had to fulfill before joining him with ongoing the restoration.

"I'm no professional chef, but I do know my way around the kitchen." He didn't want to tell her that his grandmother had been employed at Bainbridge House as head cook and she'd taught her son and grandson to duplicate a few of the elaborate dishes she'd prepared for the owners' guests.

Viola angled her head. "If that's the case, maybe I'll have you prepare a dish and, if it meets with my approval, perhaps I'll hire you as a taste tester."

"That can't happen. I'm legally bound to stay on as

caretaker and that means I cannot work as a paid employee. What I'm willing to do is volunteer in the same way I do with helping out installing plumbing whenever Taylor needs an extra hand."

"You're a licensed plumber?"

Dom smiled. "That's me." His smile vanished. "Does that shock you?"

"I don't know you well enough to be shocked by you, and knowing you're able to install plumbing is something I plan to keep in mind if I come up with a future project."

"Do you care to enlighten me about your future project?"

"I can't right now. I'm still thinking about a few things, but I probably won't be able to make up my mind until after we finish the tour."

Dom liked that she was being mysterious because it indicated she wasn't impulsive by nature.

And despite his initial reaction to seeing her for the first time, Dom realized he liked Viola Williamson. In fact, he liked everything about her, especially her outspokenness. They could become friends, enjoy each other's company without the pressure of more involvement. Although he did not view himself as hired help, Dom could not forget that Viola owned a portion of the estate on which he lived.

"Do you think you could find your way back to the library without my help?" he asked, smiling.

Viola pulled back her shoulders, bringing his gaze to linger on the outline of her rounded breasts under a white tee. "Is this another test? And to answer your question… Yes, I can find my way back without your help."

Dom bowed, arms extended at his sides. "Lead on, Ms. Williamson."

While Dom was mildly shocked when she did navigate the many turns that led back to the library, walking behind her allowed him an unobstructed view of her curvy, compact body in fitted jeans. It had taken only seconds for his brain to register the physical reaction within his own body before he mentally stomped it down. The silent voice in his head told him Viola was strictly off-limits. Instead, he planned to enjoy her company and if, or when, their friendship ended, he would go on with his life without regrets.

## *Chapter Three*

Viola set the platter with a carved roast chicken on the table in the dining area at Taylor and Sonja's condo. She'd returned to the library minutes before Sonja, claiming fatigue, had decided to quit for the day. Viola had told her friend that she would come by later and share dinner with her and Taylor. What she hadn't revealed was that she'd planned to cook for them. Viola knew Sonja was tiring easily because of her pregnancy, and that her brother was up early and at Bainbridge House before the contract workers arrived. Because she wasn't working, Viola did not mind helping the couple to do what she did best: cook.

Taylor spread a napkin over his lap. "You know you didn't have to do this."

Viola smiled at her brother whose face and body had sold millions of magazines whenever his image graced the covers. She'd recalled her mother crying, something Elise rarely did in front of her children, when Taylor dropped out of college at nineteen to embark on a modeling career. Tall, dark, and handsome, Taylor had earned millions during his five-year stint before returning to college to earn an engineering degree. Taylor, the eldest, and the first of the Williamsons' adoptees, was the best brother Viola could have wished for. He'd become her superhero sans cape.

"I know I don't have to do this, but I wanted to. It's going to be a while before the kitchens at Bainbridge House are up and running, and that means I have to keep up my skills."

Sonja smiled. "There's no way you'll ever lose your skills, Vi, not with your training and experience."

Viola sat, reached for her napkin and placed it over her lap. "And I don't intend to lose them because I'm going to cook for you guys several times a week." She held up a hand when Sonja opened her mouth. "Please let me finish, Sonja, before you go off on me. I'd also like you two to sample some of the dishes I'd like to offer the guests at the hotel." What she didn't tell them was that Dom had also volunteered to sample her dishes.

"You won't get an argument from me," Taylor quipped.

"Taylor Edward Williamson!" Sonja said, giving him an incredulous stare. "There's no way I'm going to allow my friend to cook for us as if we're too helpless to fend for ourselves."

Viola knew Sonja was annoyed with her fiancé whenever she called him by his full name, but she did not want to be in the middle or witness a confrontation between her best friend and beloved brother. "I'd never think of you two as helpless."

Taylor lifted the platter for Sonja to serve herself. "Listen to her, babe. You're still in bed when I leave in the morning, and there are some nights when I come home that you're asleep before seven. Not only do you complain that you're always tired, but you also admitted there are some nights when you're too tired to cook so you order in."

Viola gave Sonja what she considered her death stare. "Did you neglect to mention this to me?"

"Taylor talks too much," Sonja mumbled under her breath.

"My brothers and I were raised to be open with one another. Taylor only said it because he's concerned about you and your baby," Viola said as she filled her plate with chicken, garlic mashed potatoes and wilted spinach.

Taylor had caught up with her before she'd left Bainbridge House to confide that if Sonja had agreed he would've married her as soon as she'd revealed she was pregnant, but his fiancée wanted to wait until December because she'd always wanted a Christmas wedding. And she knew Taylor's wanting to marry Sonja right away and not wait for December was his fear that history would repeat itself. His biological father—a man he hadn't known—had abandoned his mother when she'd become pregnant with his child. He'd lost his biological mother before he'd celebrated his third birthday, and was placed in foster care with an aunt who had neglected him until social services had assigned him to Elise and Conrad Williamson.

Sonja blew out her cheeks. "Okay. I'll let you cook, but only until I'm not so tired." She took a bite of chicken and then moaned softly. "I don't know how you make your chicken so moist and tender. You'll have to teach me so I can pass the family recipe along to my son or daughter."

Viola shared a wink with Taylor. She was looking forward to spoiling her niece or nephew; that is, if Elise didn't pull rank as the grandmother. "I turn the oven up to around 400 degrees to crisp the skin, baste it with garlic butter infused with olive oil, then reduce the thermostat to 200 and let it bake for two to three hours. The longer, the better. It's usually so tender that it will fall apart and make carving easy."

Taylor swallowed a mouthful of potatoes. "I wouldn't mind if you cook for me every night."

"Spoken like a man who can really burn some pots," Viola teased.

"I can, but not like this, Viola," Taylor countered.

"Don't play yourself, brother love. You cook better than any of our brothers."

"But not better than my sister."

"That's because of my training."

Elise had taught all her children to cook, but it was Viola who had excelled. Before she'd celebrated her fourteenth birthday, she'd known she wanted to be a chef. It was as if she'd been drawn to kitchen at an early age when she sat on a stool to watch her mother prepare their meals. Not only had Elise homeschooled her four sons and daughter, she'd also taken time to make them breakfast, lunch and dinner.

Taylor's dark eyes in an equally dark complexion met hers. "Do you regret leaving the restaurant when you did?"

Viola lowered her eyes to focus on the food on her plate for several seconds. "At first I did, because I believed the manager when he'd said I was up for a promotion whenever a position became available in a few months. But then I realized I'd heard the same promise before." She gave Taylor a steady stare. "It was as if he'd rehearsed the line. That's when I told myself never again."

"So, you're not sorry you left?" Sonja asked.

"No. And now that I've seen the kitchens at Bainbridge House, I can't wait to begin ordering the appliances and equipment to furnish them. Taylor, I'm going to need the dimensions of all the spaces before I can order sinks, stoves, refrigerators and freezers."

"I have copies of the plans at the château, so when I go there tomorrow, I'll text them to you."

"How did it go between you and Dom this morning?" Sonja questioned after she'd swallowed a mouthful of potatoes.

"Okay."

Taylor looked at Viola and then Sonja. "Am I missing something?"

"No," Sonja and Viola chorused in unison.

"It's just that I thought Vi was going to go for his throat when he insisted she call him Dom and not Dominic," Sonja said after Taylor continued to stare at her.

Viola shrugged her shoulders. "Maybe he was teased as a boy about the Italian Christmas song 'Dominick the Donkey,' so he prefers Dom."

"I never thought of that," Sonja said softly.

"Did he give you a hard time, Viola?" Taylor asked.

"Why would he give me a hard time?"

"Because if he had, then your brother would probably punch his lights out," Sonja said before Viola could reply to Taylor's query.

It was Viola's turn to ask, "Am *I* missing something?"

"Your brother thought there was something going on between me and Dom when he saw us hugging. He approached the man with all sorts of threats and innuendoes about me carrying on an affair with him."

Viola narrowed her eyes at Taylor. "No, you didn't."

"Yes, he did, Vi. Dom had hugged me because I promised not to tell anyone about his family's secret and that's when my then boyfriend misconstrued the friendly gesture for something else."

Viola did not want to believe Taylor would jump to conclusions about a woman who had confessed her love for him and if Sonja hadn't intervened she was certain they would not be making plans to marry. "What did you find out about his family?" she questioned.

Sonja leaned back in her chair. "I'm not going to tell you."

Taylor shook his head. "Let me warn you that my sister is like a dog with a bone. When she gets it, she refuses to let go."

Sonja also shook her head. "Bone or no bone, I'm not telling."

Viola affected a smug grin. "Maybe I'll ask him when I see him again this weekend."

"What's happening this weekend?" Taylor asked.

"He's offered to take me on a tour of the property."

Taylor blinked slowly. "That's it?"

"What else did you think it was?" she asked her brother.

"I don't know," Taylor mumbled.

"It's not a date, Taylor," Viola countered. "If I've inherited property with a house with more than a hundred rooms sitting on three-hundred-fifty-plus acres, I think it's time I become familiar with it. And I'm certain once Tariq and Joaquin join us, they will be afforded the same consideration."

She and her brothers owned one-fifth equal shares in the estate that, once fully restored, would be valued at a half-billion dollars. Elise had told them at Easter that even before her husband retired and sold his private equity company, he'd filed permits and approval for variances to convert the property from residential to commercial. But despite his talk about initiating the restoration, golf had taken precedence over everything.

Sonja gave Taylor a long, penetrating stare. "What is it about you and Dom where you have to be so defensive? Why don't you like the man?"

Taylor sat straight. "Did I ever say I didn't like the man? In fact, I happen to like him a lot."

"Based on your reaction to his showing me around, it sounds as if you don't, brother love," Viola quipped teasingly.

"Well, you're wrong, little sis. He's volunteered to help with installing plumbing, and his work is equal or better than the ones I have on payroll. He doesn't waste time talking and, whatever task he's given, he's able to finish it in record time. If I had another three or even five plumbers like him, I would be a very happy man. Even the project manager talks about how good he is."

"So, you don't have a problem with him hanging out with your sister?" Sonja asked.

Viola glared at her future sister-in-law. Why did Sonja make it sound as if she and Dom were a couple? That was something she would never permit to happen. She had been forthcoming when she'd told Dom her sole focus was to become executive chef for Bainbridge House, and that she wasn't looking for a relationship.

"I think, at twenty-eight, I shouldn't have to ask any man, especially my brothers, whether I can or cannot hang out with someone. Besides, you and Taylor know I strike out big-time when it comes to relationships. Enough about me. What about our family secret, Taylor? Do you believe Dom knows Conrad's kids were adopted?"

Taylor's expression stilled, becoming serious. "Why should he?"

"Because he was close to Daddy. He told me they used to talk to each other a couple of times a month before our father retired, and a lot fewer once Daddy sold his company. Dom claims he never met Momma, so he's probably unaware of her racial identity."

Sonja touched her napkin to the corners of her mouth. "I know you guys were all adopted, and even if you don't tell anyone else, it isn't going to remain a family secret for long."

"You're probably right, but it had become *our* secret," Viola said emphatically. She gave Sonja a direct stare. "The fact that we were homeschooled shielded us from other kids teasing us about not being biological brothers and sister. We were all legally adopted on the same day, and that's when we decided we didn't have to explain to anyone, even though we all looked different, that we weren't siblings, because we claimed the same last name. And when our parents took us out to eat and we called them Momma and Daddy, folks would give us all kinds of crazy looks. I think people forget that Mia Farrow, Angelina Jolie and Madonna adopted children of different races and ethnicities, so I don't know what the big deal was."

"Viola's right," Taylor confirmed. "If folks don't believe Viola is my sister or that Patrick, Tariq and Joaquin are my brothers, then that's their problem."

"I agree," Sonja said. "Thankfully, things are changing with the proliferation of blended and mixed-race families. The only beef I had with your sister is that she didn't tell me her brother was supermodel T.E. Wills."

Viola affected a screw-face expression. "That's because T.E. Wills is his past and I wanted you to meet the engineer, not the model. And now, fast-forward several months, you're engaged and planning for a wedding and a baby."

Sonja shared a smile with her fiancé. "Everything did happen rather quickly, didn't it, *papi*?"

Taylor's dark eyebrows slanted in a frown. "Not soon enough. I told you I don't want to wait until Christmas for us to marry."

"Please don't stress her, Taylor," Viola warned her brother. It wasn't the first time she'd cautioned Taylor not to put any pressure on his then girlfriend because if he did he would lose her. "Sonja's not going anywhere, and neither are you, so cool your jets, brother, and let your future wife do it her way. After all, you are living and working together, so what's the problem?" Pushing back her chair, Viola stood. She knew it was time for her to leave so her brother and his fiancée could discuss their future. "I'm done here. Taylor, do you think you can handle cleaning up?"

Taylor also rose, smiling. "Of course." Rounding the table, he pulled Viola close. "Thanks for helping Sonja," he whispered in her ear.

Viola kissed his stubble. "Anytime, brother love. And I mean what I said about cooking and bringing food over." She patted his back. "It's time I leave because I need to check out a few things in Momma's fridge and pantry before I go shopping for perishables."

"Are you coming to Bainbridge House tomorrow?"

"No. I'm going to stay away until the weekend. That's when I'm really looking forward to touring the entire estate."

Taylor nodded. "It's probably going to take more than one weekend for you to see everything, and that includes the house. Some of the rooms on the second floor are now cordoned off since the walls between many of the suites have been removed to expand them to accommodate as many as four guests at any given time."

Viola smiled. "Even if does take more than a couple of weekends to see all the property, it doesn't matter. I have nothing but time on my hands." Suddenly her smile faded. "I know I'd asked you before, but it still bothers me that Daddy had only mentioned the property to Momma, and she in turn didn't say anything to us until months after the reading of his will. And whenever I ask Momma about it, she claims she doesn't want to talk about it. Has she said anything to you why?" She knew Elise was closest to Taylor and had confided things to him she'd been reluctant to discuss with her other children.

"Not about that. But I suppose Dad had his reason for asking Mom to delay telling us. Well, it doesn't matter because we're going honor his wishes and restore Bainbridge House to make it a showplace again." Taylor kissed her forehead. "Drive carefully."

"I will." She'd been known to drive too fast, and in the past she'd earned several speeding citations.

Easing out of Taylor's embrace, Viola scooped her crossbody off a chair in the family room and walked out the condo.

Sharing dinner with her brother and best friend had been enjoyable. Growing up in a large family and eating meals together was something she'd missed once she'd left home to attend culinary school, and then when she'd lived alone in her Greenwich Village apartment. She'd craved independence, and knew she could survive on her own, but coming home to an apartment void of human contact was a constant reminder of the adage "Be careful what you wish for." She'd lived in the two-bedroom apartment for three months and then decided to advertise for a roommate; she'd rented the extra bedroom to a nurse who worked the night shift, which had worked well for both.

Viola had experienced mixed emotions when she'd had to give up her apartment because she liked living in New York City and had come to crave the nonstop energy of the city regardless of the time of day. She loved strolling through the streets of the Village to take in the sights, and stop and browse in small shops offering everything from vintage books, antiques and clothing. She'd found a flapper dress from the 1920s she'd wanted to wear to a Halloween party hosted by the restaurant's executive chef at his Brooklyn Heights town house. She'd purchased the dress, a matching headband and an onyx necklace to complete her vintage outfit.

Viola had gotten along well enough with her coworkers to host a Sunday brunch buffet at her apartment. The gathering had been small, with less than a dozen people including the restaurant's waitstaff, her roommate's colleagues, and a few of the neighbors on her floor.

She'd also invited Sonja and had noticed a few of the men had tried hitting on her, yet had known their efforts were in vain. Her friend had confided in her about her first marriage in which she'd become a virtual prisoner when her husband's jealousy had forced Sonja to methodically plan her escape from a man who had emotionally abused her for years. Sonja had sworn her to secrecy and Viola had kept her secret until she'd been forced to tell Taylor about her best friend's toxic marriage to save their relationship.

She made it to Sparta and took a shower, changed into sweats and then opened her laptop to search for the appliances she needed to update the kitchen. It took hours for Viola to research and print out specs and dimensions for several commercial turbo ovens and broilers. Patrick hadn't given her a budget and she wondered if he would go along with her proposed purchases—many items began at five figures. Her CPA brother had earned a reputation of questioning every expenditure submitted for approval and eventual disbursement; she had to convince him whatever she ordered was necessary for a fully functioning commercial kitchen. And Bainbridge House had not one but three kitchens to restore and equip.

Viola's eyes were burning when she finally logged off and stacked the pages on the printer tray in a neat pile. She changed out of her sweats and into a nightgown and then settled in bed to watch the Hallmark channel. It was a movie she'd seen before, but Viola never tired of watching her favorites over and over. And she wasn't ashamed to admit that she was addicted to romance novels and any movie of the same genre. While she had gotten used to her brothers teasing her about reading the books and watching the movies, she wasn't comfortable admitting to them that their sister was unlucky when it came to love and therefore lived vicariously through the books and films.

It was as if she didn't have the wherewithal to reject a man who expressed an interest in her; she hadn't been perceptive enough to suspect his ulterior motive. And in her naivete, she'd failed to pick up on the signs until she'd found herself in too deep. In the end, she concluded it was because she'd grown up with four older brothers who protected her that she'd come to believe most men were like them.

A wry smile flitted over Viola's features when she thought about Dom Shaw. If they were to interact with each other, it could only be as friends, which suited her well because she'd never had a guy friend. And as a friend, there wouldn't be any pressure for them to become friends with benefits. For her, offering or agreeing to benefits was not an option at this time in her life. She was more than willing to put romance on the back burner since her singular concentration and motivation was to become the executive chef at Bainbridge House.

Viola adjusted the pillows behind her head and focused on the flat screen. She picked up the remote and programmed the television to shut down in two hours. There had been times when she'd fallen asleep while the television watched her instead of the reverse. Fortunately, the movie was one of her favorites. She liked the lead actress.

Viola reached over and turned off the bedside lamp

as the movie ended and she settled down to fall asleep. She didn't have to wait long as her breathing deepened and Morpheus wrapped her in a comforting, dreamless slumber.

## *Chapter Four*

Saturday was a typical autumn day in the northeast—cool in the morning with warmer temperatures in the afternoon, and cool again at night, which forced Viola to dress in layers. Dom had informed her that he got up early, yet she hadn't wanted to arrive at Bainbridge House before seven. A few minutes after eight, she maneuvered through the electronic gates and along the stretch of cobblestone roadway while taking note of the age-old trees beginning to change color in the autumnal equinox.

Each time she came to the property, Viola felt as if she'd stepped back to an era when those with unlimited wealth sought to flaunt their social status by erecting structures in the grand style of European mansions. It wasn't just the French-inspired château built on a hilltop overlooking an expanse of verdant lawns and gardens. It was also the interior of the house, with its many rooms, the steep-pitched roofs and turrets, the outbuildings with their tiled roofs that called to mind the fairy-tale kingdoms illustrated in the children's books she'd read over and over until she'd memorized every word.

As she parked, the front door opened and Dom walked out dressed entirely in black: jeans, long-sleeved tee and boots. The somber color made him appear taller and thinner. He came down the steps and met her as she stepped out of the car. Bright sunlight glinted off the gray strands in the raven-black hair fastened at his nape.

He smiled, minute lines fanning out around his eyes, and she returned his smile with a friendly one of her own. "Good morning."

"That it is," Dom confirmed, his smile still in place.

Viola wondered if he was referring to the weather or if he was glad to see her. She'd hoped it was the former because she did not want to fantasize that he'd been waiting to see her again. Although, if she were honest with herself, she had looked forward to seeing him again. Despite her reluctance to become even remotely involved with a man, Viola could admit there was something about Dom she found not only attractive but captivating, and it had to do with the soft timbre of his voice. The cadence was measured, as if he'd thought about what he'd wanted to say before opening his mouth.

"What have you planned?" she asked.

He glanced up at the bright blue sky dotted with fluffy clouds. "I figured we'd start with exploring the grounds before you tour the house."

Viola nodded. "How long do you think that will take?"

"Probably a couple of days."

Her eyebrows lifted. "That long?"

Dom nodded. "Three-hundred-fifty-plus acres is equal to about five miles. And given the number of buildings, gardens and open pastures, it isn't something you can gloss over quickly. It usually takes me three days to mow the grass, and then several more to weed and prune the flower beds, vineyard and the orchard."

Viola had noticed the lawns were cut with the precise meticulousness usually found in professional baseball stadiums. "Where are we going first?"

"I'd like to take you to the barn and stables before they're demolished and rebuilt."

"When was the last time they were used?"

"It's been decades."

She asked Dom a litany of questions because she knew so little. Taylor had been so involved with the team of contractors, they'd rarely spoken to each other about the ongoing progress.

Dom cupped her elbow and led her in a westerly direction away from the house. Before he dropped his hand, the scent of his cologne wafted to her nostrils and she found the notes of bergamot and sandalwood sensual and hypnotic.

"Were there horses on the estate while you were growing up here?"

"No. My grandfather told me the horses were gone by the late 1940s. The cost of feed and vet bills had prohibited them from keeping the animals on the property."

"How many horses did they have at any given time?"

"There were stalls for six, so I assume they had at least that many."

"What about the barn?"

* * *

Dom knew Viola would ask him countless questions before she was able to see the entire estate. Most he would be able to answer and some he couldn't or wouldn't. He was the fourth-generation Shaw to grow up at Bainbridge House and, as such, he had been privy to the lives and secrets of the wealthy family that had become the darling of New Jersey society before the twentieth century. However, there was one secret he'd confirmed with Sonja Rios-Martin which she'd promised never to divulge. Although he believed Sonja, Dom still wondered how long it would take for someone else to uncover what had been buried for more than one hundred years, once Bainbridge House was open for business.

He slowed his stride to keep pace with Viola's shorter legs. "Taylor said he would rebuild the barn and stables because they were in the original plans, but right now he's uncertain whether he's going have animals other than horses on the property." As the chief engineer, Taylor had scheduled Monday morning staff meetings to update the crews on various projects, and had requested Dom attend.

"What other animals are you talking about?" Viola asked.

Dom gave Viola a sidelong glance, admiring the loose curls falling over her forehead. "Ducks, sheep, chickens, cats and dogs."

She stopped, and he also stopped to face her. "You're talking about farm animals."

"There was a time when the cooks at Bainbridge House didn't have to purchase chickens, ducks or lamb because they were raised here. The ducks and chickens became a part of the dinner table once they stopped laying eggs, and it was the same with the lambs after they were weaned. The sheep were let out in a pasture where they were four-footed lawnmowers. The dogs had become companions for the horses and the cats kept the rodents at bay."

Viola flashed a wide smile. "The only things missing were cows for milk and beef."

"I was told there was a time when they did have goats, but that experiment didn't last long because they would chase the sheep and get into it with the dogs."

"I love goat's milk. There's nothing better than goat cheese, or chèvre, whether it's soft fresh or hard aged."

Dom winked at her. "Spoken like a true chef."

A beat passed. Viola sobered. "If Taylor's going to rebuild the barn, then I'm going to ask him to set up enough space to house chickens and ducks for their eggs. Freshly laid eggs taste so much better compared to those in supermarkets."

"I assume you speak from experience."

She nodded. "After I graduated from culinary school, I enrolled in a couple of six-week courses in France, Spain and Italy to familiarize myself with their regional cooking. The instructors recommended using fresh chicken or duck eggs for various recipes if they were available."

Dom did not intend to involve himself in the plans the Williamson siblings had for Bainbridge House. He was an outsider and that was where he intended to remain. While he did not mind volunteering to help install plumbing, anything else was outside his essential responsibility of protecting and maintaining the property. He had learned from his father and grandfather that there were distinct societal boundaries between his family and the Bainbridges, and he'd tried not to blur the lines. However, his life had changed after his father and stepmother relocated to Arizona and he'd taken over the position as the caretaker for the property.

"So, you are really serious about raising chickens on the estate?" Dom asked Viola.

"Very serious," she replied, smiling. "If there were animals on the property more than a hundred years ago, then I have to assume it was self-sustaining when it came to preparing meals for the Bainbridge family and their guests. That was farm-to-table eons before lots of restaurants adopted the practice."

"You're right about that. There were several acres with a vegetable garden, but it went to seed a long time ago."

Viola took off the sunglasses and placed them on the top of her head. "Taylor had mentioned something about an orchard."

Dom found himself unable to pull his gaze away from the hazel eyes that reminded him of smoky quartz and peridot. "Yes."

"Yes what, Dom?"

He blinked as if coming out of a trance. The brilliant morning sunlight had turned her into a statue of gold, and he'd found himself reacting to her like a teenage boy coming face-to-face with the girl he'd been worshipping from afar. However, he wasn't fifteen, but a thirty-five-year-old divorced man who hadn't lived a monkish existence. He didn't know what it was about Taylor's sister that had him thinking about her when he least expected, but he doubted whether her brother would appreciate him coming on to his sister despite Dom's declaration that he only wanted friendship from her.

"Yes, there is an orchard. It's on the east end of the estate."

"Can we see it now?"

"I can get the ATV if you don't want to walk."

Viola gave him an incredulous look. "How far is it?"

"Give or take a couple of miles."

Her mouth curved into an unconscious smile. "I don't mind walking."

"Are you sure?"

A frown replaced her smile. "Dom, please. I used to live in Manhattan where I walked every day to get around, so a couple of miles is not a challenge."

Dom had asked her because there were days when he rode the all-terrain vehicle whenever he surveyed the entire estate after thunderstorms or blizzards. Downed tree limbs, broken windows and missing roof tiles had become a priority to keep the estate from going into disrepair.

"Let's go, princess," he mumbled under his breath.

She blinked slowly. "What did you call me?"

Dom affected a sheepish grin. "Nothing."

"Yeah, right," she drawled. "I don't know what it is, but something is nagging at me that you were closer to my father than you're willing to reveal."

"Why would you say that?"

"Because Daddy used to call me princess."

Dom met her eyes, his gaze unwavering. "That's something I wasn't aware of." Although he'd recalled Conrad referring to his sons as princes and his daughter as his princess, he'd never gone into detail about them. "I did do some part-time work for your father."

"What type of part-time work?"

"Investing."

"You're saying you were involved with my father's investment and hedge fund company?"

"Why, didn't your father tell you about me?" He'd answered her question with one of his own.

"Not only didn't he tell me about you, I had no idea that my father owned this property until my mother mentioned it once we all got together this past Easter. Taylor said Momma had hinted about some property in Daddy's family, but other than that, all of us were clueless until she told us about Bainbridge House. But you still didn't answer my question."

"And that is?"

"How were you involved with my father's investment company?"

"When your brother Patrick left to get involved in wine growing, Conrad asked me if I would be interested in taking on a few of Patrick's clients."

"How did you go from plumbing to finance?"

Suddenly it hit Dom. It was apparent Viola could not imagine that he was familiar with something other than pipes and drainage systems. "The same way you went to culinary school to become a chef."

Viola went completely still. "You graduated college?"

Dom curbed the urge to laugh when he saw her stunned expression. "Does that surprise you?"

A rush of color suffused her gold-brown complexion as she lowered her eyes. "I… I…" she stammered uncomfortably, "I'm just confused."

"About what, Viola?"

"Why are you working here instead of at an investment company?"

"Why would I when Bainbridge House is my home? And I happen to like my work."

"You like living here—alone?"

Dom smiled as he angled his head. "Very much."

"You're a recluse."

"Not quite," he countered.

"Does that mean you invite women here to keep you company?"

His eyebrows lifted. "Are you asking because you're curious or are you interested in keeping me company?"

"What!" The single word exploded from Viola.

"Forget I asked," he said. Dom didn't know where that had come from, yet after saying it, he knew it was impossible to retract the question.

Viola gave him a long, penetrating stare. "Consider it forgotten."

Dom didn't know why he'd asked Viola if she was interested in him except, unconsciously, he did want her to be. And despite his pronouncement that he wanted them to be friends, he knew he hadn't been completely truthful with her or himself.

Aside from being attracted to Viola's natural beauty, he liked everything about her. She was confident, outspoken, and that meant he didn't have to guess what she was thinking. Those were traits missing in the women with whom he'd had relationships. He also wanted her to be comfortable enough with each other to spend some quality time together. And for him, quality time meant dating without the possibility of taking their friendship to another level. Dom knew their sleeping together would not prove advantageous to either of them if they broke up and still had to see each other because they worked and lived on the same property.

Dom forced a smile. “Where we’re going, the ground is a little uneven, so I want you to watch your step. I can’t have you falling down and turning an ankle.” He extended his hand and Viola took it, his fingers closing over hers. They walked together, holding hands as the sun rose higher in the sky along with the increase in temperature.

He led her to an open field blooming with a riot of autumnal wildflowers in every hue. Within minutes, they were surrounded by a hodgepodge of hedges with a mix of trees and shrubs.

“I know Joaquin is going to be in his element once he sees this,” Viola said as she stopped and stared at the flowers. “He’s a landscape architect,” Viola added when Dom gave her a direct stare. “He lives in Los Angeles and he’s designed lawns and gardens for a number of A-list Hollywood actors.”

“Has he committed to come on board for the restoration?” Dom asked.

“Yes. But only when he completes two more commissions. You’ll get to meet him, Patrick and Tariq this Christmas.”

“Is that when the Williamsons get together?”

“Yes,” she repeated. “We always celebrate Easter, Thanksgiving and Christmas as a family, no matter where we are in the world. However, this year is going to be different because my mother will be on a cruise for Thanksgiving, but she’ll be back in plenty of time for Christmas.”

Dom tightened his hold on Viola’s delicate fingers as they made their way over an uneven section of land scheduled to be landscaped before the ground froze. The rutted terrain gave him the perfect excuse not only to touch Viola, but to also inhale the sensual fragrance of the perfume wafting from her petite body.

"How was it growing up with four brothers? Were they the types to scare away any boy that appeared remotely interested in their little sister?"

Viola laughed softly. It was a question she'd been asked whenever people discovered she was the only girl, and the youngest, in a family of five. "Not really. My mom homeschooled us, so we didn't have classmates. Once we were older and got our licenses, we would drive to the mall or into town and occasionally hang out at the spots favored by other teenagers. Although most of the kids considered us outsiders, we did manage to make a few friends at the local high school. A boy asked me to prom because he'd broken up with his steady girlfriend, but when she discovered he'd asked me, she made up with him."

"So, you never went to prom?"

"No. What about you, Dom? Did you have a traditional education?"

"Yes. I was bussed to a school district a couple of miles from here. I skipped a couple of grades and graduated at sixteen. I was too shy to ask some of the older girls to prom, so I didn't go."

"At what age did you attend college?"

"That's a long story."

The seconds ticked by and with the silence it became obvious to Viola that Dom did not want talk about it. She'd been told she was like a dog with a bone, unwilling to let go of something whenever she sought answers to her questions. But this time she knew when to let the proverbial bone go. In the short time she and Dom had been together, they tended to verbally spar and snipe at each other. And that wasn't conducive if they hoped to become friends.

"You asked about my brothers," she continued as if there hadn't been an obvious lapse in their conversation. "Taylor is the oldest, and an engineer. Patrick is next, and an accountant. By the way, did you ever meet Patrick?"

Dom shook his head. "No. Conrad told me about him after Patrick quit the firm and moved to California."

Viola realized Dom had never met any of her siblings until Taylor had assumed the responsibility of chief engineer for the restoration project. "Then there's landscape architect Joaquin and, finally, Tariq, who is a vet with a specialty in equine veterinary."

Dom whistled softly. "Now I know why Conrad wanted his children to inherit this property."

"What do you think would have happened to it if he'd decided to sell?"

"Several developers did approach him about selling because they wanted to put up condos or single-family homes, but Conrad refused to sell because the estate was a part of his family's legacy."

Viola took the sunglasses off her head and placed them on the bridge of her nose. "A legacy which he'd kept hidden from his kids."

"I suppose he had his reasons," Dom said.

"Did he ever tell you why he'd decided to raise his family in Belleville instead of moving us here?" she asked as she glanced up at Dom's profile, noticing he was squinting against the brilliant rays of the sun.

"No, he didn't. Conrad and I got along only because I'd learned early on not to cross the line from business to personal. The one time I did ask him something that he considered too personal, he told me outright it was none of my business. That was enough for me not to do that again."

"That's because there was Conrad the businessman and Daddy the family man, and he made certain to keep them separate."

Viola had learned as a child that there had been two sides to Conrad Williamson. He was no-nonsense when it came to his business matters and the complete opposite when it concerned his private life. He put in long hours at his Manhattan office during weekdays, rarely coming home in time to share dinner with his family. However, on weekends, anything resembling business was forgotten. That was the time he was father and husband with total devotion to his wife and children.

"I suppose that's why Taylor gives his work crew Fridays off during the summer months, so they can spend that time with their families."

Viola smiled. It was obvious some of their father's traditions had rubbed off on Taylor. She tripped over a tangle of exposed roots and would've fallen if Dom hadn't tightened the grip on her hand. "Why is the land so uneven here?"

"This section of the estate was filled with trees that were damaged during a number of severe storms. Many of them couldn't be saved, so Conrad told me to have them cut down and hauled away. Next month, an excavation company will remove the tree roots and stumps before a landscaping company will lay sod to level it off."

"You couldn't save any of the wood?"

"No. Most of them were too old and filled with rot."

There was so much for her to learn about the Bainbridge property, and it was obvious she needed to become knowledgeable before the château opened as a viable business venture. Sonja had revealed it would take months before she could put together a comprehensive history of generations of Bainbridge family members. She had discovered a Bible dating back to the sixteenth century that had recorded births and deaths, which meant searching for and reviewing genealogical records going back centuries.

Viola stumbled again and she gasped when Dom's free arm went around her body and under her breasts. Heat flared in her cheeks from utter embarrassment and the reaction of her body pressed intimately against a man disturbed her—but in a good way. The gesture was innocent enough, but it was a reminder of how long it had been since she'd felt cradled in a man's embrace.

"I'm okay now."

Dom stared at her under lowered lids, the corners of his mouth curving in a smile. "Remember, I did tell you that we didn't have to walk."

She wasn't about to admit to him that he'd been right because she'd never been one to accept defeat. If someone told her she couldn't do something, she did everything in her power to prove them wrong. She was very competitive, even an overachiever when playing with her brothers. Whether it was tennis matches or swimming laps in the family's in-ground pool, her sole goal was winning, and often she did. It had been the same at cooking school.

She'd been one of twenty-two women enrolled at the

Culinary Institute of America's Hyde Park campus that year and she'd graduated with honors, coming in second in her class. But despite the accolades and growing numbers of women graduating from renowned culinary schools, they still weren't thought of as equals to their male counterparts. Although she'd been hired to work at a Michelin-star restaurant, Viola had been passed over for promotion in favor of a male chef, not once or twice, but three times, despite her training and experience.

Dom reluctantly dropped his arm and smiled. The soft crush of Viola's body had elicited memories of how it felt to hold on to a woman. She'd accused him of being a recluse, and that was what he'd become since his last relationship. In the ensuing months, he'd consciously purged all memories of the woman who'd, in a moment of madness, had him planning a future with her. However, fate had intervened when he'd discovered she was still sleeping with her ex-boyfriend. Once again, distrust had reared its ugly head and Dom swore an oath—never again.

He had to admit to himself that despite her delicate appearance, Viola Williamson had grit. His initial impression of her was that she was not only spoiled but had been pampered by Conrad. If he had to assign an adjective for her attitude, it would be somewhat snobbish. Growing up privileged, she'd believed, as the caretaker for her family's property, he probably wouldn't have earned a college degree.

He had grown used to women questioning him about his choice of vocation, which in turn had led him to categorize them as superficial and small-minded. One had even told him that if he lived on an estate then he should've owned it rather work as a handyman. What they did not understand was that Bainbridge House was his home just as it had been to more than four generations of Shaws. Even when he left the property for extended periods of time, he couldn't shake the feeling of homesickness.

"Wow," she whispered.

Viola's soft gasp shattered his musings, and he knew what had captured her rapt attention.

The land sloped into a valley where a lingering fog shrouded the guesthouses dotting the landscape like miniature dollhouses. "Most people seeing them for the first time react the same way as you."

"I told Taylor I'd planned to move into one of them because I don't want to work *and* live at the château. But I had no idea they would look like this. They are a lot larger than I imagined them to be."

"They are quite spacious."

"What a perfect spot to build guesthouses. The mist makes this valley looks like a watercolor painting."

Dom had to agree with Viola. Living in the valley was like being in another world where one was cut off from the main house. Once he returned to his house at the end of the day, it was his sanctuary, where any and everything outside his front door ceased to exist.

"The fog usually doesn't burn off until midmorning, and that's a plus with cooler temperatures during the summer. Each house sits on a half acre, so that provides a modicum of privacy from the next one."

"It is possible to look inside one?"

Dom shook his head. "Not at this time. After Taylor had the property wired for surveillance videos by a security company, he said he didn't want anyone to have access to the guesthouses until they're scheduled for rehab. They'll need updated electrical wiring, plumbing, and complete kitchen and bathroom makeovers. Right now, he's concentrating on the exterior of the château before the cold weather sets in, and renovating the second-floor suites has also become a priority."

"What about your guesthouse?" Viola questioned. "Is it up to code?"

It had taken years before he'd been able to renovate the spacious two-story, three-bedroom stone house with its tiled roof for his personal comfort. "Yes. It's about another mile to the orchards, so we should head out before it gets too hot. There's a golf cart there that we can take to ride back to the main house."

## *Chapter Five*

Viola was glad Dom had suggested riding in the golf cart, not because she was tired, but because she feared falling and injuring herself. The one time she'd fallen on the tennis court after running to hit Patrick's vicious backhanded volley, she'd broken her wrist and spent the entire summer with her left hand in a cast. Unused to the inactivity, she'd pouted, watching her brothers play basketball, swim and challenge one another for dominance when shooting pool. The accident had also changed her because she'd begun spending more time in the kitchen with her mother; it was when she'd decided she wanted to become a chef.

"Where do you keep the equipment for the property?"

"There are two large buildings that were carriage houses and garages not far from the bridle path. The roof tiles are an exact match for every other structure on the estate and that's where the mower, tractor, snowblower, ATV and other farm tools are stored."

Viola knew it would take a while before she would become familiar with the three-hundred-fifty-plus acres. Unlike Dom, who had grown up at Bainbridge House and admitted he was familiar with every room and hallway in the château and the land on which it stood.

"This is really a lot to take in."

"Yes, it is," Dom agreed. "If you look at the original blueprints, you'll see that the property is divided into four quadrants. North, south, east and west, with the château dissecting east and west. The guesthouses, orchards, vineyard and duck pond are in the east, and the vegetable garden, stables and barns are in the west. The formal gardens are in the south quadrant and the golf course is in the north end."

She tried to imagine what the estate would look like after a snowfall when it would resemble a winter wonderland. She was looking forward to becoming involved in a Christmas-themed wedding, even if it did not snow.

The ground leveled off and, fifteen minutes later, they reached the orchard with its apple, pear and cherry trees.

She picked up a large light-green apple among several that had fallen to the ground. "This Granny Smith is perfect for pies."

Dom looked up at the tree with its low-hanging fruit. "There's enough here to make hundreds of pies."

Viola used her fingers to brush off a light layer of dirt on the apple's bruised skin. "What do you do with them after they fall off the trees?"

"I give them to a man that owns several horses."

"Some of these trees don't look very old."

"That's because they're not. My father planted them about ten years ago. Dad is what you would call a modern-day Johnny Appleseed. When he wasn't working, he spent all his free time here. He even planted some of the cherry and pear trees."

Viola glanced up at another tree with apples she recognized as Fuji. Walking around the orchard, she saw ripening galas, Golden Delicious and McIntosh apples. She walked over to Dom, who'd crossed his arms over his chest. "Should I assume you take care of the orchard, too?"

Smiling and nodding, he said, "Yes."

Viola cradled the Granny Smith, her imagination going into overdrive. "I'm going to need your help."

"With what?"

"I want to pick as much of the ripe fruit as we can, because I can use them to make pie fillings, sauces, jellies, jams, preserves and marmalades. What's the matter?" she asked when he continued to stare at her.

He blinked, as if coming out of a trance. "I'm just stunned that you thought of that so quickly." He snapped his fingers for emphasis.

"I sleep, dream and breathe food, Dom. I save bones to make stock and broth rather than throw them away. It's the same with folks in the South using every part of the pig from the rooter to the tooter. They'd learned to use tough cuts of meat to make delicious, wholesome soups or stews and other dishes that were passed down through countless generations that now are listed on menus of many restaurants."

A hint of a smile curved the corners of his mouth.

"Are you talking about soul food like neck bones, oxtails and ham hocks?"

Viola liked it when Dom smiled. It softened the sharp angles in his lean face at the same time deepening the lines around his green eyes. "You know about soul food?"

"I know I like to eat it," he countered.

Viola decided to test him. "What's your favorite dish?"

"Shrimp and grits, while red beans and rice comes in a close second. And whenever I make the shrimp and grits, I always add andouille. I'm proud to say they're always lip-smacking good."

She scrunched up her nose. "Showoff."

Dom affected a smug expression. "When you got it, flaunt it."

"When are you going to make some for me?"

Sobering, he went completely still. "You want *me* to cook for *you*?"

"Yes. I need you to show me what you've got."

Dom knew he was being challenged, and by a professional chef no less. He wanted to laugh since he knew there was no way he could begin to compete with Viola. However, what he didn't have in experience or training, he had in confidence. He knew he was a good cook—a trait he'd acquired from his paternal grandmother, Josephine Shaw née McNeill. His grandparents had been employed at Bainbridge House as cook and caretaker respectively, and Josephine had insisted he learn to cook. Even after so many years, he still missed hearing his grandmother's voice and inhaling the lingering scent of her favorite French perfume she'd received from her employer's wife every Christmas. Josephine hadn't waited for special occasions to wear the fragrance and would apply a small dot behind each ear after her morning bath.

Dom never knew his mother; she'd died from a pulmonary embolism before he'd celebrated his first birthday. His grandmother had assumed the responsibility for looking after him and she'd become the only woman in his life until he was twelve when his father married a divorcée with a son three years Dom's junior. It had taken him a while to warm up to his new stepmother, but it'd been the complete opposite with her son. He'd become an older brother to a kid who'd followed him everywhere. Even as adults they remained close, Dom standing as best man at Evan's wedding and godfather to his twin sons.

"Okay," he said softly. "What do you want me to make?"

"Shrimp and grits."

"All right. What if we get together one day next weekend? You can select the day and time."

Viola hesitated and then said, "I really prefer Sunday brunch. How's eleven?"

Dom wanted to tell Viola that he, too, liked Sunday brunch. "Eleven it is."

"I'll bring dessert and mimosas."

He chuckled under his breath. Although he wasn't partial to wine, he did make an exception when it came to champagne. "That sounds like a plan."

Viola laced her palms together in a prayerful gesture. "I have to hold off gathering the fruit until I buy a canning kit."

"Don't worry about the fruit. I'll pick them for you."

“You don’t have to do that, Dom.”

“I know I don’t, but I want to help you out. Some of the fruit is ripe enough to be harvested now. There’s also a bramble on the other side of the orchard with raspberries and blackberries. I don’t know how much is left because of birds and rabbits feeding on them.”

Viola set the apple on the ground. “Perhaps there’s enough left for me to pick and use for sorbets.”

“You’ll need gloves. The thorns are wicked.”

“I’ll buy several pairs when I order the canning unit. I’ve seen enough today.”

“Are you coming back tomorrow?”

Viola shook her head. “No. I hadn’t planned on it, and I need to do some shopping.”

Reaching into the front pocket of his jeans, Dom took out his cell phone. “Give me your cell number and I’ll call to let you know when I’ve harvested some of the fruit.” She recited the numbers and he programmed them into his contacts.

Dom smiled. They may have gotten off on the wrong foot several days ago, but it now appeared they could have an easygoing friendship. “The golf cart is over near the vineyard.”

He led Viola to where acres of withering vines had once yielded grapes for the wine bottled as Bainbridge Cellars. Although he rarely drank wine, some of the bottles stored in the château’s basement had been highly prized for wine produced in a state not known for wine growing.

Dom periodically weeded the vineyard as he had the orchard, flower beds and the bramble to keep them from becoming overgrown. He had also called his father and done extensive research on insecticides to control certain species of insects.

Dom assisted Viola into the golf cart, then rounded it to sit next to her, and started up the engine. He made certain to avoid the ruts as he maneuvered onto the bridle path where at one time the hooves of horses had worn down the earth; now he made certain to mow the path every two weeks to prevent it from being overgrown with grass and weeds. Some of the other roads on the estate worn away due to age or the weather were systematically paved to permit a smooth ride.

Except for him and his father, his grandparents had been the last of what had been decades of live-in servants working for the Bainbridge family. And he never tired of listening to Josephine's lilting Irish brogue when she talked about emigrating from Ireland as a young girl and finding employment at a New York City shirtwaist factory. She'd worked there for three years before she was able to secure a position as a kitchen maid at Bainbridge House. At nineteen, she'd fallen in love with and married Michael Shaw, and then moved from the servants' quarters into the guesthouse delegated to the estate's caretaker.

"The next time I come, I'd like to see the duck pond and the golf course."

Viola's voice shattered Dom's musings. "We can do that either before or after brunch."

"Probably before."

He smiled. "I was hoping you would say that. After grits and mimosas, we probably won't feel like moving around too much."

"You're right about that. By the way, how often do you cook for yourself?"

Dom gave her a sidelong glance before returning his gaze to the road. “Every day. Why did you ask?”

“I just thought you’d cook enough to last for several meals.”

He slowed the cart as the château came into view. “Is that what you do?”

Viola shifted on the worn leather seat. “Now I do. After I gave up my apartment and moved in with my mother, I prepare enough to last us for at least three days. I’ll roast a chicken or small turkey and use the leftovers for lunch in a soup or salad. My mother really likes my meat loaf, so I make that at least once every couple of weeks. I usually make rice, mac and cheese, and occasionally potato salad for side dishes. My mother prefers fresh fruit and veggies, so that is something that must be made daily. And reheating the food in the microwave is a real time-saver.”

“What do you do during your spare time? Or do you have spare time?” he asked, correcting himself because he didn’t want Viola to think he was being facetious.

“We drive and shop.”

He blinked slowly. “You drive and shop?”

“Yes, Dom. We drive to flea markets and outlets to browse and pick up something we like. We even managed to take in a state fair where I bought a beautiful handmade quilt made in the flying geese pattern.”

Dom wanted to tell Viola that his grandmother had put together a collection of quilts that he’d wrapped in tissue paper and stored in one of the spare bedrooms. Josephine had learned to sew as a young girl, which had led her to seek employment in the dress factory. During her downtime, she could be found sewing as she listened to the radio or watched her favorite television program.

"What else do you collect?" he questioned.

"Pen and ink sketches. That's how I met Sonja. I was browsing art stalls at a street fair, looking to buy some to decorate the entryway in my apartment, when Sonja whispered to me that they were overpriced. Then she took me to a hole-in-the-wall art store near the South Street Seaport, and I found what I wanted for about half the price I would've paid the street vendor. That was the beginning of our friendship."

"And now she's engaged to your brother."

"Yup. I've always wanted a sister, and now I'm going to have one after Sonja marries Taylor." Viola paused. "Do you have any siblings?"

"I have a stepbrother, but we never call each other that. When my father married his mother, he legally adopted Evan, so he's also a Shaw." Dom maneuvered next to where Viola had parked her car. "Don't move. I'll help you out."

Viola waited for Dom to come around and assist her. He advanced a rung on her approval ladder because not only did he hold doors open for her, he was willing to help her in and out of the golf cart.

She'd grown up watching her father seat her mother at the table, open and hold doors for her, and help her in and out of her coat. A practice he'd instilled in his sons. Even Sonja had confided to her that Taylor had impeccable home training. Viola had told Sonja that their father had been raised by a societally conscious aunt who'd deemed etiquette and education equally important.

"Thank you," Viola said softly after Dom had helped

her alight. *Why couldn't I have met you when I was interested in having a relationship?* she mused.

Dom opened the driver's-side door to the Subaru, waiting until she slipped behind the wheel. Reaching into his pocket, he took out a remote device. "I'll open the gates for you," he said before he closed the door and moved away from vehicle.

As Viola left, her head was filled with their conversation. She'd enjoyed the time she'd spent with him. She liked his quiet confidence, and he had not come across as cocky or arrogant. He obviously had above-average intelligence to have accelerated two grades to graduate high school at sixteen. To say she was shocked was putting it mildly when he'd admitted working for her father's investment company. He had a background in business, yet he appeared content to perform the duties of a caretaker.

She had asked him a lot of questions, but there was one she hadn't. Had Dom asked Conrad about his children and the older man had shut him down? Is that what Dom had alluded to when he'd told her Conrad had said it was none of his business? And they also had something else in common. He had an adopted sibling.

It still nagged at Viola that her father had been so secretive when it came to Bainbridge House yet he wasn't reticent in revealing that he had been raised by an unmarried aunt after his wealthy parents had died in a boating accident. He did admit that his aunt had never wanted to marry or have children, and there were times when he'd believed she'd seen him as an inconvenience imposed on her very active social life.

She was only ten minutes into her ride to Sparta

when Dom's name and number popped up on the navigation screen. Smiling, Viola tapped the screen.

"Are you calling me to make certain I didn't give you the wrong number?"

There was silence and then he laughed softly. "Is that what you do, Viola? Give dudes the wrong number when you don't want to be bothered with them?"

"I've been known to do that a few times."

"I never took you for a naughty girl."

She laughed. "I can be very naughty when I want to be. I've been told they are a lot more fun than good girls."

Viola bit her lip, wondering where that had come from. She usually didn't engage in witty repartee, especially with men. She had always been uncomfortable with flirting. She had missed that phase in her adolescence because of her homeschooling. And whenever she'd observed the groups of boys and girls at the mall or their favorite hangout spot in town, she'd envied the easygoing interaction between the sexes.

"So I've been told," Dom said. There was a hint of laughter in his voice. "I'm glad you gave me the correct number, or I would've been forced to ask Taylor for it."

She sobered quickly. "I'd prefer you don't use my brother as a go-between unless it has to do with the restoration."

There came another noticeable pause. "Point taken. I called because I forgot to thank you."

"For what?"

"For a most enjoyable morning."

Viola laughed softly. "That goes double for me. It was very enlightening."

"Now that we both agree, I'm going to hang up."

"Goodbye, Dom."

"Later, Viola."

She tapped the screen, disconnecting the call and chiding herself for questioning why Dom had called her. Was she so distrusting of men that she viewed them as having ulterior motives? Viola had only had two of what she considered serious relationships, and it was the first that had been imprinted on her memory like an indelible tattoo. During her sophomore year at the Culinary Institute, she'd found herself involved with another student. They'd talked about marrying and opening a restaurant together until he'd confessed to sleeping with another girl and getting her pregnant. The revelation had come within months of their graduation. Viola had been so devastated by his duplicity that she'd taken the summer off, flown to Europe and enrolled in several cooking courses. Putting thousands of miles between her and the States had been the perfect balm for her to put heartbreak in the rearview mirror and concentrate on honing her craft.

Viola tightened her grip on the steering wheel. She had to force herself not to exceed the speed limit; she couldn't wait to get back to the condo and search for the items she needed to turn the harvested fruit into jellies and jams.

She parked in the garage and entered the condo through the door from the laundry room. Ideas were still tumbling over themselves in her head when she took off her boots and left them on a thick rubber mat. Twenty minutes after changing into a tank top and cut-offs, she sat on a chaise with her laptop.

Once she'd committed to coming aboard to supervise the kitchen, Patrick had called her to say she could purchase whatever she needed to make the kitchens fully functional. It had taken her a while to process that her nitpicking, penny-pinching brother was giving her a blank check, while Taylor had complained about Patrick questioning every expenditure he'd submitted to structurally restore the château. Now she would take Patrick at his word when he'd stressed the word *needed.*

Viola had learned at an early age that her brothers not only doted on her, but also let her get away with things she shouldn't because they didn't want backlash from Elise, who'd tended to be overprotective when it came to her daughter. But Viola had also learned, as she'd matured, not to push them too far since they would collectively stop talking to her. Having her brothers shut her out had been emotionally crushing for Viola, so the pouting and hissy fits had become less and less until they'd stopped completely.

She powered down the laptop, reached for her cell phone and went downstairs to the kitchen to prepare lunch. Opening the refrigerator, she checked the vegetable drawer and took out a plastic container with finely shredded green, red and napa cabbage at the same time she heard a familiar ringtone. She closed the door with her hip and scooped up the cell phone off the countertop.

"Hey, Sonja."

"It's official. I'm pregnant."

Viola couldn't stop grinning. "Congratulations! When's your due date?"

"Late May or early June."

"We're going to have to celebrate."

"That's what Taylor said, but right now I don't think I can get up the energy to get dressed to go out."

"What if I fix a special dinner for you and Taylor?"

"You really don't have to do that, Vi."

"Yes, I do. I'll come over tomorrow and make Sunday dinner. Just tell me what you want to eat."

"Right now, I'm craving soup."

Viola smiled. "What kind of soup?"

"It doesn't matter, Vi."

It was apparent Sonja was craving comfort food. "Then soup it is."

"Thanks, Vi."

"There's no need to thank me. I'm going to make certain your baby is going to enjoy whatever his or her mother eats, because Titi Viola intends to become their mama's private chef."

"And I'll wind up so spoiled that I probably won't want to look at another pot," Sonja said, laughing.

Viola also laughed. "Not to worry. I experience withdrawals whenever I'm away from a stove. I never knew when I made the decision to become a chef that it would take over my life. I love everything about it, from prepping to plating. Even my mother said she created a cooking monster once she'd allowed me to assist her in the kitchen."

"You have a gift, Vi, and you're going to make a name for yourself once Bainbridge House opens for business."

Viola wanted to tell Sonja it wasn't so much about making a name for herself as autonomy. And unlike the former boss who'd tended to overlook her skills, she didn't want to make the same mistake once she hired her staff. There were cooks who began as kitchen help and eventually rose through the ranks to become executive chefs in the very kitchen where they'd begun their tenure. She also wanted to make certain female chefs were also well represented at Bainbridge House.

"I'll see you guys tomorrow."

She ended the call and concentrated on gathering the ingredients she needed to make a slaw with spicy Thai vinaigrette. Once she'd become proficient re-creating popular French and Italian dishes, she'd begun experimenting with Asian recipes, and whenever she made the slaw for her friends or family, there were never any leftovers.

Viola nodded. Not only would she make soups for Sonja, but she'd also treat her and Taylor to an Asian-themed dinner. She activated the Notes feature on her cell phone and entered the ingredients she needed to purchase from the supermarket for Sunday's dinner.

## *Chapter Six*

"Damn, Viola. What do you have in here? Rocks?"

Viola smiled as Taylor hoisted the picnic hamper onto one shoulder. "Stuff."

Taylor glared at her. "This stuff better be worth having to deal with aching muscles later on."

"Quit jawing, brother love. You must be getting old and soft because it's not that heavy. I managed to put it into the car without throwing out my back." She'd loaded the hamper with cookware and containers filled with the ingredients she needed to cook enough for Taylor and Sonja to last them several days.

"I'm hardly old," Taylor mumbled under his breath.

"If not old, then soft," Viola countered.

"I won't need to work out if I lift *stuff* weighing a hundred pounds every day."

She followed her brother up the stairs and into the

condo Taylor had rented for Sonja once she'd agreed to accept the position as the architectural historian for the restoration project. He had given up his own Connecticut rental to move into their mother's Sparta condo while Elise lived in the family's Belleville, New Jersey, home until she was able to sell it.

Everything changed once Taylor and Sonja became a couple and he moved out of his mother's unit and in with Sonja. Viola felt as if the Williamsons were playing musical chairs with their residences after she hadn't renewed the lease on her apartment and gone to live with her mother.

Viola, Taylor, Tariq and Joaquin had all agreed to eventually make the estate guesthouses their permanent residences, unlike prior Bainbridge generations who had designated the entire second floor in the château solely for members of their extended family, which included parents, children, grandparents, grandchildren, aunts, uncles and cousins.

The one time she'd asked Sonja about Conrad's ancestors, Sonja had determined that Charles Garland Bainbridge was a self-made millionaire who had accumulated his wealth investing in steamship travel, real estate and electricity. Charles had purchased the château from an impoverished French nobleman, disassembled and transported the building across the Atlantic by steamship, and then had it reassembled on a hilltop in northern New Jersey.

Viola glanced around the kitchen with its open floor plan. "Where's Sonja?" Viola asked Taylor.

He set the hamper on the floor next to the cooking island. "She's upstairs working on the computer, and she's been at it for hours."

"Doing what, Taylor?"

"Updating that damn inventory of thousands of plates, spoons and heaven knows what the hell else, when she should be resting, because she's always complaining that she's tired. And whenever I say anything to her, she claims I'm trying to control her life."

"If you're telling her when to rest, then Sonja's right about you attempting to control her."

Taylor threw up both hands. "Now you're taking her side?"

"It's not about sides, Taylor, and you know I don't like being the go-between for you—or any of my brothers—and your partners. I'm going to say this once. As a pregnant woman, Sonja's body will tell her when she's fatigued or when she needs to eat. Have you forgotten that her ex controlled every phase of her life? Please don't let history repeat itself when you try and pressure her to do something she doesn't want to do, because you'll lose Sonja *and* your baby."

A deep frown settled into Taylor's handsome features. "That's never going to happen."

Viola's eyebrows lifted slightly. Taylor was exhibiting behavior she'd rarely witnessed. He always appeared calm and in control and not prone to outbursts. This made her wonder if his assuming complete responsibility of restoring the estate and the reality that he was going to be a father was affecting his emotional well-being. "Because you say so?" she questioned.

"No!" he snapped angrily. "It's because I promised Sonja that I would always be there for her and not desert her like my father did to my mother the minute he found out she was carrying his baby."

"When are you going to let that go, Taylor? You

never knew your father and neither did I, and we all agreed once we were adopted that Conrad was our father."

Elise had put all her children in therapy to deal with the circumstances that had led them to becoming a statistic in the foster care system. She'd wanted them to know where they'd come from, though it had never been her intent to completely erase the tragic circumstances surrounding the early years of their lives.

"Sonja knows you would never desert her, Taylor," Viola added in a quiet voice. "But she will continue to have flashbacks about what she went through with her ex-husband if you treat her as if she's unable to make her own decisions about her body."

"I just don't want her to overdo it."

"I know you're concerned about her because of the baby, but—"

"It's not only the baby, Viola," Taylor interrupted. "I'd be concerned even if she weren't pregnant. I keep telling her that the projected timeline for completing the restoration is two years, so there's no need for her to rush with cataloging everything."

"You may have two years, but Sonja doesn't. I can understand her wanting to complete her project before she has the baby, because then the focus and priority will not be classifying patterns on plates or forks."

Taylor ran a hand over his face. "I'm going to try to do better."

"Don't try, Taylor. Just do it."

"Thanks, baby sis."

She smiled. "For what, brother love?"

"For the pep talk and for reminding me what Sonja went through with her jackass ex."

"There's no need to thank me. You've helped me out enough when I had problems with some of my jackass boyfriends."

Taylor was the only one Viola had felt comfortable enough with to unburden herself about the men in her life, especially the ones she'd believed were Mr. Right when in reality they'd been Mr. Right Now. It had taken a while for her to figure out that not all men were like her father or brothers. It hadn't been once burned twice shy, but twice burned thrice shy. After her last relationship fizzled two years ago, she'd promised to give herself at least five years before contemplating another. It was now two down and three to go.

"Do you need my help with anything?" Taylor asked.

"I don't think so," she said. "But I would like you to hear me out about a few ideas I have for some of my proposals."

"Talk to me."

Viola unlatched the top of the hamper and removed containers of food she'd prepped earlier that morning, setting them on the countertop. She told Taylor about wanting to harvest the fruit and berries and can them for future use in the hotel's kitchens. "Those I can now will have to be used within a year, so what we don't use, you can give your workers. But then there's next fall's harvest. I want to put together welcoming baskets for our guests who check in, filled with sample jars of jams and jellies, along with sample soaps, lotions, notepads and pens. We could also stock the same items in the gift shop with Bainbridge House labels." She paused. "Then there's something else."

Taylor angled his head. "What else do you want, Viola?"

"I'd like to erect at least two greenhouses near the vineyard to supply the kitchens with fresh fruits and vegetables year-round."

"Did Sonja mention greenhouses to you?"

"No," Viola answered quickly, wondering if Taylor thought they were coconspirators. "She's never mentioned the word to me."

"I ask because when I took her to Bainbridge House for the first time, she said we can save a lot of money growing our own produce in greenhouses year-round and offer farm-to-table dining. She claims when she was in Europe, she'd eaten at restaurants that provided meals with locally sourced food."

Violet laughed. "I can't believe how much we think alike."

Taylor also chuckled. "Order whatever you need, baby sis."

Viola blew him an air kiss. Taylor was the only brother who referred to her as his baby sister. "Thank you, brother love. Now, do I have a limit as to how much I can spend for the greenhouses?" The protocol was for her to submit her requests to Taylor for his approval, and he in turn would submit them to Patrick for payment.

"Nope. For some unknown reason, Patrick has loosened the purse strings where you're concerned, while I must give him a detailed written requisition for every expenditure before he will approve it."

"So, that's why he didn't ask me to give him a projected budget."

"He told me, and I quote, '*if Bainbridge House is to become a luxury hotel, then Viola should have whatever she wants or needs to achieve a five-star dining establishment.*'"

Viola's jaw dropped. "Our Patrick said that?"

Taylor nodded. "That, he did. I kept asking myself where is the Patrick I know and who has taken his place."

"Word," Viola drawled. "He never approves anything that's more than three figures unless you quote him verse and chapter and why you want him to pay for it. Maybe Andrea is rubbing off on him."

"Please don't mention her name around Mom. I don't know why, but she really doesn't like the girl."

"No comment. I've said more than I want about future in-laws, because you know how I hate being in the middle of family squabbles, and I refuse to take sides where it concerns Patrick and his fiancée."

"Point taken, and I'm sorry I involved you again with—"

"Don't, Taylor. There's no need to apologize."

He nodded, smiling. "Okay. What's on today's menu?"

Viola removed a small wok and a bottle of peanut oil from the hamper. "Asian fusion. I prepped and marinated everything in advance to cut down on wait time to eat."

"Did someone mention eat?"

Viola turned around when she heard Sonja's voice. Dressed in sweats, with her hair styled in a ponytail, her friend appeared not much older than a college student. "Yes, I did."

Sonja approached Taylor and brushed a kiss on his cheek. "Why didn't you tell me Vi was here?"

Taylor met Viola's eyes over Sonja's head. "I didn't want to bother you."

Sonja kissed him again. "You're never a bother."

Viola lowered her head, hiding the smile parting her lips. It was obvious Taylor had overreacted—once again. Hopefully, after their talk, he would see things more clearly when interacting with his future wife.

"You told me you wanted soup, so I made black-eyed peas with ham, split pea soup also with diced ham and white bean, sausage and kale. I used reduced sodium chicken broth to counter the salt in the ham. This is all for later in the week."

Sonja approached Viola and hugged her. "You're the best. Do you need help with anything?"

She pointed to quart jars filled with soup. "You can put those in the fridge. I'll need a baking sheet, Dutch oven, a large skillet and large salad bowl."

"I'll get the pots and pans," Taylor volunteered. "After I set the table, I'm going into the family room to watch baseball."

Viola exchanged a wink with Sonja. Taylor would be the last to admit it, but he was a sports junkie. If he wasn't attending a baseball, basketball or hockey game, he was an armchair spectator.

"What on earth did you bring for today?" Sonja asked.

"I remember you talking about missing New York City Chinese takeout, so I decided to bring a little Asian fusion to north Jersey, beginning with an Asian slaw with Thai vinaigrette. I cut back on the spice because I didn't know if you could tolerate it in your condition."

Sonja placed a hand against her belly over the sweatshirt. "So far, so good, when it comes to spicy foods, but I try not to overdo it because the last thing I need is heartburn."

Viola set a bamboo steamer on the countertop.

"We're also going to have pork and scallion dumplings, sticky hoisin spareribs, dim sum pot stickers, General Tso's chicken tenders, Mongolian beef meatballs, and fried rice."

"Hold up!" Taylor called out. "Who's going to eat all this food?"

"You, me and Sonja will have some today, and you and Sonja can enjoy leftovers during the week. These are some of the items I want to list on the bar menu as appetizers. And if it's all right with you, I'd like to make them for your work crew as a preholiday appreciation party."

"It's more than all right with me. Just do your thing, baby sis."

Sonja stored the last jar in the fridge and closed the door. "Have you made up your menus?"

Viola tapped her forehead with a finger. "Many of the ideas are still in here. I'd like specific menus for breakfast, lunch and dinner. The proposed bar and lounge food will be limited to appetizers and small plates. I'm seriously thinking about offering a breakfast and lunch buffet because there's no need for a full waitstaff during those hours. Dinner will be table service and that's when I'll need most of my waitstaff. I also want to offer high tea in the solarium."

When she'd asked Taylor for the dimensions of the kitchens, he had sent her the blueprints of the château's interiors. She'd been astounded by the number and size of the rooms, thinking of many of them as conspicuous excess. Charles Bainbridge had apparently succeeded in his goal to flaunt his wealth with a lifestyle mirroring European royalty.

Taylor took down a stack of plates from an overhead

cabinet. "Do you plan to serve those little sandwiches without the crust?"

Viola knew exactly what her brother was referring to because the one time he'd attended a high tea, he'd complained incessantly about eating cucumber sandwiches. He'd claimed cucumbers belonged in salads not between slices of white bread. "I will make traditional high tea finger sandwiches with egg salad, smoked salmon, shrimp, chicken, ham and Brie. I will also include strawberries topped with clotted cream, macarons, tea cakes, tartlets, and bouchées with tarragon and mustard lobster, and wild mushrooms, garlic and thyme."

"What are bouchées?" Taylor asked.

"They are puff pastries with savory fillings."

"That sounds a lot more appetizing to me than cucumber sandwiches. Now if you were serving sliders, I'd sign up for high tea."

Viola rolled her eyes at him. "I am not going to serve sliders. What I don't understand is why you didn't try the other sandwiches." She washed her hands in one of the double sinks and dried them on a paper towel before slipping on disposal gloves.

"I wasn't willing to risk it. For me, it had become one and done. Speaking of done, I'm done here so, if you don't need me, I'm going to watch the game."

"How did it go with Dom?" Sonja whispered to Viola after Taylor left the kitchen.

Viola gave Sonja a puzzled stare. "What are you talking about?" she asked.

"You said Dom was going to take you on a tour of the estate. I just want to know if…" Her words trailed off. "You know?"

Viola knew exactly what Sonja was implying, but decided she wasn't going to make it easy for the architectural historian. "No, I don't know. Spit it out, Sonja."

"Do you like him?"

"Like him how? As a friend or someone I could possibly get involved with?"

"The latter."

Viola flashed a Cheshire cat grin. "I'm sorry to pop your matchmaking bubble. We've decided on friendship."

"You actually talked about that?"

"Yes. Why does that surprise you, Sonja?"

She blinked slowly. "I don't know."

"You should know I'm not one to hold my tongue. I must admit, we did verbally spar with each other the first time we met, but yesterday turned out well."

"When are you going to see him again?"

Viola couldn't help but laugh. "What's up with the inquisition?"

Sonja affected a sheepish expression. "He seems like a nice guy, so I was hoping something would happen between the two of you."

"Nothing's going to happen. Dom has trust issues. So do I."

"He told you that?"

Viola nodded. "Yes. Apparently, it was the result of a bad marriage, and you know that I keep hooking up with users. I must have a big red Use Me on my forehead because every man with whom I've become involved has tried to take advantage of me. And the downside is that I didn't realize it until it was too late."

"Look on the bright side, Vi. You were smart enough not to marry any of them."

"Thank goodness for that." There had been a time when Viola had fantasized about falling in love and marrying, but that was before she'd become extremely competitive *and* career driven. "Do you want me to fix something for you before we sit down to eat?"

"Nah, I'm good. I had a bowl of fruit a couple of hours ago. I try to have small snacks in between my regular meals." She rounded the cooking island and sat on a stool. "I'm going to sit here and watch you work your magic."

"I thought you were going to be my sous chef," Viola said teasingly.

"Girl, please. It takes me forever to peel and slice plantains because I'm afraid of cutting myself. I've seen you wield a knife and I'm always amazed when you slice and dice something as small as a garlic clove."

Viola removed a bibbed apron and bandana from the hamper. She covered her hair and then slipped the apron over her shirt and jeans. "It takes a lot of practice. You just need to make certain to keep your fingers out of the way. What's happening with your wedding plans?" she asked, steering the topic of conversation away from herself.

"Taylor and I have finally decided to marry a week before Christmas. I did call my mother to let her know to send out save the date cards to the family. I'll email your mother tomorrow and give her the same information."

"That gives us exactly twelve weeks to finalize everything. Do you think Taylor will be able to complete his projects before that?"

Sonja blew out a breath and shook her head. "I don't know. He claims a lot of the space on the first floor and more than half the suites on the second floor will be completed before that time."

Viola made a mental note to remind Taylor that the kitchen had to be updated and ready weeks before the wedding so she would be able to use it. She didn't want to wait until the last moment to find out that there was something wrong with the plumbing or that the stoves and ovens didn't work. She didn't want to micromanage her brother and trusted Taylor knew what had to be operational at least two weeks before his wedding.

She emptied a plastic bag with the shredded green, red and napa cabbage into a large bowl and then added sliced green onion, chopped green pepper, kosher salt and finely ground pepper to the slaw. "I'm not going to add the vinaigrette until just before serving it."

Sonja propped an elbow on the countertop and rested her chin on the heel of her hand. "I didn't know you were familiar with Asian cuisine."

"I met a chef at a cooking show whose parents owned an Asian fusion restaurant on Long Island. When we started talking, he said he wanted to branch out on his own, but wasn't certain what type of restaurant he wanted to open. When I asked Kenzi what dishes he liked to eat and he said Italian, I offered him a proposition. If he taught me Asian dishes, I would return the favor and teach him what I knew about Italian cuisine. In other words, it became a win-win for both of us."

"How long did the lessons last?"

"Almost two years."

"What I don't understand, Vi, is why didn't he enroll in a cooking school?"

"He didn't want his parents to know that he was planning to leave the family business to go out on his own. They'd expected him to take over the restaurant once they retired."

"Did he leave?"

"I don't know. I lost contact with him. He used to come to my apartment during my days off and we would alternate lessons. One day I waited for him to come and when I called his cell, the recording said his mailbox was full. I called him the following week and that's when I found out the number was no longer working. I didn't have an address for him, and he never told me where his parents had their restaurant."

"Do you think something terrible happened to him?"

"I don't know, Sonja. What I do know is that I'll never forget him because he taught me so much about Asian cuisine that would've taken me years of traveling to different countries to learn. My cell phone number is the same and so is my email address. If he wants to contact me then he can."

"Oh my goodness. That smells delicious."

Viola had just removed the cover of the container with the Mongolian beef meatballs. "It's the grated garlic and ginger. Whenever I make them into little cocktail meatballs, they disappear as soon as they're set out on a table."

Sonja lowered her arm. "Now you've got me thinking about what I'd like for the wedding menu."

"What about it?"

"If we have a cocktail hour, then it can be Asian-inspired with everything we're having today. Can you make sesame prawn toasts?"

Viola nodded. She'd learned to make the popular dishes featured in most Chinese takeout restaurants, including chow mein. "Yes. Are you sure that's what you want?" she asked.

"Yes. I've thought about the main menu, and I really don't want the ubiquitous prime rib, chicken or fish entrées."

"You and Taylor have plenty of time to decide on what you want to serve your guests."

"What if we decide to have a buffet instead of a sit-down dinner?"

"A buffet will offer your guests a lot more variety," Viola said. "You can have Southern, Caribbean, Italian, and even Middle Eastern dishes. It's your call, Sonja."

A beat passed. "I want the buffet."

Viola was hoping Sonja would select a buffet. It would give her the opportunity to showcase her knowledge of different cuisines. "I will need your final head count before I plan the menu."

Sonja nodded. "I'll make certain to keep you updated after the response cards are returned. Once I hear back from your mother, I'll order invitations. I also forgot to tell you that I've decided to hire an event planner. There aren't enough hours in the day for me to work and plan a wedding. And it's not right to impose on you when you'll have enough responsibility planning and preparing food for our guests and families."

"I'm also going to hire a couple of assistants," Viola admitted. She'd given it a lot of thought once she'd realized it would be impossible for her to supervise the kitchen at the same time she would stand as maid of honor. And that meant she had to hire someone with a few years of experience to work unsupervised.

"I feel so helpless sitting here watching you cook,"

Sonja said after Viola had preheated the oven to bake the ribs.

Leaning over, Viola handed Sonja a pair of disposable gloves. “You can line a baking sheet with parchment paper for the meatballs. They’ll bake at the same temperature as the ribs.”

Seventy-five minutes after walking into the condo, Viola sat at the table with Taylor and Sonja, and she knew her teacher would be proud of his student. Everything was delicious. A ripple of excitement eddied through her. Catering the wedding reception would bring her a step closer to the time when Bainbridge House opened for business and she would be listed as the hotel’s executive chef.

Unknowingly, her brother and Sonja had become taste testers for her Asian fusion dishes and had given her rave reviews. Her thoughts shifted to Dom. In another week, she would taste test and rate his shrimp and grits. She still hadn’t decided what to prepare so that he could evaluate what she intended to include on the hotel’s menus.

## *Chapter Seven*

Dom joined the work crew in the small ballroom where Taylor held his regularly scheduled Monday-morning meetings. A table in the center of the room was covered with tubes of plans and several laptops. As a volunteer, he wasn't mandated to attend, but Taylor had invited him, and Dom found it the best way to stay informed as to the progress of the restoration. If Taylor had a two-year timeline to complete the restoration, Dom also had the same timeline. He then had to decide whether to stay on as caretaker or leave Bainbridge House forever.

Robinson Harris entered the room and stood next to Taylor. Dom had learned the two men had worked together at a Connecticut engineering firm and Taylor had brought the architectural engineer on board as the project foreman.

Taylor cleared his voice. His jeans, sweatshirt and

work boots made him indistinguishable from the other contract workers. "I'm going to keep this short this morning." He smiled when murmurs filled the room. "Yes, I know I can be rather long-winded, but today it's different. Firstly, I'd like to let everyone know we are ahead of schedule with expanding more than half the second-floor suites. All the windows on three of the floors have been replaced and that only leaves the ones in the turrets, which are on special order and are expected to arrive sometime early next year." He paused and exchanged a look with Robinson. "I also want to inform everyone that I'm getting married in December, and we plan to hold the wedding here at Bainbridge House."

Dom applauded with the others as Taylor and Robinson exchanged fist bumps. Within seconds, however, Dom sobered, wondering how Taylor planned to hold a wedding at the château when there was so much more work to be done.

"I know most of you are wondering why Sonja and I made the decision to have our wedding here," Taylor continued, "but I can't think of a better venue, especially during the most festive time of the year. We're going to have twelve weeks to make repairs to the small ballroom, solarium, the great room and the first-floor kitchen. Robbie will oversee updating the elevator, so guests won't have to trudge up the staircase with their bags. And before the hotel opens officially, we plan to install a second elevator."

One of the electricians raised his hand to get Taylor's attention. "You're renovating twelve of the thirty rooms on the second floor. Will that be enough for your guests?"

Taylor smiled. “I’m almost certain it will be. The larger suites can accommodate up to four people and the smaller ones, two. I know this is short notice, but if anyone wants overtime then see Robbie and he’ll sign you up. Thank you, folks. Dom, please don’t leave. I’d like to talk to you about something.”

Dom waited until the others left before approaching Taylor. “Congratulations on your upcoming wedding.”

“Thanks. When I mentioned holding the wedding here, I noticed most of the men were shocked.”

Dom wanted to tell Taylor he was shocked when he’d first seen Sonja wearing a diamond ring on her left hand. It was days later that Taylor had revealed he and Sonja were engaged, but wanted to wait for a while before setting a date for their wedding. “I must admit, I was also shocked. I thought you would have waited for the grand opening before getting married.”

“I’d thought so, too, but unforeseen events call for quick decisions.”

Dom did not have to be clairvoyant to know what Taylor was alluding to. Sonja was pregnant. “Congratulations again.”

Taylor ran a hand over his face as he exhaled an audible breath. “Thanks. I want to talk to you about my sister.”

Dom went completely still. He did not want a repeat with Taylor where it had to do with Viola. He hadn’t backed down when Taylor had accused him of coming on to Sonja, and he had no intentions of backing down again. He did wonder what Viola had told her brother about their time together.

“What about her?” He knew he sounded defensive yet was past caring how Taylor interpreted his response.

"I'd like you to help her put up a couple of greenhouses near the vineyard. She's gotten it into her head that she wants to grow her own produce for farm-to-table dining."

Dom relaxed. So, it wasn't about his interaction with Viola. "I agree with her. Why should she buy produce from farms when she can grow what she needs right here?"

Taylor's inky-black eyebrows lifted in an equally dark face. "You agree with her?"

"Of course, Taylor." He wanted to tell the man that he should give his sister credit for her forward thinking. Locally sourced organic foods were a plus when served at gourmet dining establishments.

"Well, I guess that settles it. You're the point person for this project. However, I'd like to warn you that my sister can be very opinionated about a few things."

"If it pertains to food, then I have no problem with that. And if she doesn't cross the line to tell me how to install an irrigation system, then we're good."

Taylor folded his arms over his chest. "I think she may have just met her match," he said under his breath.

"I would like to get one thing straight between us before I begin working with Viola."

"What's that?" Taylor asked.

"I don't want a repeat of what you and I had about Sonja. I live here and I don't want you in my face about what goes on between me and your sister."

Taylor stared at the toes of his work boots. "I suppose you're never going to let me live that down."

"That's where you're wrong," Dom countered. "I'm done with that."

Taylor's head popped up. "Good. Viola is a grown

woman and I've learned not to get involved with her relationships with other men. Unfortunately, there was one time when I had to intervene and after that I promised myself never again."

Dom wondered what could've been so extreme that Taylor had had to come to the defense of his sister. "She's lucky she has a brother willing to protect her."

"Brothers," Taylor said, smiling. "I'm known as the nice brother. Tariq, Patrick and Joaquin will challenge professional wrestlers in a free-for-all even if they know they're going to get their asses kicked."

Dom chuckled. "Well, damn."

Taylor smiled. "Whenever all of us get together, it can get a little raucous. You'll get to meet them sometime before the wedding."

"They sound like fun."

Taylor shook his head. "It all depends on what you mean by fun. Thanks again for agreeing to work with Viola."

"No problem, Taylor. Send me a text if you need me for something." All the work crew had walkie-talkies to communicate with one another. Dom was the exception because of his status as a volunteer.

Dom left the château and headed for the building to get the riding mower. He needed to cut the grass on the golf course and then pick ripened pears and apples before it got too hot. He also wasn't ready to tell Taylor that he and his sister had already made plans to work together harvesting fruit. Other than cooking for each other, setting up the greenhouses would give Dom another excuse to spend time with Viola.

Three hours later, Dom propped a ladder up against several trees in the orchard and managed to pick enough ripened apples to fill two bushels and another for pears. Later in the week, he planned to tackle whatever was left on the cherry trees. Flocks of birds and a pack of squirrels had come to eat as much of the fruit as their tiny bellies could hold while a family of rabbits feasted on whatever had fallen to the ground.

Taylor mentioning his brothers reminded him of the time when Viola had asked if he'd met Patrick. He hadn't lied to her when he'd said no, but also hadn't admitted that he was aware that she and her brothers had been adopted by Conrad and his wife. He didn't know the circumstances surrounding their adoption and, when he'd asked Conrad about it, that was when he was told it was none of his business. Dom wanted to tell the estate's new owners that not sharing DNA did not make one any less family. His father had adopted Evan, and they couldn't be any closer if they'd shared the same bloodline. There were a lot of families with closely held secrets, and the Shaws, Bainbridges and Williamsons were no different.

When Viola parked in front of the château, Dom was waiting. He'd called her to inform her he'd opened the gates and would be at the château when she arrived.

She smiled up at him as he opened the driver's-side door for her. Dark tailored slacks had replaced the jeans and she had also exchanged her sweater for a tangerine-orange peplum blouse. She'd tried on several pairs of shoes before deciding on black ballet flats. But just for good measure, she had put a pair of boots in the trunk.

Seeing Dom after a week was a stark reminder of how attractive he was, and when he stared at her with those large green eyes, she felt as if he could discern how much she really liked him. He was the first man with whom she'd felt comfortable enough to be herself. With Dom, there was no pretense or censoring herself.

Extending his hand, he helped her out, steered her around to the other side of the Subaru, and opened the passenger's-side door. "Please get in. I'm going to drive home."

Viola reacted like an automaton as she slipped onto the seat and secured her seat belt. Dom got in the driver's seat and adjusted the seat to accommodate his longer legs. "No golf cart today?"

He smiled and fine lines fanned out around his luminous eyes. "Nope."

"Why not?"

He gave her a quick glance before starting the engine. "Because we're going to take a different route today, and the golf cart is too unsteady to navigate the bumps and potholes."

"When are they going to fix the roads?"

"That's not going to be for a while. Trucks carrying heavy loads will just cause more damage during renovations to the guesthouses. Once the entire estate is landscaped, then the paving company will come in and pave the roads."

Viola realized Dom was right about the uneven landscape. The Subaru's suspension enabled the vehicle to glide over some of the deep ruts. "I'm trying to imagine how this property would've been before the invention of cars, when horses and wagons were used to transport people and goods."

"There's no doubt an estate this size employed a full staff to keep everything in pristine condition."

"How much do you know about the Bainbridge family?" Viola asked Dom.

"I know only what has been passed down through generations. I'm certain Sonja will uncover a lot more than what I've heard."

"I'm sure she will.

Dom nodded. "There's several bushels of fruit waiting for you at my place."

"I thought you were going to wait for me to pick them with you."

"You wanted to wait until today to pick apples while wearing Cinderella slippers."

Viola stared, unable to believe he'd just said that. "Do you realize how sexist that sounds?"

"Don't get your nose out of joint, Viola. You can't deny that your shoes are better suited for dancing than traipsing through an orchard."

"For your information, I do have boots in the trunk. What's the matter, Dom? Cat got your tongue?" she taunted when he didn't respond.

"I'm sorry," he mumbled under his breath.

"Oh, no, Mr. Shaw. Say it like you mean it." In that instant, she'd learned something about the man sitting beside her. He didn't like losing.

"I am sorry, Miss Viola Williamson, for sounding sexist. Is that humbling enough for you?"

Crossing her arms under her breasts, Viola glanced out the passenger's-side window. Fast-moving dark clouds swept across the sky, blocking out the sun. "I'll think about it." She didn't intend to let him off that easily.

"While you're thinking about it, we're here."

"Please pop the trunk. I need to get the basket with the wine and dessert."

"Don't worry. I'll get it."

Dom knew he'd made a serious error in judgment with the remark. He knew Viola wasn't one to hold back when speaking her mind, and Taylor had warned him that she was opinionated. But Dom wanted them to get along without engaging in a power struggle for dominance. Perhaps he'd been alone so long that he had to relearn how to relate to not only a woman but an independent one who didn't need a man to validate her. He parked behind his pickup, which had seen better days. Every time he'd planned to sell it for scrap, something wouldn't allow him to part with it.

"How old is that truck?" Viola asked.

"Older than you."

"I'm twenty-eight."

"I did say it's older than you. In fact, it's older than both of us."

"Does it run?"

Dom laughed as he undid his seat belt. "Lollipop runs whenever she feels like it."

"Why do you keep it?"

"It has sentimental value. I'd learned to drive an automatic, but not one with a stick shift. My dad refused to buy me a car because he said if Lollipop was good enough for him, and she was still running, then she was good enough for me. And because I didn't want to rely on him to chauffeur me around, I decided it was Lollipop or nothing. However, whenever she breaks down, I manage to fix her."

"Why haven't you restored the body?"

Dents, holes and rust had worn away most of the original red paint. "I can only fix what's under the hood. I know nothing about body work."

"If I owned her, I would have the body restored."

Stretching out his right arm, Dom rested it over the back of Viola's seat. He hadn't realized he was holding his breath when she turned to stare at him and found himself mesmerized by the green and gold glints in her eyes. "You like old cars?"

She smiled, bringing his gaze to linger on the sensual curve of her sexy mouth. "I like anything old. Old cars, clothes and classic black-and-white movies. My mother claims I was born too late because I would've done well back in the days of the Roaring Twenties. I was invited to a Halloween party, and I managed to find a beautiful flapper dress with the required accessories. I'm just waiting for the time when I can wear it again."

Dom met her eyes. "I'm certain if you'd lived here during that time you would've felt right at home. I have photos of some of the grand parties once held at Bainbridge House. One of these days, I'll get them out and let you see them. I'm going to warn you that if you like old, then you'll probably like most of the furnishings in my place."

Dom got out and glanced up at the darkened sky. The wind had also picked up and he wanted to get inside before it began raining. He removed the basket from the trunk, closed it, and then came around to assist Viola. Holding her small hand, he led her up the path to his home. In that instant, he realized he'd been waiting, counting down the days when he would have the opportunity for her to see where he lived. He opened the door and stepped aside for her to enter the house that had become his sanctuary.

He'd spent several years renovating it to his specifications. It had begun with removing walls to create an atmosphere of openness. Then he'd gutted the kitchen to install new cabinets, an island and breakfast bar, banquette and state-of-the-art appliances. He had also put in a bathroom between the kitchen and pantry. His next project was to update the mud and laundry room with new lighting.

Viola hadn't known what to expect when she walked into Dom's house. A basket of dried herbs sat on a large, round pedestal table in the spacious foyer, which opened into the living room with a sofa and overstuffed chairs covered with fabrics she recalled seeing in some of the homes and shops she'd visited while abroad. Roughhewn side tables were also from a bygone era.

"It's beautiful," she whispered as she stared at the tightly packed built-in bookcase. Model ships lined one shelf, another with bottles of spirits, and two with a collection of fragile crystal stemware. She moved closer to the bookcase, peering at framed black-and-white photographs of people wearing clothes spanning nearly a century.

"It's not too outdated for you?" Dom asked behind her.

"No. I love it. Your furniture reminds me of what I saw when I visited some of the homes in Paris."

"You've got a good eye because all of the furniture in this house was imported from France. The exception is the kitchen, which I had to update."

Viola traced her fingers over the floral fabric on a

club chair with a matching footstool. "This upholstery looks new. When did you replace it?"

"Two years ago. Once I decided I wanted an open floor plan, that's when the furniture also underwent a makeover. I was offered a tidy sum from an antiques dealer for the tables, but I couldn't part with them because it would be like selling a piece of my family's legacy."

"How long has your family lived in this house?"

"I'm the fourth generation caretaker to have occupied this house."

Viola gave him a long, penetrating stare and tried to process the length of time his family had occupied the same domicile. "That long?"

"Yes, Viola. It's been that long. Do you find that shocking?"

"Yes and no. If my father had decided to raise us at Bainbridge House, then it would be the same as with your family." A slight frown appeared between her eyes when Viola tried imagining living in the same house where great-grandparents several generations removed had resided. "It appears as if your family and my father's have been inexorably intertwined for generations. I wonder how often that has occurred."

"It's probably more common in other countries where positions are passed down through generations than here in the States. If someone is a butler on an estate, then it was probable that his father or grandfather were also butlers."

Viola wanted to remind Dom that he also was a carryover from prior generations of caretakers. She still couldn't wrap her head around the fact that he had earned a college degree yet was content in his role as caretaker on an estate where the new family did not share the bloodline of the last surviving heir.

"I need to take the dessert out of the basket because it needs be refrigerated."

"What did you make?"

"Tiramisu."

Dom pressed a fist to his mouth. "No, you didn't say tiramisu," he mumbled.

Viola blinked slowly, unable to gauge his reaction. Did he or didn't he like the coffee-soaked sponge cake made with mascarpone? "Are you lactose intolerant?"

He lowered his hand. "No. Not when I use heavy cream to make shrimp and grits. Unknowingly, you made my favorite dessert."

"Lucky me."

Dom winked at her. "Lucky us. I think we're going to make a good team."

It took a full thirty seconds for Viola to process his statement. Was he talking about them bypassing friendship to become a couple? And she had to ask herself, was she attracted to Dom Shaw in a way a woman was to a man?

The questions bombarded her until she wanted to yell out for them to stop. Viola wasn't opposed to a friendship that could evolve into a relationship with Dom, but the timing was wrong. And it was timing that had gotten her into trouble with the men from her past. Some women had a hard-and-fast rule to never kiss on the first date, while others had a designated period for sleeping together.

However, for Viola, it had been the trifecta of naivete, immaturity and impulsivity that had clouded her judgment; she'd believed it wasn't their intent to take advantage of her. Unfortunately, that was what a few had done. They'd taken advantage of her generosity and used her to benefit and advance their personal agendas.

Viola blinked as if coming out of a trance. "A good team how?"

"It appears as if we're on the same page. We like the same dishes and neither of us want a committed relationship."

"Right." She wanted to correct him and say it wasn't that she didn't want a relationship, but she did not *need* a relationship. From the time she'd decided to become a chef, her goal was to become an executive chef, unaware it would become a reality by the time she turned thirty. And now that she'd locked in like a guided missile on supervising her kitchen at Bainbridge House, it was too late for her to change course.

Outside, a rumble ended with a loud clap of thunder and the rhythmic sound of rain hitting the windows. "It looks as if we'll have to postpone the rest of our tour," Dom said as he headed for the kitchen.

Viola followed, glancing around the expansive space that doubled as the dining and family room. It was separated by a rustic rectangular table with seating for six. The arrangement of a chaise, armchairs and love seat allowed for unobstructed viewing of the large flat-screen television mounted over the wood-burning fireplace. A smile spread over her features when she saw the pool table. Her father had taught all his children to play, but it was Joaquin with his incredible hand-eye coordination who was so good that he could've become a professional billiard player.

She walked into the kitchen and stopped. Dom had mentioned updating the kitchen, but she wasn't prepared for sage-green kitchen cabinets with brass handles and knobs, recessed lights, natural plank flooring and a granite-topped mahogany table doubling as an island. The kitchen combined the elements of modern and rustic with double wall ovens, a microwave and a built-in stainless-steel refrigerator and dishwasher.

The trio of pendants over the island were reminiscent of Victorian-era gaslights. The kitchen was a chef's dream with plenty of granite countertops, a six-burner stove with a grill and range hood and twin sinks. A banquette under an oval stained-glass window provided the perfect space to eat breakfast or end the day with coffee and dessert.

"It's beautiful, Dom." She turned to face him. "I could really do some serious cooking in here."

The galley kitchen in her mother's condo, although equipped with state-of-the-art appliances, was too small and limiting when compared to the one in her Greenwich Village apartment. The lack of countertop space was her pet peeve. Even Elise had admitted downsizing from a farmhouse kitchen to the one in the condo had taken some getting used to.

"You can use the kitchen to do your canning because I'm up and out around seven and only come back for lunch, and then I'm gone again until six or sometimes even later. It will save you time hauling fruit back to your place, and I will show where you can store the jars until the château's kitchens are up and running."

Viola knew Dom was right. She would have had to take the fruit to her mother's condo, prepare them for canning, and then bring them back to Bainbridge House. What Dom was offering her was a win-win. He led her to an area off the kitchen with three doors and opened the first one. "There's enough room in here for at least one hundred jars."

She walked into a pantry with facing floor-to-ceiling shelves of groceries ranging from canned goods to labeled containers of rice, flour and sugar. Three large woven baskets at the far end of the room were near to overflowing with apples and pears. "There may be enough space for a lot more than a hundred jars."

"So, it is a deal?" he asked, smiling.

Viola smiled and curbed an urge to do the happy dance. When she'd contemplated supervising her own kitchen, the notion of owning property and sourcing food from her property was beyond anything she could've imagined. She was not only one-fifth owner of an estate but, for the first time in her life, she was in control of her own destiny.

The ripples of excitement coursing through her surpassed what she'd experienced when informed she would become a new hire at The Cellar, but the eventual disappointment, frustration, and disillusionment had weighed on her psyche like a leaded blanket. She had known her situation wouldn't change unless she'd taken steps to change it. Under another set of circumstances, if she hadn't been given the opportunity to join her family's business venture, she would have become another unemployed chef. Becoming a part owner of Bainbridge House had changed the course of her life.

"Yes," she said after a pregnant pause.

"I'll move everything to one wall, so you'll have room to store the jars."

"What's behind the other doors?" Viola asked.

"The middle one is a bathroom. I use it to shower when I come home after working rather than go upstairs. I'd always wanted a bathroom and laundry room on the same floor. The door in the corner is connected to the side door and doubles as a mud and laundry room." Dom closed the door and held out his hand. When she placed her palm on his, Dom gave her fingers a gentle squeeze as they returned to the kitchen.

"That's convenient. Will the other guesthouses be configured like this one?" Viola wanted to know because she'd planned to make one her permanent residence.

"No. You will have to decide whether you want to change the floor plan or keep the original design."

"I'm not going to make that decision until I see one," Viola said. Although she liked the changes Dom had made to his home, she wanted to wait because it wasn't imperative she move out of her mother's condo and onto the estate.

"Taylor told me about your greenhouses project."

She felt her pulse quicken. Taylor had followed through on his promise that she would get her wish to grow her own produce. "What did he say?"

"He said I should help you select what you want. Once they're installed, I'll be responsible for setting up the irrigation system. You're going to have to let me know whether you want them now or you want to wait until next spring."

Viola worried her lower lip. She did want the greenhouses; however, Dom asking whether she wanted them installed now or months from now had given her food for thought. If the hotel was nearing completion, she would've said now. But that was almost two years away.

"I'm not sure," she replied truthfully. "I want to use one greenhouse strictly for herbs and veggies, and the other for fruit trees. I'd like to plant additional apple and cherry trees, while adding peaches and different varieties of lemons and limes."

"What about oranges and grapefruit?"

"So, you really want Florida up in here," she teased.

"And don't forget Hawaii with pineapples," Dom countered, winking at her.

"Mexican avocados."

"Oh, no. You really had to go there."

"Yes, I did, Dom. What else do you have?"

A beat passed. "Kiwi from New Zealand."

Viola slowly shook her head. "Now I know you're really bugging." She sobered. "I think I'm going to wait before I decide what to grow in the greenhouses until I talk to Joaquin. I'll call him later to get his opinion on what type of structure and their dimensions."

"That sounds like a good idea. Now, princess, are you ready to eat?"

Viola did not know why, but this time she did not take offense when he called her princess. "Yes, I am."

## *Chapter Eight*

Viola sat at the banquette, opposite Dom, studying his impassive expression and wondering what was going on behind the green orbs as he stared at her over his flute of champagne. She had decided to substitute the mango for the traditional orange juice in the mimosas.

Not only had she enjoyed the time they'd spent together, but what he had prepared had surpassed her expectations. His grits were creamy with a hint of cheese, topped with grilled barbecued shrimp, spicy, diced andouille and chopped green onions.

"What's my grade?" Dom asked Viola.

Picking up the flute, she took a sip. "Definitely an A."

"Plus or minus?"

"Just a straight-up A. It is something I will definitely add to my Sunday jazz brunch menu."

"You plan to have Sunday jazz at the hotel?"

"Yup. There are a lot of folks who like listening to jazz while enjoying brunch. I used to attend quite a few of them when I lived in New York. I'm also projecting that some people who don't plan to check into the hotel may just want to come to eat, drink and listen to live or prerecorded music. And I'm going to give you credit for the shrimp and grits when it's listed on the menu as 'The Dom.'"

Dom stared at her, his expression mirroring astonishment. "You don't have to do that."

Viola speared the last remaining seedless grape from the fruit cup Dom had prepared as an appetizer and popped it into her mouth. "Yes, I do," she said after swallowing it. "In fact, I plan to name most of the dishes on various menus."

"How many menus do you anticipate having?" he asked.

"There will be breakfast and lunch buffet menus along with the bar. I also plan for an extensive dinner menu and a specialty Sunday brunch. Taylor makes the best chicken and waffles I've ever tasted, so they'll be listed as 'The Taylor.' Don't you think it's easier to order The Dom or The Taylor without the waitstaff having to write down shrimp and grits or chicken and waffles? And I want to go completely new school with orders recorded on devices and transmitted directly to the kitchen. Speaking of the kitchen, can you give me an update on what's going on with the one on the first floor?" she asked without taking a breath.

Viola pushed the half-filled flute away from her plate. She'd had two glasses, one more than she would normally drink, and she was feeling the effects of the bubbly wine. Her talking nonstop was what Elise called run-on sentences, and it was a habit she had worked hard to overcome. However, whenever she was excited, she tended go on and on to get her thoughts out before she was interrupted or forgot what she wanted to say.

Dom felt Viola's excitement as surely as if it were his own. He knew Viola was anxious to have the château's kitchen completely renovated before her brother's wedding. Once Taylor had made the announcement that he was to marry on the Saturday before Christmas, many of the contractors had signed up to work overtime. Dom had also pitched in, working alongside plumbers installing new commodes and bidets in the bathrooms that had been expanded to include freestanding shower stalls.

"The last time I looked in on it, I saw that the stoves had been removed. Taylor told me your appliances cannot be installed until they run new gas lines and upgrade the electrical grid."

Viola nodded. "I feel better knowing that some progress has been made. Some of the ovens are on back order, scheduled for delivery late October or early November. So, do you think the modifications will be done by that time?"

"I'm almost sure it will be. A lot of progress has been made in a very short period, Viola. And now that Taylor is getting married in three months, the pressure's on everyone to kick everything into a higher gear. He's offering the crew overtime pay to come in earlier and work later to accomplish what needs to be completed before his big day."

"How is it, working for my brother?"

"He's the best. He doesn't raise his voice and I've never seen him rattled unlike some supervisors I worked for when I was trying to get my plumbing license." Dom held up a hand to stop her when she opened her mouth. "And before you ask…" he said. "After graduating high school, I went to a technical school to become a plumber. Not only did I like working with my hands, but it also paid well."

"Are you also putting in extra hours?"

"I do whenever I have the time. Maintaining the property is my priority, and everything else is secondary."

"Taylor is lucky to have you."

Dom stared at Viola and, for a long moment, she looked back at him. He didn't think he would ever tire of them sharing the same space. There was something about her presence that made him feel at peace. When she'd asked him if he liked living alone and he'd said yes, he hadn't lied to her. He liked not having to answer to anyone, that he could go about his chores without having to punch a clock. When it came time to mow the grass on the estate, he had the option of attempting to do it in one day or stretch it out into three or even five, which translated into one acre per day.

He was paid well as the caretaker and, other than purchasing essentials, he was able to save and/or invest most of his salary. And whenever he wanted to go to Arizona to visit with his family, he'd only had to call Conrad to let him know.

Dom had stamped down the urge to laugh when she'd asked if he invited women to the estate to keep him company, because it was something he hadn't anticipated her asking. There had been a time when he had, yet it had been more than a year since he'd felt the need to have a woman invade what he considered his sanctuary. It just wasn't his home that had become his place of safety, but the entire estate.

He had gone through a lot of soul searching the instant Conrad revealed he was retiring and selling his investment company. Conrad had asked Dom if he'd wanted to keep his two clients, and if not, they would be included on the client list sold to the new owners. Because Dom had formed a close relationship with the young woman who'd inherited money from her grandfather and the middle-aged man who had won millions in a state lottery, Dom had said he would continue as their investment broker. The commissions he'd earned, he deposited into his own retirement account.

Dom had been in Arizona visiting his father when he'd gotten the call from Elise that Conrad had passed away. The time he'd spent with his father had been to get his advice as to whether he should give up the position as caretaker for Bainbridge House and move on with his life. James Shaw hated giving advice, but he'd told Dom to take a year to weigh his options. That, if at the end of a year, he still wanted to give up the position, it was something he should discuss with Conrad. Neither of them had known that within days of their conversation Conrad would pass away.

Dom loathed talking to Conrad's widow about the possibility of giving up his position as caretaker. He didn't want to discuss business with Elise while she grieved a man who had been her husband and partner for almost fifty years. However, everything changed when she'd called and asked that he open the gates to the estate because she wanted her children to see what they would inherit.

Dom hadn't left his house during their visit. Conrad's

admonishment still stung after so many years that Dom had no wish to directly interact with the man's family. The last time he'd had an in-depth conversation with the property's owner, Conrad had said he'd submitted an application and had received approval from the local zoning board to convert the estate from residential to commercial.

Now that Taylor had projected it would take two years to complete the restoration before the grand opening, Dom had promised himself that he would stay on until then. Two years was more than enough time for him to plan the next phase of his life.

"Who taught you how to cook?"

Viola's question shattered his reverie. "My grandmother. She was employed as a cook for the Bainbridge family."

"I can't believe I'm dealing with a ringer."

"Why would you say that?" he asked her.

"Because if your grandmother was a cook, then her skills were no doubt comparable to a professionally trained chef. And that means you're no novice, Dom Shaw."

Dom noticed the rush of color suffusing Viola's face, indicating she was probably annoyed with him. "She taught me enough so I wouldn't have to depend on someone else for a meal. There's no way I could even begin to compete with her, or you. There are certain dishes I feel I've mastered because they're my favorites. The first time I attempted to make shrimp and grits, it wasn't fit for human consumption. The grits were stiff as drying concrete and the shrimp were rubbery and overcooked. But I wasn't going to let it get the best of me, so I tried several different recipes until I found one that I really liked. After making it a couple of times, I felt as if I'd hit the jackpot."

"You're right, because it was scrumptious."

Pressing his palms together, Dom inclined his head. "Thank you, Chef Williamson."

A hint of a smile played at the corners of her mouth. "No, thank you for a wonderful meal." Her smile faded. "You say you're the fourth generation caretaker."

Dom nodded. "That's true."

"When was the first?"

"I think it was sometime before the Great War."

"That was more than a hundred years ago."

"Bainbridge House will celebrate its sesquicentennial in twelve years."

Viola traced the whorls on the fork handle with her forefinger. "She has held up well for her age."

"That's because she has always been lived in until the 1960s." Dom knew instinctually that Viola was going to ask more questions about the Bainbridge family, questions to which Conrad should've been forthcoming with his children. "When did you decide you wanted to be a chef?" he asked matter-of-factly.

"It was the summer I turned twelve. I fell and broke my wrist playing tennis, and spent the next two months in a cast. That's when I spent most of my time in the kitchen watching Momma cook. There were two things my mother always did for us. And that was homeschooling and cooking. Although she'd hired a housekeeper, she wouldn't allow the woman to prepare our meals."

"What was she afraid of?"

Viola rolled her eyes upward. "Please don't get me started. We used to tease her, saying Miss Amelia wasn't going to poison us. Momma would change her mind about some things, but having someone cook for her kids wasn't one."

"Did you like being homeschooled?"

"It was all I'd ever known. It took me a long time to realize the school bus wasn't going to stop at my house and take me to a school."

Dom stared at the crestfallen expression on Viola's face and then burst into laughter. "Please don't tell me you have issues because you never got to ride on a school bus."

Viola narrowed her eyes, reminding him of a cat ready to attack. "That's not funny."

He sobered quickly. "I'm sorry for laughing. You're right. It's not funny. How did your mother manage to homeschool five kids?" He knew he had to choose his words carefully or Viola could possibly misconstrue his intent.

"As a certified and licensed K-through-twelve teacher, Momma made it look easy. She'd set up the library like a one-room schoolhouse. And because Taylor, Patrick and Joaquin are so close in age, they were given the same instruction. Taylor and Patrick excelled in math, while Joaquin was the science phenom. Tariq, who is six years younger than Taylor, excelled in math and science. Everyone had a hobby, and for me it was books. I loved rainy days because when we couldn't play outside, I'd hang out in my bedroom and read. There were times when I'd stay up most of the night reading and couldn't get up in the morning in time to have breakfast with the rest of the family. It was only when I began falling asleep in class that Momma wanted to know what was going on. Then, one night, I fell asleep

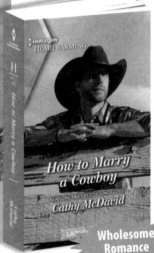

with a flashlight under the blanket and when she came in to check on me, that was all she wrote."

"What did she say?"

Viola's lips twitched as she struggled not to laugh. "It's not what she said but what she did. She hid all the flashlights."

"Busted!"

This time Viola did laugh. "Big-time. We knew Tariq was going to be a vet because he had a habit of bringing home stray dogs and cats. We had a menagerie with birds, fish, cats, dogs and rabbits. Once the rabbits began multiplying like crazy, Momma said they had to go. Tariq cried when they were given to a local pet store. Years later, he found a snake and snuck it into the house. It got loose, and that was the only time I remember seeing Momma go ape shit. She was deathly afraid of snakes. She cussed up a storm, shocking everyone, because we'd never heard her use profanity and she wouldn't allow anyone to use it in her home."

Dom found himself totally engrossed in the pranks executed by the Williamson children. "Did they ever find it?"

"Yes. It took hours of searching the entire house before it was discovered behind a basket in the laundry room. Daddy made Tariq put it a box and then drove to the woods where they released it. Tariq never brought another animal in the house after that because he lost his driving privileges and spent the next month grounded."

"Should I assume there was never a dull moment in the Williamson household?"

"Never. Things did change once we started leaving home to attend college. I was the only one left when Momma issued a mandate that everyone was expected to come home for Easter, Thanksgiving and Christmas. She didn't care if you were in Siberia or Timbuktu. You'd better be in Belleville in time to celebrate those family holidays." Reaching for the napkin beside her plate, Viola touched it to the corners of her mouth. "I've given you a rundown of the Williamsons, so now it's your turn to tell me about the Shaws."

Dom slumped lower on the cushioned bench seat. "The Shaws were not as dramatic or animated as the Williamsons. My father met my mother in high school. He was a senior and she was only a freshman. Her parents wouldn't let her date him because they felt she was too young."

"How old was she?"

"Fourteen. She'd skipped a grade and going out with a seventeen-year-old was not something her parents approved of. However, James Shaw was not to be denied. He waited for Donna to graduate and then they ran off and eloped. Her mother never forgave James because she'd planned for her daughter to go to college to become a nurse.

"Meanwhile, Dad had taken over as caretaker after my grandfather fell, hit his head and lingered in a coma for several weeks before he passed away. My mother got pregnant and had me, but I don't remember her because she died from a pulmonary embolism before my first birthday. That's when my grandmother did double duty as cook and babysitter. She was the only woman in my life until I was twelve, when Dad met and married a divorcée with a young son. It was a happy and sad time for my father because his mother passed away a year later."

"Did you get along with your stepmother?"

Dom grimaced as he gathered his thoughts. “Yes and no.” He exhaled an audible breath. “It took me a while to trust her because she was super sweet, and it was hard for me to accept someone could be that nice. One day Dad took me aside and told me my mother was his first love and she would always hold a special place in his heart. He claimed he hadn’t planned to fall in love again, but he was glad he had because Hallie was an incredible woman, and he hoped I would see in her what had made him want to marry her.”

“What happened after that?” Viola questioned.

“I still wasn’t ready to welcome her into my life with open arms until the day she took me and Evan shopping and a man shoved me because he claimed I was blocking the aisle. Hallie went after him like a mama bear protecting her cub. She dared him to push her son again and, after a stare-down, he apologized and walked away. The fact that she’d called me her son and was ready to fight some stranger twice her size to protect me spoke volumes. I waited a few days and then asked if she wouldn’t mind if I called her Mom. She didn’t answer me because she was crying so much that I thought I’d said something wrong. The next day she gave me greeting card that read ‘from a mother to her son’ and that’s when she did become my mother in every sense of the word.”

Viola closed her eyes at the same time she bit her lip.

Dom knew the story had obviously affected Viola when she laced her fingers together to conceal their trembling, and he wondered if she was reliving her own experience once she’d accepted Elise Williamson as her mother.

Dom hadn’t known that Conrad’s children were adopted until he'd eavesdropped on a phone call his father was having with Conrad. James had accused the man of caring more for five strangers than his own kin. The conversation ended abruptly when James realized he wasn't alone and hung up.

Viola opened her eyes and gave him a steady stare. "I'm glad things worked out between you and your mother."

"She's wonderful, Viola. She and my father are living their best life at a Tucson retirement community. Dad was forced to move to a drier climate because of his seasonal allergies and worsening asthma."

"How's your brother?"

"Evan is a lifer stationed in Germany. I was best man at his wedding and am godfather to his twin sons."

"So, you're Uncle Dom."

"Yup. Even though I haven't seen them in a couple of years, we manage to keep in touch electronically."

A smile curved Viola's mouth when she realized Dom talking about his family had given her a glimpse into who he was. He'd lost his mother and both grandparents. His parents lived almost three thousand miles away and his brother at least six thousand. Yet he appeared to have adjusted to being separated from his loved ones, while she knew it would be difficult for her to have her siblings living so far away. Even when Taylor had lived in Connecticut, she could either drive or take the Metro-North to reconnect with him in about an hour.

"What are you thinking about, Viola?"

"You."

His eyebrows lifted. Apparently, he hadn't expected her to be so candid. "What about me?"

"I was thinking about how much I've enjoyed spending time talking with you. And, of course, the shrimp and grits were divine. I'm going to admit they were even better than the ones I had in Charleston, South Carolina."

"You're kidding me?"

"No, Dom. I'm being truthful. You are an incredible cook."

He inclined his head. "I thank you, and I know Grandma Jo is up there smiling at the compliment."

"Was your grandmother from the South?"

"No. She was born in Ireland and came to this country as a young girl. That's a story I'll tell you about at another time. You've given me an A for the shrimp and grits, and I'm going to give you an A-plus for the mimosa. Adding mango is a very nice change from the orange juice." Dom drained his glass. "Now, what do you plan to make next week?"

Viola thought about repeating some of the dishes she'd prepared for Taylor and Sonja. "Do you like Asian food?"

Dom reached across the table and held her hands. "No fair, princess. Why are you going there? If this were truly a competition, I would fail miserably."

She tried pulling her hands away, but he applied more pressure to her fingers. His grip was firm without causing her pain. "It's not a competition, Dom. I just need you to tell me whether you like or dislike a particular dish. And if you don't, then why."

Viola stilled. "I don't want the menus at Bainbridge House to offer what I think of as conventional hotel food. Although we'll want everything about the hotel to be high-end, and give our guests the option of ordering what they could find at Le Bernardin, I also want to create dishes that will remind someone of their grandmama's cooking."

"Give me an example."

Viola paused, searching her memory for a dish she was certain to be a hit for someone who hadn't eaten it before. "Most people are familiar with lasagna. There is a meat version and a vegetarian one. Have you ever heard of or eaten *pastelón*?"

Dom released her hands. "No. What is it?"

"It's Puerto Rican lasagna. Sonja made it for me once and it was so good that I wanted to eat the entire pan in one sitting. She got the recipe from her mother who, in turn, had gotten it from her mother. I want recipes that have been passed down through generations of mamas and grandmamas."

"I can help you out if you want family recipes. My grandmother wrote down her recipes in a notebook and it's packed away in a trunk with a few things I didn't want to throw away."

"That's what I'm talking about, Dom. Familiar dishes made with locally sourced ingredients have to be a win-win."

"The *pastelón* sounds interesting. Why don't you make it for next Sunday? In fact, you can come here early, and I'll watch you put it together."

"I have to ask Sonja whether she will give me the recipe."

"If she does give you the recipe and you put it on the menu, what will you call it?"

"Probably just *pastelón*."

"It sounds…sexy."

Viola couldn't stem the laughter bubbling up in her throat. It was the first time she'd heard someone say a dish was sexy. "It's more like extreme deliciousness. The filling is a sweet-and-salty mix. And the *sofrito* is to die for."

"I've heard of *sofrito*, yet I have no idea what goes into it."

"It's an infusion of spices that's used in a number of Latin recipes. By the way, do you have a blender or food processor?"

"I have both."

"That's good. I'll need to blend the ingredients to make the *sofrito*."

"So, do we have a date for next Sunday?"

"Yes, Dom. It's a date."

"And don't forget you can have the run of the kitchen during the week to can your fruit. *Mi casa es tu casa*."

Viola had accepted Dom's offer to use his kitchen because it meant she didn't have to transport baskets of fruit to her mother's condo and then transport glass jars back to the estate to store them for future use. "You may come to regret those words," she teased.

"I doubt it," Dom said, smiling. "If you're not able to make it home, I can put you up in one of the spare bedrooms. You'll also have access to the upstairs bathroom."

"That's not necessary. If I can't make it home, I'll stay over with Taylor and Sonja."

Dom lifted his shoulders. "Just offering."

"I appreciate the offer." Viola didn't want to read more into his suggestion that she spend the night at his house. "I'll probably get here around eight and stay until the early afternoon."

"You can stay as long as you like. I usually come home for lunch and then I'm out again. Let me know what day you're coming and I'll set a basket in the kitchen for you. Each basket weighs about twenty-five pounds, and I don't want to be responsible for you lifting one and possibly straining your back."

Viola knew he was right. One wrong move when lifting could possibly incapacitate her for weeks or maybe even longer. "Thank you. I have a few things to pick up tomorrow, so I'll be here Tuesday morning, and I'll probably be gone before you come back for lunch. I'd appreciate it if you can set out the pears first because they're a lot more delicate than apples and will ripen quicker."

Grinning, Dom gave her a snappy salute. "Yes, chef."

Viola gave him a warm smile. She'd observed two sides of Dom's personality: brooding and playful, and she much preferred seeing the latter. "I think it's time we have coffee and dessert."

She cut generous slices of tiramisu, and placed them on dessert plates as the tantalizing aroma of brewing coffee filled the kitchen. It was only after they'd sat to eat the custard-filled cake and sipped rich dark roasted coffee liberally laced with sweet cream that Viola had become cognizant of the atmosphere of domesticity surrounding her and Dom—something that had been missing with other men with whom she had been involved.

Dom's offer to cook for her during her first visit to his home, and then giving her an open invitation to come whenever she wanted, would take some getting used to. Maybe he felt since her family owned the house and the land on which it stood, she was entitled to that privilege. Viola hoped that wasn't his only rationale because, as friends, she believed they should be comfortable enough with each other to volunteer to do something without entertaining an ulterior motive.

In the few weeks since their initial meeting, she had discovered he was the opposite of some of the pompous idiots who had been a complete waste of her time, which was a reminder of the adage "act in haste, repent at leisure." Perhaps the difference was they'd established their association from the onset. They would be friends. And it would be the first time that she would have a guy friend other than Kenzi Yamamoto.

The rain had slacked off when Viola helped Dom clean up the kitchen. At first he'd refused her help, but after she'd insisted, he'd relented. "I'm going to head out now," she said as she picked up her empty basket.

"I'll drive you back."

Viola shook her head. "That's not necessary. I know how to find my way back to the main gate."

"Okay. I'll open the gate remotely. The next time you come, I'll program the code for the gate into your phone. I'm going to contact the security company to ask them to give me an access code for you. Once you're connected, they will ask you for a personal password and you can give it to me or Taylor for safekeeping."

"That means I won't have to bother you whenever I need the gates opened."

Dom took a step, bringing them only inches apart as he stared at her under lowered lids. "You may be a lot of things, Viola, but I doubt if you'll ever be a bother."

Viola knew if she didn't put some distance between her and the enigmatic man with whom she'd spent most of the afternoon, she would say something she would later regret. "Thank you again for a wonderful time." That said, she turned on her heel and walked out of the house. She willed her mind blank as she got into the car and reversed the distance until she drove through the gates and left Bainbridge House in the rearview mirror.

"I'm losing it," she whispered.

The instant Dom had moved so close to her that she could feel his breath on her face, she'd wanted him to kiss her. Viola knew she had to be careful, very careful, not to step over the line so that she communicated she wanted something more than friendship, because Dom had been explicit when he'd said he didn't want a relationship.

She activated the Bluetooth and tapped a programmed number. It rang three times before Sonja answered.

"What's up, Vi?"

"Did I wake you?"

"No. I took a nap earlier this morning. Right now, I'm in the kitchen getting ready to feed my face. Are you coming over to have dinner with us?"

"No. I was just at Dom's place. He made shrimp and grits for brunch." There was silence on the other end of the connection. "Sonja, are you there?"

"I'm here. I'm trying to process what you just said about you and Dom."

"I told you we're friends."

"Oh-kay," Sonja drawled. "If you say so."

"I say so. I didn't call to talk about Dom. I want to ask you if you're willing to part with your family's *pastelón* recipe."

"Normally, I would say no, but since I'm carrying

a Williamson, that makes you family. So the answer is yes."

"Thank you, thank you, thank you. I want to learn to make it and eventually list it on the hotel's dinner menu."

"Say no more. I have the recipe on my computer, and I'll email it to you. Whenever you make it, I want you to save me some. I know if I make it, I'll inhale the whole damn pan and then blow up like a pufferfish. And if you want my *abuela*'s recipe for *pasteles* and *perñil*, I can send those to you, too."

Viola laughed. "Are you hinting that you want me to prepare dishes that you find at the homes of Puerto Ricans during Christmas?"

"I'd be lying if I said I wasn't."

"I don't mind making the *pasteles*, but only if you're willing to help me."

The one time Sonja had given her several *pasteles* she'd made with her aunt for a Christmas dinner, Viola had become hooked on the tamales filled with pork, chickpeas, olives, capers, yucca and other spices. Sonja said it had taken them two days to make nearly one hundred *pasteles*, which they'd stored in the freezer for future meals.

"I'll help you, but we won't need to make too many because I'm not sure whether Taylor will like them," Sonja said.

"It doesn't matter whether he will or won't. I can always heat them up and have one or two for a meal whenever I don't feel like cooking."

"When don't you feel like cooking, Viola Williamson?"

"There are a few times when I decide to take a break. I'm taking a break now that I'm not working."

"That's different, because you've chosen not to work at a restaurant until Bainbridge House is completely restored. Think about it, Vi. You need a break so you can concentrate on creating your menus and how many employees you're going to need to run the kitchens and dining rooms."

Viola knew Sonja was right. She had time and she intended to take advantage of it to make certain the restaurants were fully functional even before the grand opening. "When I make the *pastelón*, I'll make one for you in a loaf pan. That way you can cut it into individual portions, and then you can eat some and freeze the others."

"I'll have to hide them in the back of the freezer because if your brother finds out they're here, they'll be gone in a couple of days."

"Thanks again for offering the recipe."

She rang off and then tapped the screen for Joaquin's number. There was a three-hour time difference between New Jersey and LA, and she had made it a practice never to call him too early because as a night owl he tended to sleep in on weekends.

"Hey, Viola. Long time, no hear."

She smiled. "Stop with the lies, brother. We spoke to each other a few weeks ago when I told you that I was joining the rest of you guys in the restoration project."

"That's right. I forgot about that. I still can't believe you're going to become an executive chef at your age."

"Believe it, Joaquin. By the time the hotel opens for business, I'll be thirty, and I will have almost ten years behind my name. I'm calling you because I want to put up a couple of greenhouses on the property. One will be for herbs and veggies and the other for fruit trees."

"We must be twinning, Viola, because I was thinking of putting up one to cultivate plants and flowers. If Bainbridge House is going to be a wedding venue, then a prospective bride can either select her bouquet from flowers grown on-site or pay exorbitant fees to have orchids and other exotic flowers flown in from overseas. Can you wait for me to come in for Taylor's wedding and we can decide then what we'll need?"

Viola's smile was dazzling. "Yes!"

"Good. Now tell me if our big brother is exhibiting any wedding jitters?"

"He's cool, Joaquin. I think his involvement with the restoration is keeping him grounded."

"That's good news. I'm going to miss seeing the family for Thanksgiving, and I also wanted to meet the woman who convinced Taylor to turn in his bachelor card."

"She didn't have to convince Taylor of anything. He was the one doing the chasing until she stood still long enough for him to catch her."

"There's no doubt she's very special."

"She is," Viola confirmed. "I'll talk to you later," she said when she heard raised voices in the background. It was obvious Joaquin wasn't alone.

"Later, Viola. Love you."

She smiled. "I love you more."

Viola tapped the screen, ending the call. She enjoyed talking with Joaquin. He was always upbeat regardless of what was going in his life. He'd invited his friends to his home to host an uncoupling party after what had been a volatile marriage and the finalization of a contentious divorce. Joaquin had recently celebrated his thirtieth birthday and was enjoying life as an unencumbered bachelor.

If Joaquin was looking forward to coming to New Jersey to celebrate Christmas with the family, it was the same for Viola. It wasn't until everyone was together under one roof that she understood the full meaning of family—a family that had chosen to make her a part of their lives.

## *Chapter Nine*

Dom slipped behind the wheel of the battered pickup, turned the key in the ignition and smiled as the engine roared to life. "That's my girl, Lollipop. I knew you weren't ready to join the scrap heap."

Laughing to himself, he shook his head, not wanting to believe he was talking to the truck. Perhaps it had something to do with Viola's wanting to see Lollipop restored to her original condition. As a child, he'd seen photos of the brand-new tomato-red vehicle his grandfather had purchased for his son. It was a gift for James Shaw once he'd learned to drive a tractor. However, the pickup's better days had long since passed by.

Initially, Dom had turned down his father's offer to give him the truck because, once he'd taken driver's education in school, he didn't want to use two feet driving a standard-shift vehicle. However, he had relented and learned to drive Lollipop since some of the kids at the high school were driving their parents' old cars, many with rust, countless dings, peeling paint and front- and rear-end damage.

Shifting into Reverse, he backed out of the driveway and headed for the large pond where several families of swans had taken up residence. At one time there were more geese than swans, but the more aggressive swans had forced most of the geese to find another place in which to breed and raise their young. Last year, a small flock of geese had returned to the pond, but like the swans, they were migratory and flew south to escape the cold winter weather. Underground streams flowed continuously into the pond, preventing the surface from freezing over even when temperatures dropped into the teens. And not having to interact with the waterfowl during the winter months allowed Dom to clean up their nesting areas.

Although there were wild grasses, insects and berries in and around the pond to feed the birds, every couple of weeks Dom brought leftover rice, bird seed, shredded lettuce and kale, and defrosted peas and corn to supplement their diet. He was aware of the habit of people feeding bread to ducks, yet it was something he'd refused to do. Bread did not provide the nutrients waterfowl needed to remain healthy. He'd also made it a habit to return to the pond every other day from late April to early June to see if the pen, or female swan, had begun laying. Once the eggs hatched, he'd sit and watch the cygnets with their drab gray or brown feathers settle onto the backs of their mothers as she took them on a ride on the pond.

He'd learned as a young boy that swans mated for

life, bonding even before they reached sexual maturity, but as he'd grown older, he'd realized it wasn't the same for humans. Yet he still wanted it to be true. Dom had gone into marriage believing he and Kaitlyn would spend the rest of their lives together, but what had been a fantasy turned into a nightmare. Her deceit made him wary of forming emotional relationships with women, he opting instead not to commit.

Dom hadn't known Viola long enough to judge correctly whether he now wanted more than friendship because he'd found her irresistible. It wasn't just her natural beauty, but the confidence she exhibited, as if it were inherently hers from birth, and wore like a badge of honor. He knew it had to do with her upbringing because Taylor had exhibited the same confidence when interacting with the contractors.

And when Dom compared his working interaction with Taylor with his and Conrad's, Dom didn't want to believe Taylor had been raised by the same man, a man who seldom smiled even while he'd expected his demands to be followed without question. Then he recalled Viola saying, *"There was Conrad the businessman and Daddy the family man, and he made certain to keep them separate."* Just once, Dom would've liked to have met the family man.

He arrived at the pond and got out with the large plastic bowl filled with nutritious food for the birds. Several geese left the water to come on land to inspect what he'd brought for them. He was aware they typically fed twice a day—morning and late afternoon—and roosted in open water at night. Dom quickly emptied the bowl and then got back into the pickup before the swans and geese descended on him. The first time he'd lingered too long, he'd had to run to avoid being attacked and perhaps injured by the swans' serrated beaks. It had been a frightening reminder of Alfred Hitchcock's classic film *The Birds*.

Sitting in the truck, Dom watched the birds eat the feast he'd scattered on the ground. A large cob pecked at one of the smaller geese and, within seconds, fights broke out among the birds. Just as quickly, the competition for food ended with the geese retreating to the safety of the water.

"Bully!" Dom whispered.

The adult male swan with pure white plumage had established himself as king of the pond. The cob attacking the much smaller bird reminded him of a boy who had tormented him relentlessly in high school. Not only had he been younger than his grade counterparts, Dom hadn't obtained the bulk of those playing sports or working out. With Dom standing five-ten and barely weighing a buck fifty soaking wet, he had little recourse when a boy on the lacrosse team had made Dom his personal punching bag. When he'd come home with bruises and the occasional black eye, he'd lied to his parents saying he'd been hurt playing sports rather than admitting he'd become a bully's target.

All of that changed once J.J.—Jack Jameson—had come to his rescue. Jack's father had been a semiprofessional middleweight boxer who'd taught all his sons the sport. Jack had invited Dom to come to his house, where the elder Jameson had set up a room like a boxing gym. Dom had always been a quick learner and, within weeks, he'd established quick footwork, a jab, and a stunning right hook. His lessons with J.J. had been their secret, and the next time the bully approached him,

Dom was ready. He was able to sidestep the bully's fist and, two punches later, the bullying was over. In twenty years, he'd grown two inches and gained nearly thirty pounds. This past year, he'd lost half that weight because he preferred walking to riding when touring the estate. The only time he drove the golf cart, ATV or Lollipop was to haul equipment—or bird feed.

Dom's friendship with J.J. had continued beyond high school. Jack had taken over as owner of the family-owned pub that had fallen in disrepair, along with several other businesses in the downtown area. Dom had assisted Jack with completing the application and accompanying financial documents to apply for a community development grant to renovate the eating establishment. Once Jameson's reopened, locals and out-of-towners alike filled booths, tables and the mahogany bar to drink potent concoctions, watch sporting events on the many television screens, and dine on delicious quintessential pub food that had made Jameson's a go-to hangout for generations.

Jack had sent him a text two days ago, inviting him to stop in and share a few drinks. Dom had replied he was working on a new project and would see him once he'd finished. His new project had been assisting plumbers install new vanities, commodes and bidets in the château's second-story bedroom suites. Now that it was nearing completion, he planned to go Jameson's and reconnect with his old friend.

Dom reversed direction and drove back to the house, leaving the pickup there before he set out on foot to retrieve the all-terrain-vehicle and drive over to the open pasture to check the fence line. This area of the estate had been used for horses to run and graze, and history would repeat itself once the Williamsons filled the paddocks with the magnificent animals. Charles Garland Bainbridge had used the château for his family's summer retreat, while generations later, his property would be open year-round as a hotel and wedding venue.

Viola parked behind Lollipop and shut off the engine. She'd come to Dom's house on Tuesday because she'd dedicated Monday to gathering all the ingredients and equipment to begin her canning project. She regarded prepping as the epitome for culinary success. Even when cooking for family or friends, Viola not only planned her menu days in advance, but also marinated, cut, diced and chopped meat, veggies and fruit, and stored them in the fridge the night before. She'd packed all she would need to can jars of cinnamon pears, apple pie filling and applesauce.

As promised, Dom hadn't locked the front door, and it took Viola four trips to unload the trunk of the car to carry six boxes of a dozen jars each into the house, along with a large pot and the equipment required for canning. She had also packed the ingredients to prepare a soup-and-salad lunch.

She had been truthful when she'd admitted to Dom that she could do some serious cooking in his kitchen. It was nothing short of a chef's kitchen with everything she would need to prepare dishes that required lots of steps and ingredients. There was ample countertop space, two deep sinks, double wall ovens and a stove with half a dozen burners and grill.

Elise had taught her how to can tomatoes, pickles, and freshly shucked corn for relish, and a variety of peppers. Her task had been to examine each canning jar to make sure it was in good condition and had no cracks or chips on the rim. Her mother had drilled it into her head that the jars had to be labeled and dated, and used within a year. Once they were emptied, they were never to be used again.

Viola had decided to use a no sugar recipe for the pears. She lost track of time as she hummed along to the tunes on her phone's playlist as she washed, peeled, cored and halved the pears. She then placed them into a stock pot with water and lemon juice to prevent browning. The basket of pears yielded fourteen jars, which she'd let cool before taking them to the pantry.

Once Dom picked more, she would make cinnamon pears. She intended to use them when they were perfectly ripe. The slight tartness was achieved by using cinnamon RedHots. Cinnamon pears, like all canned fruits and vegetables, had to be stored in a cool, dark place.

"Honey, I'm home!"

Viola felt her knees buckle and she would've fallen if Dom's arm hadn't circled her waist to keep her upright. "You almost gave me a heart attack sneaking up on me like that."

"I'm sorry about that," he whispered in her ear.

With his chest pressed against her back, not only was he close, but much too close for her to draw a normal breath. She'd fantasied about him holding her and, without warning, it had come true. However, if he continued to hold her, Viola was certain she would embarrass herself and beg him to kiss her.

"Please let me go, Dom." She shivered slightly when he pressed his mouth to the bandana covering her hair before he dropped his arm. "You're just in time for lunch."

* * *

Dom took a backward step and stared at Viola when she turned to face him. He hadn't known what to expect when he'd walked into the kitchen to find her humming and cooking. The scene of domestication had been like a punch to the gut and that was when he'd realized what he wanted, needed, and had been missing.

He wanted Viola for more than friendship. He'd denied it, yet knew unequivocally that he needed companionship, that she had become a constant reminder of what had been missing in his life. He'd been living a monkish existence on an estate that had become a self-imposed monastery.

Before Taylor had arrived to oversee the restoration, weeks would go by without Dom speaking to another person. And that didn't include talking with his father. His life as he'd known it since accepting the responsibility of caretaker for Bainbridge House was his to do with as he pleased. If he chose not to get out of bed—then he didn't. He lived his life not by a clock but with the rise and set of the sun. But that freedom had also brought loneliness.

His eyes traced the arch of Viola's eyebrows, the length of her lashes, which were long enough to graze the tops of her cheekbones, and the short, pert nose she would occasionally scrunch up in a way he found so endearing. Viola's mouth. Dom had consciously pushed back all thoughts of kissing her to discover if her lips were as soft as they appeared. And then there was the curvy petite body that made him want to remove her clothes, carry her upstairs to his bedroom, and make love to her until their lovemaking erased the distrust that wouldn't permit him to allow a woman to share his life.

"You really didn't have to fix anything. I usually have leftovers for lunch."

Viola rested both palms against his chest. "I didn't bring leftovers for myself, so I made curried butternut squash and pear soup with a Roquefort pear salad."

Dom covered the hands resting on his chest. "Well, well, well. Aren't we fancy?"

"It's not fancy, Dom. I decided to use the squash before it spoiled. My mother still believes she's shopping for a big family rather than just the two of us. I also brought over some pork chops I plan to grill with an apple-pear topping."

"You're staying for dinner?" He was hard-pressed not to smile. Sharing one meal with Viola was nice. Two in the same day was spectacular.

"I will if you want me to."

Dom gently squeezed her fingers. "Of course I want you to. Do I have time to shower and change?"

"Yes. Don't rush. I still need the pears to simmer a little longer before I put them in the blender."

He kissed her forehead. "Thanks, babe."

Dom left the kitchen and headed for the staircase to the second floor. He had been surprised to find Viola's car in the driveway because he'd deliberately returned later than usual and assumed she wouldn't be there; but she had been, and he knew it was something he could get used to—very quickly.

He walked into the bathroom, closed the door, stripped off his clothes and left them in a wicker hamper before stepping into the shower. Dom released the elastic from his hair before he shampooed it and then soaped his body. Twenty minutes later, damp hair framing his face and ending at his shoulders, and dressed in gray sweatpants, black tee and white Converse sneakers, he went downstairs to join Viola in the kitchen.

Viola's head popped up when she saw movement out of the corner of her eye. She went completely still as she stared at Dom. He looked different, and it was then she realized it was his hair. Unbound, it looked like coal-black ribbons.

She recovered quickly, smiling. "Lunch is almost ready. Please sit down."

Dom approached her. "Do you need my help?"

She shook her head. "Nope. I've already set the table." Viola had put out napkins, salad forks, soup spoons, salad tongs and a ladle.

"Are you sure there isn't something I can do?"

"Yes. You can sit down, and I'll serve you."

His eyebrows lifted. "You know I could get used to this."

"Used to what?"

"Being served."

Viola flashed a sassy smile. "You served me Sunday, so I'm just returning the favor."

"I hope this is not tit for tat."

Viola wanted to tell Dom that he shouldn't compare her to his ex or some of the women with whom he'd been involved. She opened her mouth to come back at him, then thought better of it.

"No, it's not tit for tat. And I don't play games," she said instead.

Dom gave her a long penetrating stare. "And neither do I."

"Then, please sit down."

Viola felt as if she'd been holding her breath before Dom walked to the banquette and sat. She opened the fridge, removed a bowl with the salad, and set it on the table. She then repeated the action when she set the soup tureen on the table. "Water or green tea?"

He paused then said, "Green tea—please."

She was hoping he would say that. "Green tea it is."

She removed a colorful hand-painted pitcher from the fridge and a gasp of surprise slipped past her lips when Dom came over to take it from her. His hand grazed hers and she felt a jolt race up her arm much like an electric shock. Dom leaned forward and she closed her eyes, inhaling the clean masculine scent of body wash. It became a battle of wills when she didn't release the handle.

"Let it go, Viola."

She complied, wondering if they would repeat the same scenario every time they cooked for one another.

Viola picked up a small bowl with frizzled onions and joined Dom on the banquette. She removed the top of the tureen, ladled soup into a bowl and handed it to him. "I halved the amount of curry because I wasn't certain whether you would like it."

"I really like curry chicken and goat."

She filled her own bowl with the butternut squash and pear soup, topping it with the onions. "Where did you eat curry goat?"

"I make certain to order it whenever I go to Brooklyn."

Her hand stilled when she picked up her napkin. "What do you know about Brooklyn?"

Smiling, Dom spread his napkin over his lap. "You

think because I live here, I wouldn't know anything about Brooklyn?"

Viola lowered her eyes. "I… I just thought maybe you wouldn't be familiar…" Her words trailed off. Not only had she embarrassed herself, she'd also prejudged Dom.

"It's okay, princess. I do know what goes on in the outside world beyond these gates. And to answer your question about Brooklyn, I have a friend who lives there, and we usually get together a couple of times a year to reminisce. He was the one who turned me on to beef patties, curry goat and oxtails."

*I did misjudge him*, Viola thought. "You talked about tweaking your shrimp and grits recipe until you got it right. It was the same for me with oxtail stew. I was familiar with the Southern version, but once I tried Jamaican oxtail, I knew I had to learn to make it."

"How many tries did it take?"

"Two."

"Only two?"

Viola swallowed a mouthful of soup. "Yes. The first time I made it, I realized an ingredient was missing. Then I called someone who had attended culinary school with me, whose parents had emigrated from Jamaica, and told him what I'd used to make the stew. That's when he told me to use browning, which is a thick soya sauce."

"Wouldn't it have been easier for you just to research the recipe online?"

"That's not what I do, Dom. I will taste a dish and then try and figure out what ingredients go into it. And once I do, then I will tweak it to make it my own."

"Once you added the browning, did it taste like authentic Jamaican oxtail stew?"

She smiled. "Yes, it did. I vary the heat from the Scotch bonnet, depending upon who I'm cooking for. I once hosted a small gathering at my apartment and served finger foods."

"What did you make?"

"Miniature oxtail, beef and chicken empanadas. Mongolian beef meatballs. General Tso's chicken tenders. Jalapeño popper deviled eggs. Taiwanese-fried chicken chunks with basil. Bite-sized sticky hoisin spareribs. And Asian slaw with spicy Thai vinaigrette."

"Oh—my—goodness," Dom drawled. "If I'd known you then, I definitely would've been a party crasher."

"Don't worry, Dom. Once the kitchen is operational, my first project will be to put together a little something for Taylor's work crew. *And* his volunteer," she added quickly.

"I'm glad you added me, because if you hadn't, I definitely would've crashed the party. By the way, this soup is delicious. Even though I like vegetables, I've never been a fan of squash."

Viola took another spoonful of the creamy soup. "What else don't you like?"

"Rhubarb. It's too bitter for my palate."

"It can be tart and that's why sugar is added to most recipes using rhubarb. Like you, I'm not too fond of it."

"At least we can agree on something."

"That's not the only thing we agree on, Dom. After all, didn't we agree to be friends?"

Dom set down his spoon. In hindsight, if he could've retracted that statement he would have. He'd only known

Viola a few weeks, but he realized she was someone with whom he would seriously consider developing a relationship. It no longer mattered that she was Conrad Williamson's daughter. And it was irrelevant that she was a millionaire and soon-to-be executive chef at a French-inspired château listed on the National Register of Historic Places. He also knew if he told his father about Viola, James Shaw would warn his son to stay away from her—that the enmity between the Shaws and Bainbridges ran too deep for him to get involved with Conrad's daughter.

"You're right," he said after a pregnant pause. "We did agree to be friends."

Reaching for the pitcher, Viola filled her glass with the pale green tea. "Do you want to talk about your college days or is that topic taboo?"

## *Chapter Ten*

"No, it's not taboo," Dom said quietly.

He told Viola about growing up on the estate and feeling isolated from other kids despite attending the local public schools. And then there was his age. He'd been two years younger than his peers and that had made him an anomaly when the other senior boys were driving and dating.

"You didn't have any friends?"

He almost laughed when he saw her expression mirror distress. "I made a few. The only one who literally had my back was J.J.—Jack Jameson. His family owns a pub in town and now J.J. runs it. He's been bugging me to come spend time with him and I've decided to take him up on the offer. I'd like you to come with me and then I can show you around town."

"Okay."

"It's not a date," he said quickly.

Viola's lips parted when she smiled. "I know that, Dom. Friends hang out together, while those in relationships date."

His smile matched hers. "I just didn't want you to think I was sending mixed messages."

Viola was unaware that he did want to date her. There were things he wanted to do with and for Viola that he hadn't been able to experience with other women in his past. He also wanted a relationship free of the manufactured arguments that had been so prevalent during his marriage.

"You asked if I'd attended college after graduating high school." She nodded and he continued. "I decided not to go at that time because I didn't know what I wanted to study. I went to a technical school to become a plumber. After a period of apprenticeship, I got my license and was hired by a local plumbing company. Then one day I got a call from the owner not to come to work because he was being shuttered because he hadn't paid his taxes. I was twenty-four and unemployed, and my father issued an ultimatum. Either go to college or join the military. That's when I decided on college.

"I applied to several colleges and left home for the first time when I enrolled in The College of New Jersey and shared an off-campus apartment with another student. I was an incoming freshman, while he was junior. I still hadn't decided on a major until I took an economics course. I majored in economics as an undergrad and finance as a graduate student."

"When did my father find out that you had a business background?"

"When my dad couldn't stop bragging that I'd graduated with honors. Dad is also proud that I was the first Shaw to graduate college."

"He has every right to be proud of his son."

Dom recalled his somewhat acerbic relationship with Viola's father. "Once Patrick told Conrad he was quitting to become a winegrower, your father decided he needed someone he could trust. That's when he approached me and asked whether I would come and work for him. He knew I was paid from an irrevocable trust, and if he'd put me on his payroll, it would forfeit any claim to the trust. He got around that by issuing quarterly bonus payments."

"How was it, working for my father?"

"We were respectful of each other because I didn't work in the office. Most times, we communicated by phone or electronically. He'd occasionally come here to inspect the property. I knew he was checking up on me, but then, it was his right as the owner."

Viola's eyelids fluttered. "Something keeps nagging at me that you and my father didn't get along."

Dom had to call on all his self-control not to divulge the details of the oftentimes volatile confrontations he'd had with Conrad. He knew the hedge fund owner would never have hired him if he hadn't needed him. But necessity sometime brought warring factions together.

"You said it best, Viola, when describing your father."

"He was that bad?"

"It all depends on what you call bad. I don't believe I would've lasted two weeks if I'd had to work in his office. We would've been like oil and water." Dom was sorry he'd said what he had when seeing Viola's crestfallen expression. "I'm not saying your father was an—"

"You don't have to apologize for him," Viola said, cutting him off. "Daddy was who he was at his office. I've worked for enough executive chefs to understand what you're talking about. They would shout and bully everyone in the kitchen because they could. Some of the cooks would take it and others would take off their aprons and walk out in the middle of dinner hour, leaving the place short-staffed. Even that wasn't enough for the boss to change his dictatorial behavior. I've sworn an oath never to belittle my staff because I've been on the receiving end more than once."

"What did you do?"

"Pretended I didn't hear it and went on about my business. The one time I complained to my father, he offered to give me the money to start up a restaurant. I turned him down because I felt at the time that I hadn't had enough experience."

"Now you do."

Viola nodded. "I feel confident that I have what it takes to run my own kitchen. However, I do have two years in which to get it together. Once the appliances are installed in the first-floor kitchen, I will begin testing different recipes to determine what I want on the menus."

"How long do you think that will take?"

"At least a year. Then I'll concentrate on hiring staff. I'll need line cooks, sous chefs, a waitstaff, dishwashers, and a butcher."

Dom was momentarily speechless in his surprise. "You intend to butcher meat on-site?"

"Yes. What better way of making certain it's fresh, and the beef and lamb must have only been grass-fed.

I don't want to serve steak tartare with beef that isn't organic. I also want a room to age steaks."

"So you want to operate a totally organic kitchen."

"That's my goal," Viola said.

He picked up his glass and took a sip of tea, finding it not only delicious but refreshing. "I like the tea."

"I used passion fruit to sweeten it."

"Nice." Dom paused to take another sip. "I'd like you to answer a question for me, Chef Williamson."

"Talk to me, Shaw."

He couldn't help smiling. There were times when he didn't know what would come out of Viola's mouth. "How would you prepare prime rib in advance of a banquet?"

"I precook them the night before in Alto-Shaam ovens, which just happen to be on back order. They are electric ovens that have heating elements around the entire box. The doors have rubber seals and latches like refrigerators, and have two thermostats and a timer. I will set the first thermostat at 225 degrees, according to a formula that calculates the time necessary to cook the roasts to a particular doneness. Each oven can hold up to twelve roasts."

Dom was totally intrigued by what she was saying. "What happens with the second timer?"

"Once the first one hits zero, the second thermostat will come on and the roasts are held at 140 degrees. This is above the temperature danger zone, so the roasts are safe and hot, but don't cook any further. If I put the roasts in at midnight for the next day, they will stay at the same level of doneness for an entire day. There is only ten percent of shrinkage if cooked at the lower temperature when compared to about thirty percent if cooked at 325 degrees. When cooking fifteen to twenty full seven-bone roasts each day, that's a savings of a lot of money."

"Live and learn."

"Other than taste testing my recipes, if you want to help out in the kitchen, I'm willing to tutor you."

Dom wanted to ask Viola what it was about him that made him seemingly so available to her *and* her family. First Conrad and now Viola. He shook his head. "I don't think so."

"Why not?"

"Because working together would ruin our friendship. There may come a time when we may stop being friends, and that would complicate matters."

"Why would we stop being friends?"

He knew it was time for him to let Viola know how he felt about her. "Because right now I don't want to be your friend."

"Why?"

"Because I want something more."

Her hands were shaking and Viola laced her fingers together under the table so Dom wouldn't notice how much he'd unnerved her. She couldn't believe he'd just professed what she'd felt when they'd shared brunch. But there was always the nagging thought that she did not want to become involved with a man. That she wanted to wait until after her kitchen was up and running smoothly. However, that was a lie. She had time—at least another two years.

Then there was the man sitting across the table from her. He'd claimed he wanted friendship and now he wanted more, while if she were honest, she would admit she wanted a second chance to experience a relationship with a man who was looking for more than what he could get from her. Who wanted to give to her as well. She had always been the one giving, and receiving disappointment and heartache in return.

"And the more is a possible relationship?" she questioned.

He stared at her, unblinking. "That's exactly what I'm saying. I know you haven't had the best experience with men, and it's the same with me and women, but I'm willing to try again, but only if you're willing."

She stared at him through her lashes. "What if it doesn't work out, Dom?"

He gave her a half smile. "We won't know that if we don't try. And it may not work out even if we do."

"If it doesn't, then I don't want any hard feelings between us."

"We're both adults, Viola, so there shouldn't be any reason why we should act like kids bent on revenge after a breakup. I know how much setting up your kitchen means to you, so no pressure when we're not able to see each other."

Viola wanted so much to believe she could have an open and mature relationship with Dom. *What are you waiting for? You have nothing but time to get it right.* The voice in her head taunted her as she thought about whether she was ready to get involved with a man that went beyond friendship. However, Dom wasn't just any man. He was someone who knew what she wanted and had professed he would not hinder her achieving her goal.

The seconds ticked before she removed her hands from under the table and extended the right one. "Deal."

Dom didn't take her hand, but stood and came around and gently eased her off the seat. She knew he was going to kiss her and in that instant she wanted him to. It was as if she'd been waiting eons for this moment, waiting for a man to relate to her as his equal.

His hair grazed her cheek when he lowered his head and brushed a light kiss over her parted lips. "I think that's a much more pleasurable way of sealing our deal," he whispered. He kissed her again, this time with more passion as his arms went around her waist and pulled her body flush against his.

Viola nodded like a bobblehead doll and then buried her face against his neck. She sucked in her breath, holding it for a moment before letting it out slowly. Everything seemed so right. She felt so right in Dominic Shaw's arms that she knew it was where she belonged.

"Dom?"

"What is it, babe?"

"I don't want to rush this."

"There's no need for us to rush into anything."

"Thank you."

He pressed a kiss to her ear. "No, thank you for agreeing to put up with me. I'm going to be honest when I say there are times when I'm not the easiest person to get along with."

"No one's perfect," Viola countered. "I've been known to occasionally push a few buttons to get what I want. And no, I wasn't spoiled," she added.

As much as Viola enjoyed being in Dom's arms, she knew if she didn't put space between their bodies, she would beg him to make love to her. Her celibate body wasn't just hungry for lovemaking but starving, and she knew it would have to wait a while longer before it would be sated.

"Dom?"

"What is it, babe?"

"We need to finish lunch."

"To be continued."

"Yes," she said in agreement. "To be continued."

Dom folded his body down to the chaise in the family room, reached for the television remote on the side table and began channel surfing. It was Friday and it had been raining for the past two days; meteorologists reported a stalled weather system along the mid-Atlantic was predicted to drop up to three to four inches of rain in the region, with possible flooding along coastal areas. The inclement weather had forced him indoors when he'd planned to pick what was left of the apples.

It had been a week since he'd asked Viola whether they could take their friendship to another level. After she'd left to return home, he'd berated himself for going against everything he'd wanted or needed when initially he'd told her that there could only be friendship between them. Then, like turning on the proverbial dime, he'd professed to wanting a relationship. He hadn't expected her to agree, but now that she had, he had to deal with his impulsivity—a trait with which he was totally unfamiliar. He had always been the one to study a situation for an appreciable length of time before reaching a decision. Viola had asked him to take whatever they had slowly and that was what they'd done.

He'd just settled back to watch a channel featuring a polar bear with her three newborn cubs when his cell phone rang. He picked it up and smiled. It was Viola.

"How are you holding up in this messy weather?"

"I'm not," she replied. "I'm about to go stir-crazy. When I lived in the city, I used to go to the movies on rainy days."

"Isn't there a movie theater in your mother's development?"

"Yes. But it's closed for renovations."

"Well, the cinema here at Bainbridge House is open for business. I have an extensive selection of movies, and the staff offers popcorn." Viola's lilting laugh caressed his ear. "And there's no charge for admission."

"That's an offer I can't refuse. What time is the first showing?"

Dom glanced the time on the phone and then estimated how long it would take Viola to drive from Sparta. "Eight."

"Okay. I'll should be there in about thirty minutes."

"You should think about bringing an overnight bag, Viola. I don't feel comfortable with you driving home so late in this weather."

There came a noticeable pause. "I thought the hotel was still under construction."

He heard an undercurrent of laughter in her voice. "It is, but there is a guesthouse with some availability and excellent room service."

"That sounds inviting. What other perks is the guesthouse offering?"

"Management is waiving the room fee because of the weather."

This time she did laugh. "I like the sound of that. What time is checkout?"

"Checkout time has also been waived this weekend."

"I really like what I'm hearing about your hotel."

"Should I book you, Ms...."

"It's Ms. Williamson."

"I'm booking you now. I've reserved one room with a complimentary breakfast."

"What! No lunch or dinner?"

Dom covered his mouth with a hand to muffle the laughter threatening to erupt. Her tone reminded him of a child pleading with a parent for something they truly wanted. "If you want lunch and dinner, I will make certain the kitchen staff will provide it."

"Thank you. I'm going to hang up now and pack. I'm not certain if I can arrive in time for the first showing."

"Not to worry, Ms. Williamson. We happen to have a later viewing that begins around ten."

"That will do. I'll see you later."

"Please drive carefully." Taylor had hinted to him that his sister had a lead foot when driving.

"I will. Later."

Dom tapped the screen, disconnecting the call and, within seconds, the phone rang again. Smiling, he noted the name on the screen. "What's up, buddy?"

"That's what I should be asking you."

"It's all good in the hood," Dom joked. It had been a while since he'd spoken to Marcus Younger and even longer since seeing him in person. He'd met Marcus when they'd shared an off-campus, two-bedroom apartment.

"Yeah, right, Shaw. I wouldn't call living on three hundred acres a hood even if it didn't have a blade of grass."

Dom wanted to remind Marcus that his living at Bainbridge House did not translate into ownership. "I wouldn't mind trading places with you." The Baltimore native, a member of the National Association of Black Accountants, had passed the CPA exam on his first attempt.

"And I'd be willing to trade places with you, but not without my wife and kids."

Dom smothered a chuckle. Marcus was known to say Chynna was his missing rib. "How is your family?"

"Living the dream, Shaw. Remember, I told you Chynna was flipping houses."

"How's that going?"

"Incredible. She's bought, flipped and sold three houses in a year. I managed to convince her to use the money to invest in her dream house. It's large enough so when the kids become teenagers they can have their own suite of rooms. We sold our old house to one of her cousins and moved into the new one last month. Now that we've settled in, we're inviting family and friends over for a costumed Halloween party. We're going to have one for the kiddies and another for the grown folks. I want to know if I can add your name to the guest list."

Dom didn't have to scroll through his calendar to know that he didn't have anything planned for the holiday. "I know I'm going to regret saying this. Add my name to the list."

"I was hoping you would say that. Chynna has been complaining that we don't see you enough."

Marcus's wife was right. He usually visited with the Youngers a couple of times a year, but this past year had been the exception because he'd wanted to spend more time in Arizona with his parents. Marcus and Chynna were a couple who supported each other in their endeavors. When Chynna had informed Marcus that she'd wanted to leave teaching and get into real estate, he'd become her fervent ally.

"You know I can't hang with you guys."

He'd been a groomsman in Marcus's wedding party. Their wedding and reception was held at a mansion overlooking Chesapeake Bay. The vivacity had continued well past midnight and when he'd finally climbed into a taxi to take him to his hotel, he'd literally collapsed across the bed and woken up the next day fully dressed.

"Don't worry about that, buddy. There's more than enough room in the house to put you up if you overindulge."

"Thanks for the offer to put me up, but I doubt whether I'll ever overindulge like that again." He and some of the groomsmen had challenged one another downing shots. Dom had tossed back eight and then given up.

"Shots or no shots, we want you to stay for the weekend. You can bring a plus-one if you want. The more, the merrier."

Although he and Viola had decided to date each other, he still hadn't thought of her as his plus-one. This would be the first time they would be extended an invitation as a couple. "Thanks, Marcus."

"So, I can really count on you coming?"

Dom smiled. "I wouldn't miss it." Marcus had become his sounding board during the time he'd been trying to salvage what was left of his marriage with Kaitlyn. His friend had been supportive and finally told him what he'd needed to hear: nothing he could say or do would make her happy. His advice was for Dom to give her what she truly wanted: a divorce.

"Good. I'll add your name to the list and text you the address and directions how to get here in a couple of days."

"I'll be looking for it."

## *Chapter Eleven*

Viola eased off the gas pedal as she exited the county road and slowly executed a left turn onto a two-lane road leading to Bainbridge House. Not only was the rain coming down in torrents, there was also ponding on the roadway where she'd twice hydroplaned, forcing her to decelerate to under twenty miles per hour.

She'd told Dom she was going stir-crazy because even with inclement weather she'd always found something to do or someplace to go in Manhattan. During her days off, she would go to a movie, visit a museum, browse through a bookstore or just hang out at a neighborhood Starbucks.

Viola did not want to admit to herself that she missed living in the city that never slept. It had an electricity she'd never experienced in all her travels, even though she'd instantly fallen in love with Paris and Rome. She'd spent hours at outdoor cafés drinking wine or espresso while listening to conversations in French and Italian. Elise, fluent in French, had taught all her children the language, and Viola was grateful she had because she'd been able to easily communicate with Parisians. She'd had more difficulty in Italy, but discovered many Europeans spoke and understood English in addition to their native tongue.

Viola knew she would not have accepted Dom's invitation to spend the weekend with him if she'd been employed. She'd inventoried her mother's freezer and defrosted and cooked meat with the oldest labeled dates. She'd made meat loaf, grilled pork chops, roast chicken, sausage and peppers, and steak bites, and dropped them off at Taylor and Sonja's condo. Her brother's fiancée was still experiencing bouts of nausea, and he'd suggested she work from home for the duration of her pregnancy. When Sonja complained to Viola that Taylor was being dictatorial, she knew she'd shocked her future sister-in-law when she'd agreed with him. She'd admitted to Sonja that the noise and dust had also kept her away from the work site.

She turned off onto the private road and tapped the remote device on the visor to open the gates. Dom had secured a code for her and she'd programmed it into the remote and her cell phone. A smile parted her lips when she recalled their lighthearted banter about her spending the weekend at his house. Most times, he was so serious that she was reluctant to say anything that bordered on teasing. He had admitted he wasn't the easiest person to get along with. That did not matter to Viola since she planned to enjoy whatever time they had together and, when it ended, she wanted no regrets.

She was past the point when she'd asked herself if she'd lost her mind to agree to having a relationship with a man she'd known for such a short time, because it was no different from what she'd done in her past relationships. Although she didn't believe in the rule not to kiss on the first date, she did have one for sleeping together. Perhaps it had something to do with Elise's warning that a single woman living alone had to be very careful who she invited into her home. Now it was the reverse. She was going to Dom's home to sleep under his roof and the difference was that he'd agreed to let her determine the direction of their relationship.

Did she like Dom?

Yes.

Like him enough to sleep with him?

Not yet.

Although she viewed sex as an important component of a relationship, for Viola it wasn't the glue that cemented her continuing to see someone. She'd dated the aspiring politician for several months without sharing his bed. She'd talked herself into believing he was Mr. Right until she'd discovered he was Mr. Wrong after she'd rejected his request to cater a fundraising banquet for one of his political cronies. He'd verbally threatened her. Not only couldn't she wait to get out of his apartment, she'd also blocked his number. That had been more than two years ago.

Viola drove through, then closed the gates and flicked on the car's high beams as she navigated the narrow drives leading in the direction of the guesthouses. The Subaru bounced over the ruts and she blew out her breath when the guesthouses came into view. She'd turned the wipers to the fastest speed, and it still wasn't enough to keep the water build-up off the windshield. She reached her destination, parking behind Lollipop. The guesthouse door opened even before she shut off the engine.

Dom came out of the house holding a golf umbrella to shield Viola from the downpour. The wind had picked up and the rain was blowing sideways.

He opened the driver's-side door and handed Viola the umbrella. She wore a bright yellow slicker and matching rain boots. He'd slipped a black poncho over his clothes while waiting for her to arrive. "Go inside. I'll get your bag."

"Thanks."

Dom scooped the large quilted bag off the rear seat and closed the door. The wind howled like a banshee as he went inside. He set Viola's bag on the floor and slipped out of the poncho, wiping his boots on the mat.

Viola met his eyes. "I'm sorry about dripping water all over your floor."

"Don't worry about it. It will dry. Give me your slicker and boots, and I'll put them in the mudroom."

"I should've come around to the side of the house."

"Stop stressing over a little water, Viola," he admonished in a quiet tone. When she'd asked who cleaned his house, he'd admitted he did. And he also confessed to being a neat freak, resulting from his father's asthma and seasonal allergies. "After I put your rain gear away, I'll take you to your bedroom."

Dom returned from the mudroom to find Viola at the foot of the staircase with her bag. He eased it from her loose grip and took her hand, his thumb grazing the inside of her wrist to find her rapidly beating pulse.

He lowered his head and brushed a light kiss over her mouth.

"The management will offer you clean towels and turn-down bed service every night. I'm sorry to inform you that we ran out of mints to put on the bed, so the next time you come I'll make certain we stock them. I'm also sorry there isn't a bathroom in your room. However, there is one across the hall."

"That's okay, Dom. I haven't had an en suite bath since leaving home."

"How many rooms did your house have?"

"Six bedrooms and seven baths."

"Was the housekeeper overwhelmed keeping house for a large family?"

"Miss Amelia never appeared frazzled to me. We were taught to make our beds and put away our clothes, so all she had to do was vacuum and dust. We had two commercial washers and dryers in the laundry room, and they were on from morning to early afternoon. That's when she folded clothes while watching her daytime soaps and talk shows."

Dom led Viola past his bedroom and down the carpeted hallway to one that overlooked the rear of the house. "Did she ever go on vacation?" He was intrigued to know how Conrad's children had grown up.

"Oh, yes. She'd fly down to Florida a couple of times a year to stay with her sister. Miss Amelia never married or had children, but doted on her nieces and nephews."

"What happened when she was away?"

"Momma called an agency for them to send a temp. Although I'd learned to make a bed and clean up after myself, I never got the knack of doing laundry. Once

I move to Manhattan, I paid for pick-up and drop-off service."

*That's why your father called you princess*, Dom thought. "Here's your room. If you find it too cold for your comfort, I can turn up the heat or build a fire in the fireplace. Even though the house has indoor heating, I usually don't turn it on until the temperature goes below fifty."

Viola entered the bedroom and pressed the fingers of her free hand to her mouth. She felt as if she'd stepped back in time with the magnificent mahogany sleigh bed with white lace and embroidered bedcovers. Matching lace sheers covered the tall, narrow, shuttered windows. A floral rug, hand-painted chests, an overstuffed chair covered in chintz and a bench at the foot of the bed covered in the same fabric had turned the space into a quiet retreat.

She glanced up to find Dom intently watching her. "There's no need for a fire. The room's perfect."

He let go of her hand and set her bag on the floor. "I'm glad you like it. I'll let you get settled, and then after that you can come downstairs whenever you're ready."

Viola waited until he left and closed the door to examine the space where she would spend the night. She hadn't seen any of the second-floor suites in the château because it was off-limits to everyone except the contractors. But if the furnishings in the guesthouses were this luxurious, then those in the château were either comparable or even more opulent.

Bainbridge guests, regardless of wherever they stayed on the estate, were no doubt pandered to with every amenity befitting their social status. Viola tried imagining women—dressed in the height of fashion and wearing priceless jewels, on the arms of their formally attired husbands—clutching their breasts and possibly swooning if they had glimpsed the future to discover that the mixed-race adopted children of Conrad Williamson were now the owners of the vast estate where they'd preened, dined and been entertained by live musicians in the ballrooms with marble floors and massive crystal chandeliers.

The notion that Dom was waiting downstairs shattered Viola's reverie and she began unpacking, storing several changes of clothes in a chest-on-chest lined with sachet-scented paper. She removed a cosmetic bag and walked across the hall to the bathroom. The bathroom was also furnished with antiques. A fireplace, mahogany wardrobe, an antique cross-legged table, fluted-column pedestal sink, an oversized claw-foot tub with brass fixtures, and a narrow shower stall and framed prints of pen-and-ink architectural drawings on the walls beckoned her to come in and linger awhile. She crossed the room and peered into an alcove to find a commode and bidet.

Viola took a wide-tooth comb from the cosmetic bag and ran it through her hair. She still hadn't decided whether to cut it before Sonja's wedding. If not, then a stylist could blow out the curls and pin it up for a more sophisticated look. She stared at her image in a shaving mirror resting on a mahogany pedestal, wondering who she most resembled—her biological mother or father. The year she'd celebrated her sixth birthday, she'd asked Elise why everyone in their family looked different. The exception was Patrick, who had the same red hair and blue eyes as their mother. Elise had explained as simply as she could to a six-year-old that she had chosen all her children because they did not have mommies and daddies. Some of the mothers and fathers of Viola's brothers had either passed away or been unable to care for them. That was why Elise had brought them home to live with her.

Once Elise believed Viola was old enough to understand the circumstances surrounding her birth, she'd told her everything, and then, as she'd done with her sons, Elise had her daughter see a therapist to work through whatever issues she had about becoming a foster child. The therapist had recommended Viola keep a diary to write down her thoughts. The date that proved the most momentous in her young life was when she and her four brothers stood together in a courtroom to legally become the sons and daughter of Conrad and Elise Williamson.

Even after Elise's revelation that Viola's biological mother had died in an automobile accident, and the name of her biological father was not listed on her birth certificate, Viola had no desire to look for her birth mother's relatives. She was grateful for the love from her adopted parents and thought of it as an act of betrayal if she were to connect with relatives with whom she shared DNA. She'd vowed to leave well enough alone.

Viola left the bathroom and went downstairs. The aroma of popcorn and burning wood wafted to her nostrils as she walked into the family room to see the flickering flames behind a decorative screen in the fireplace. Watching movies while eating popcorn was a reminder of what she'd shared with her roommate when both were off on the same day.

She met Dom as he came out of the kitchen carrying a large bowl of popcorn. "I love the smell of popcorn."

Dom laughed. "You sound like Robert Duvall in *Apocalypse Now* when he said, 'I love the smell of napalm in the morning.'"

Viola also laughed. "Maybe I should've said I love the smell of popcorn in the morning, afternoon and at night. It's my go-to snack food."

He set the bowl on the table next to the chaise. "For me, it's potato chips." Dom didn't want to tell Viola that once he opened a bag, he found he couldn't stop eating chips until the bag was empty. "What genre of movie do you want?"

"What choices do I have?"

Walking over to an armoire, he opened the doors to revealed shelves packed tightly with DVDs, Blu-ray discs, CDs and vinyl records in their own sleeves. "Take your pick."

"Damn!" Viola whispered as she stared at the collection. "When did you get all of these?" She picked up a shrink-wrapped record and turned it over to read the back cover. "You like Blues?"

Dom approached her. "That belonged to my grandmother. In fact, all the records were hers. Her musical preferences crossed genres. One night she'd play Muddy Waters and then on another night it would be country with Patsy Cline. She grew up listening to the radio and watching black-and-white television. Even with the advent of color TV, she preferred watching black-and-white reruns."

Viola sorted through several albums. "You know these records are probably much sought after by collectors of vinyl."

Dom took one from her and slipped it back in place. "I know, but something won't allow me to sell them. Other than photographs, they are lasting memories of my grandmother." He flashed a sheepish grin. "I know you must think of me as a sappy sentimentalist, and I'll gladly embrace that, but some things are just worth holding on to."

Viola shifted slightly to look at him. "There's nothing wrong with being a sentimentalist, Dom. I've also been accused of being one."

Table lamps and the glow from the fire cast long and short shadows over Viola's features, and never had Dom seen her look more enthralling. Everything about her ignited his senses until he struggled not to sweep her up in his arms and carry her upstairs to his bedroom. He was transfixed by the black silky curls falling around her face. Then there were her hypnotic eyes with glints of green and gold that were imprinted on his brain much like a permanent tattoo. They no longer reminded him of his ex-wife because Kaitlyn's had seldom been soft and inviting, but were frosty and angry.

Dom had come to recognize the fragrance of Viola's perfume, and if challenged, he would be able to identify her in a darkened room with a crowd of other women. And then there was her laugh. Though high-pitched, he hadn't found it annoying but infectious. His strongest fantasy was to strip Viola naked and run his mouth and hands over her silken body and feast on every inch before satiating them both.

The physical pull he felt whenever he and Viola

claimed the same space was so strong, Dom believed she'd woven some spell over him he was helpless to resist. A spell he did not want to break or escape. He did not know what it was about Taylor Williamson's sister that had turned his predictable life upside down where he feared falling in love with her. Not only did he want a relationship, but also a committed one.

"I told you before that we make a good team."

"You're right," Viola said, smiling.

"Have you decided which movie you want to see?"

She shifted her attention to hundreds of movies lining the armoire's shelves. "I can't believe you've alphabetized all of them."

"Initially, I thought of cataloging them into genres like the library's Dewey decimal system, but found that too frustrating. It was easier to alphabetize them."

"I feel like a kid in a candy store and there's so much that I can't decide what I want."

"You claim you like the Roaring Twenties."

"I do," Viola confirmed.

Dom selected a movie and handed it to her. "*Live by Night* is set in post-World War I and deals with bootlegging. Even though it's rated R for strong violence and language, I think you'll enjoy it."

"Stop it, Dom," she admonished softly. "I grew up with four brothers who weren't permitted to cuss in the house, but really knew how to let loose whenever my mother wasn't around. And believe me, I can cuss with the best of them, so an R-rated movie isn't going to make me blush."

*That's my girl*, Dom thought. It was apparent Viola was tough without sacrificing any of her femininity. He picked up the remote device off the mantel and turned on the television. "Do you want anything to drink to go along with the popcorn?"

"No, thank you."

He slipped the DVD into a component on a table several feet from the fireplace and synced it with the television. Viola sat on the chaise, and he startled her when he lifted her effortlessly, sat down and settled her between his outstretched legs. Reaching over, he turned off the table lamp and then picked up the bowl of popcorn, which he set in her lap, and then handed her several napkins.

"Comfortable enough," he whispered in her ear.

"Yes."

Although he'd watched the movie before, Dom found it more enjoyable the second time with Viola's body pressed against his. The lighting, costumes, locations and automobiles were spot-on during Prohibition with gangster-run speakeasies. Two hours had passed much too quickly as the closing credits rolled across the screen.

Dom pressed a light kiss on the nape of Viola's neck when she let out a soft moan. "What's the matter, babe?"

"I can't believe they killed Graciela."

"Given all that Joe Coughlin had done in his life, do you think he was entitled to a happily-ever-after?"

"I know he'd left the life of an outlaw behind and was willing to go straight, so I believe that was enough repentance."

Dom wanted to tell Viola that she was being naive. "You have to remember he was the son of Boston police captain, yet he had chosen to live life on the dark side, which always carries a heavy price. He'd gone to prison and that should've been enough for him to turn his life around. However, it was the pull of power and money that made him a prisoner of his own demise, and in the end, although he wasn't killed, he did lose the love of his life."

Viola sighed again. "I suppose I see it that way. He didn't lose everything because he did have his son."

"A son who will carry the sins of his father."

Viola shifted on the chaise until she was facing Dom. "Why would you say that?"

"Haven't you heard the expression that the sins of the father will be visited upon the sons?" She nodded. "Joe Coughlin made his money breaking the law robbing and murdering. And when his son is older, he will come to know who his father was and what he'd done to give him a comfortable life that he wouldn't have had if Joe hadn't been a gangster. Even if Tomas decides he wants to be an honest and respectable citizen, he'll still carry the stigma that his father was a criminal."

"So, when would it end, Dom? When would the sons have to stop making amends or repent for prior generations?"

"I don't know," he answered truthfully.

What Dom couldn't tell Viola was that her father had asked him to take on two of his clients not because Patrick quit, but out of necessity. Conrad was aware that Dom had earned degrees in economics, accounting and finance and during a rare call had asked if Dom could come into Manhattan for a meeting. After listening to the older man's proposition, Dom had turned him down, but Conrad wouldn't be denied. He'd gone into a spiel that blood was thicker than water.

It was the first time Conrad had acknowledged their kinship.

It had been a closely held secret—a secret Sonja Rios-Martin had uncovered with her meticulous research—that Melanie Shaw, a fifteen-year-old house servant, had been seduced by Charles Bainbridge and bore him a love child. A love child who was Charles's illegitimate son.

Charles loved his wife, but was obsessed with Melanie and refused to give her up. He'd set her up in one of the guesthouses and showered her with gifts of jewelry worth millions today. Although Melanie had known she would never become Mrs. Charles Bainbridge, she'd convinced him to set up an irrevocable trust that a male Shaw would become the estate's caretaker in perpetuity.

Carrying Bainbridge DNA was not a badge of honor for Dom. How could he respect a married man who had eventually fathered ten legitimate children, but had also seduced a young girl and gotten her pregnant? Instead of setting Melanie up with own her residence, away from his family, as many wealthy men did for their mistresses, Charles had continued his life of respectability when he'd moved his family to their Fifth Avenue mansion at the end of the summer season, leaving Melanie and a small staff at Bainbridge House year-round.

It was only after he'd closed the Manhattan graystone to return to New Jersey that he continued his affair with Melanie. She'd borne him a second child, who was stillborn, and then a third, who was so severely deformed Charles had ordered the midwife to get rid of it. Melanie wrote love letters to Charles that she'd never mailed and kept a journal where she'd detailed everything about her illicit affair with her boss. The journal had been hidden in a false-bottomed drawer, discovered years later by her son's wife.

Charles's sin was also Conrad's sin because Viola's adopted father believed he carried the shame of what his ancestor had done to an orphaned young girl. To atone for Charles's transgressions, Conrad had adopted five children.

"Thank you for recommending the movie. I really enjoyed it."

As much as Dom enjoyed Viola straddling his lap, he felt the flesh hardening between his thighs and knew if she didn't get up she would know just how little control he had over his body. He blew out an inaudible breath when she stood, rising with her. "Are you ready for a second feature?"

"Not tonight." Going on tiptoe, she pressed her mouth to his. "I'm going to turn in now."

Dom ruffled her curls. "Do you need me to tuck you in?" he teased.

Viola scrunched up her nose. "I don't think so."

"Do you want breakfast or brunch?" he asked, prolonging her departure because he wasn't ready to let her go.

"Breakfast, but only if you allow me to be your sous chef."

"Come now, Viola. You know you don't need to ask." He paused. "But there is something I need to ask you."

"What is it?"

"A friend I went to college with invited me to his house in Baltimore for a Halloween party. I was wondering if you'd be willing to go with me and wear your flapper costume."

Viola's eyes lit up like a child's on Christmas morning when she spotted mounds of gaily wrapped presents under the tree. "Of course! What do you plan to go as?"

"A gangster, of course. I should be able to find a suit in the store in town that sells vintage clothes and other paraphernalia going back decades."

"Joe Coughlin and Albert White's girlfriend Emma Gould will have nothing on us."

Dom felt a powerful relief that Viola had warmed quickly to the idea of accompanying him to reconnect with his friend combining a holiday celebration with a housewarming. "As soon as Marcus sends me the particulars, I'll let you know."

"Okay. Good night, Dom."

"Good night, princess."

## *Chapter Twelve*

Dom sat at the breakfast bar drinking coffee, waiting for Viola to join him. How different this morning began compared to twenty-four hours before; then he was alone and now he waited for a woman who appealed to everything he needed and had come to share a minuscule piece of his life.

He was mature enough not to delude himself into believing he could have with Viola what her brother had with Sonja. The few times he'd witnessed Taylor and Sonja together, he'd known they were destined to become a couple. The way Taylor stared at the architectural historian spoke volumes. And what he'd recognized in Taylor, he now had to acknowledge was similar to his reaction to Viola.

For Dom, there were two Violas. There was the free spirit and there was also the old spirit, and there were times when he couldn't decide which one he liked best. He felt more alive whenever she was playful, teasing, appearing as if she didn't have a care in the world. That she could go through life doing exactly what fancied her at the time. Then there was the more serious side. The young woman who liked old clothes, cars, farming and possibly a simpler way of life. However, the latter was certain to conflict with the career-driven, twenty-first-century Viola. Women in the 1920s had fought hard to secure the vote and a century later were still fighting for myriad issues that included equality in the workplace.

Viola being denied a promotion had forced her into a situation she hadn't planned. She'd wanted to advance in a Michelin-star restaurant, but when it hadn't happened, she'd quit. As a professional chef there was no doubt she could've secured a position with another eating establishment, but she would have to start at the bottom to prove herself.

Conrad's passing had given her what she'd needed to control her destiny. His wish to restore and reopen Bainbridge House as a hotel was a gift to her that she probably could never have imagined. Conrad had offered her the money to open her own restaurant and she'd rejected it. Now, he had given her a second chance to supervise the kitchens at the hotel, and she'd accepted it.

Viola had secured her future while Dom was uncertain about his own. He'd admitted to her that he liked living alone and enjoyed being caretaker for the estate. He'd said that because he'd believed that was what she wanted to hear. Yet Dom knew he wasn't being completely truthful. During his last telephone conversation with his father, he'd told James Shaw that he was now certain he was going to leave Bainbridge House once the restoration was completed. It would be the first time in a century that a Shaw would no longer be connected to the estate. He would give Taylor enough notice to hire another caretaker.

When he'd first read the Alexandre Dumas literary masterpiece *The Count of Monte Cristo* in high school, Dom had identified with the protagonist Edmond Dantès because of the word *château*. Dantès had been falsely accused of treason and sentenced to spend the rest of his life at the Château d'If, while Dom had been reminded every so often by his father that as a Shaw his future was linked to an estate on which there was a château. At the time, James Shaw had no inkling that his son did not want to spend his entire life at Bainbridge House.

Dantés managed to escape his prison after thirteen years to reinvent himself as the Count of Monte Cristo. It hadn't been the same for Dom. He'd become a licensed plumber, earned degrees in economics and business, and still he hadn't been able to escape a château to which he had no claim.

Viola had asked for their relationship to unfold slowly, unaware that in two years they would go their separate ways to live separate lives. She would become executive chef at the hotel, and he would apply for a position with an investment company.

Viola could not believe she'd slept so soundly. As soon as her head touched the pillow, it was night-night. When she woke, she found the house eerily silent, wondering if Dom had gone out since the rain had stopped. She completed her morning ablutions and, after slipping into a pair of leggings, long-sleeved tee and thick socks, she went downstairs to look for Dom. She found him in the kitchen drinking coffee.

"Good morning. Have you been up long?"

He slipped off the stool and came over to kiss her cheek. "No, and good morning. I'd thought about going out to see if there is any storm damage, but decided to wait for you."

Viola felt as if she were drowning in a pool covered with waterlilies when staring into Dom's eyes. He hadn't shaved and his stubble made him even more attractive. She still was coming to grips with what she'd been searching in vain for in other men was standing right in front of her. She heard women talk about finding their soul mate and now she knew exactly what they meant.

"I'm glad you waited, because I'd like to go with you."

He appeared shocked with her suggestion when he asked, "Really?"

"Yes, Dom. Really. First I'm going to brew a cup of coffee before I go back upstairs and put on more clothes."

Dom rested a hand at the small of her back. "I'll make the coffee while you get dressed."

Going on tiptoe, Viola kissed his stubble. "Thank you, love."

His arm pulled her closer. "Love, Viola? Do you actually believe you could love me?"

Viola wanted to tell him it was just a figure of speech then changed her mind. "Yes," she admitted candidly. "What's the matter, Dom? Do you believe you're not worthy of a woman loving you?"

"It's not about whether I'm worthy, Viola."

"Then what is it about?" she asked.

"It's about us. Don't you think falling in love will ruin everything?"

"For whom, Dom? For you or for me?" He stared at her, reminding Viola of a deer caught in the headlights. "Forget I said it."

"No. I'm not going to forget it, Viola. I just want to warn you there's going to be talk once the word gets out the caretaker and one of the owners of the estate are carrying on with each other."

Viola closed her eyes and counted slowly to three. "I don't care, Dom. Taylor and Sonja already know that I'm seeing you."

Dom wondered how many more shocks he would have to experience before the day ended. He'd already warned Taylor about confronting him regarding his interaction with his sister, but he had been unaware Viola had talked about their friendship to her brother and future sister-in-law.

"What did he say?"

"He said, and I quote, 'Viola is a grown woman and I've learned not to get involved with her relationships with other men. Unfortunately, there was one time when I had to intervene and after that I promised myself never again.'"

Color suffused Viola's face at the same she lowered her eyes. "Taylor tends to be somewhat overprotective when it comes to women."

"Good for him. Now, back to us, Viola."

"What about us?" she asked, meeting his eyes.

"If what we have does progress to love, where do you see it going?"

"I don't know, Dom. There was a time when I wanted to marry, have children and a career."

"Has that changed for you?"

"Not really," Viola admitted. "I still want it, but not necessarily in that order."

"Are you saying you want a career first then marriage and finally children?"

She nodded. "Yes."

Dom dropped his arm. "I told you before, and I promise I would never do anything to stymie your career."

"Thank you," she whispered.

He wanted to ask her about marriage and children and then changed his mind. There had been a time when he'd wanted to start a family and when it hadn't happened, Dom dismissed the notion as if it had never entered his mind.

Dom knew he was falling in love with Viola because there wasn't anything about her he didn't love. It was as if he'd been waiting all his life for someone like her to come along, yet there was an impediment he could not forget. He was the caretaker on the property she owned with her brothers. It felt as if history was repeating itself. He was a Shaw who had been denied his birthright because he was the illegitimate descendant of Charles Bainbridge.

"I'll make your coffee while you go upstairs and change," he said, rather than prolong their conversation about who they were and what they wanted. After all, they had time—plenty of time in which to map out their futures. Either together or separately.

Viola sat next to Dom in the Subaru as he drove into town. After their discussion earlier that morning she'd accompanied him in Lollipop to drive around the entire estate to look for downed tree limbs or missing roof tiles. The bed of the pickup was filled with broken branches that Dom said he would allow to dry out before cutting them into firewood.

He'd wanted eggs Benedict for breakfast and Viola had suggested they vary the popular Yankee original with a distinctly Southern take with poached eggs nestled on buttermilk biscuits and smothered with sausage gravy. She'd made the biscuits while instructing him step-by-step how to make the gravy. Viola promised she would show him how to make five other versions of the classic brunch dish after he'd taken a photo of the plate with his phone, teasing her that he was thinking about becoming a food blogger.

Now they headed into town to have dinner at his friend's pub. Dom drove so he could show her around town.

Lost in her own thoughts as they meandered along the country lanes, Viola focused on their comfort with each other. She knew calling Dom "love" held a different connotation than when she called Taylor "brother love." She knew of her deepening feeling for Dom, yet she wasn't ready to openly acknowledge them. She hadn't held back when she'd admitted she wanted marriage, children and a career, even though she wasn't ready to sacrifice one over the others.

Her mother had had all three. Elise had married, become a teacher, and had given up a traditional classroom to educate her foster children. Viola knew she could marry, supervise her kitchens and eventually have a child or children.

She shared a smile with Dom when he rested his right hand on her knee. "How often do you go into town?"

"At least once every couple of weeks to pick up what I need at the supermarket."

"You don't have a Costco or BJ's?"

"No. This part of Jersey is stuck in time where most folks don't want big-box stores, fast-food joints or Starbucks because they would put the mom-and-pop shops out of business. I'm surprised you hadn't gone into town before now to check it out."

"I spend most of my time in Sparta where I don't have to leave the gated community to find whatever I need."

"I'm going to warn you that you'll probably experience culture shock because downtown is the perfect setting for a movie set in the fifties."

"Where did kids in school hang out?"

"There's a diner most families frequent on the weekends. Jameson's is the pub that has a special lunch menu for school kids during the day. It is the go-to spot for grown folks at night. There is a movie theater with two screens. The movies are a couple of months behind what you'd find in the malls with their multiple screens, but the upside is the admission is a lot cheaper."

"How far is the mall from here?"

"Less than ten miles. We're close to the Pennsylvania border and the Delaware Water Gap National Recreation Area."

"I suppose as a reclaimed Jersey girl I need to get out more."

"Did you ever stop being a Jersey girl?"

Viola reversed their hands, hers gently squeezing his long, slender fingers. "I suppose I did when I lived in the Village. You couldn't tell I wasn't a city girl until I opened my mouth. The first time someone told me I had an accent, I took offense. To me it was like saying I came from Brooklyn where people have a distinctive way of speaking, like saying 'earl' for 'oil.'"

"Don't fight it, babe. We do speak differently from other states."

"So, you like being a Jersey boy?"

Lines fanned out around his eyes when he smiled. "There's nothing better."

"I rest my case."

Viola realized Dom had been spot-on when describing the downtown business district. Hints of cobblestone and what had been trolley tracks were visible where the pavement had been worn down. They drove past the feed and farm equipment store, drugstore, hair salon, dry cleaner's, pet grooming, hardware store and butcher shop. Dom turned the corner and there were more small shops catering to the needs of those in the hamlet with a population of a little more than thirty-five hundred.

"It's charming," she said as he pulled into a parking space behind a row of stores.

Dom cut the engine. "I knew you would like it."

Viola wanted to tell Dom that she liked him. A lot. She had never had a preference for how men wore their hair if it was clean, but she really did like the jet-black hair brushed off his forehead and secured in a bun. She'd wanted to ask him why he'd opted not to cut it, and then chided herself for trying to get into the man's personal business. She had already asked him a litany of questions, most of which he'd answered, but a few had remained unanswered.

"I hope you brought your appetite because the food at Jameson's is incredible."

"Yes," Viola confirmed.

Dom helped her out and led her into the restaurant using the rear door, and she was assaulted with mouth-watering aromas, an instantaneous reminder that she hadn't eaten in more than eight hours.

His arm circled her waist as he steered her into the dining room where patrons lined a bar, eating, drinking and watching muted television screens tuned to channels showing sporting events. The establishment featured a mahogany bar, tables and booths—the quintessential sports bar that could be found in most New York neighborhoods.

"Well, well, well! As I live and breathe, it's the return of the prodigal son!" shouted a tall man sporting a military crewcut from behind the bar. "Dominic Shaw, get the hell over here so I make certain I'm not seeing an apparition."

Dom pressed his mouth to Viola's ear. "He's the owner and he's all bark and no bite."

She moved closer to his side. "That's obvious. Go and greet your friend."

"Not without you," he said sotto voce.

Viola had no choice but to follow him to the bar. She smiled when the bartender rounded the bar and enveloped Dom in a bear hug. The two men were obviously quite fond of each other.

"Shouldn't you be in the kitchen?" Dom asked.

"I just filling in for Bobby. He's on his break right now."

"Let me go, J.J., so I can introduce you to someone."

Viola met the dark brown eyes of the man Dom

called J.J. She bit back a smile when he stared at her as if she had a third eye in the middle of her forehead. It was obvious Dom hadn't told his friend he was bringing someone with him.

"Holy crap! Please don't tell me Rhianna just walked into my place."

Viola laughed. It wasn't the first time she had been mistaken for the beautiful, talented singer. "I'm definitely not Rhianna." Dom draped an arm over her shoulders and she knew the proprietary gesture was not lost on J.J. when he sobered quickly.

"J.J., I would like you to meet my girlfriend, Viola Williamson. Viola, Jack Jameson, the esteemed owner of this venerable establishment."

J.J. extended his right hand, but not before wiping it on his apron. "It's a pleasure meeting you, Viola. I hope you're the reason why my MIA friend has decided to grace us with his presence."

Viola shared a glance with Dom. "I'd like to think so."

"This *one* is a definite keeper," J.J. said to Dom.

Viola wondered how many other women had accompanied Dom to his friend's restaurant. When she thought about it, the number was irrelevant. He'd had a life before meeting her and she believed in letting the past remain in the past. And she was somewhat surprised that he'd introduced her as his girlfriend.

"Do you think we can get a booth?" Dom asked.

"Sure. I'll have one of the waitstaff bring you your usual Glenfiddich." He beckoned at a young waiter. "Please seat my friends in a booth."

"Forget the Glenfiddich," Dom told J.J. "I'm carrying precious cargo tonight. I'll have whatever beer you have on tap."

Viola knew Dom favored scotch as evidenced by the number of bottles lining the bookshelf in the living room. All of them were unopened except for one. "Why didn't you order the scotch? I don't mind being the designated driver," she said after they were seated in a corner booth and given menus.

"I'm not that much of a drinker anymore. I'd rather collect aged scotch than drink it. The last time I drank was with Taylor when he bested me playing pool."

Viola stared at Dom, speechless. "You played pool with my brother?" she asked, recovering her voice.

"Yep. We were playing for a bottle of aged scotch and he beat the pants off me. In fact, he left his case with his cues at my place. Even though I lost, Taylor opened a bottle of your father's fourteen-year-old Balvenie Caribbean Cask and we tossed back a few. I told him he could stay and sleep it off but after coffee loaded with espresso, he managed to make it home unscathed."

Viola saw Dom in a whole new light. She had no idea he and Taylor had bonded over a game of pool. "My father also collected aged liquor. My mother boxed up the bottles and left them the garage. She says she's going to give them to Taylor after he and Sonja settle into their permanent home."

"Do you play?" Dom asked.

"Yes, I do." She wanted to tell him all of Conrad's kids played the game.

"Maybe one of these days you can show me what you've got."

She angled her head. "Are you challenging me to a game?"

"I am," he said, smiling.

"What are you willing to wager? And please don't say scotch, because don't I drink it, and I also have no intention of becoming a collector."

Dom flashed a sheepish grin as he reached across the table to grasp her hands. "Give me time and I'll come up with something we both can agree on." Rising slightly, he leaned over and pressed a kiss on her hands before letting them go. "Do you want me to order something from the bar for you?"

"I'll have a rosé." It was the first thing that popped into her head.

"Have you sampled any of the wines in the château's basement?"

"No. Have you?"

"I don't drink wine. I do make an exception for champagne. The bottles have been there for decades. Maybe you should sample one or two to see if they're palatable. When I go to the château on Monday for the crew meeting, I will pick up a couple of bottles from different years."

"If they're too acidic, maybe I can use them in the kitchen as cooking wine." Viola glanced at the menu in front of her. "What do you recommend?"

"Everything. The steak bites are exceptional."

Viola continued to peruse the menu. "Did you ever order the lamb burger?"

"No. It wasn't on the menu the last time I was here."

Her head popped up and she looked at him. "How long ago was that?"

Dom looked at Viola through half-closed lids, wondering if J.J.'s statement about her being a keeper was a reference to his bringing other women to the pub. There had been occasions when he had invited a woman to accompany him after his divorce was finalized, but less frequently over the past year. "It was sometime after Easter." A half smile lifted one side of his mouth. "And I came alone."

"It doesn't matter if you did or you didn't, Dom. I don't believe in revisiting the past. I will never ask you about the women in your past if you don't ask me about the men I've dated."

He nodded. "Will you answer one question? Then the topic is moot."

"What's that?"

"Were you ever in love?"

A dreamy expression flitted over her features. "There was a time when I'd believed I was, but when I look back, I realize it was nothing more than infatuation. Is there anything else you want to ask me?"

Dom struggled to keep a straight face. He'd been hoping she would say that. What he did not want was to compete or be compared to one of her old boyfriends. When Taylor mentioned he'd had to intervene after the breakup of one liaison, he'd wondered what had become so extreme for her brother to become involved.

"No."

Viola went back to studying the menu. "I think I'm going to order the lamb burger with hummus and a small Greek salad."

Dom nodded. "That sounds good. I'm going to have the butter steak bites with garlic string beans and a house salad."

She set the menu aside. "This place is really nice. I like the stained-glass insets around the windows."

"It is nice. It underwent a major renovation some time back. Rumor has it that it doubled as a speakeasy during Prohibition, but no one could prove it."

Viola's eyes lit up with excitement. "Where did they serve the booze?"

"I couldn't tell. Like I said, it was just a rumor."

"I did notice there were doors marked Private when we came in through the rear. Maybe that is where folks gathered to drink."

Dom's eyebrows lifted slightly. "Could be."

Viola scrunched up her nose, the gesture bringing his gaze to linger on her delicate features. J.J. had mistaken her for Rhianna and she did share similar physical characteristics with the singer: complexion, eye color and body type.

The waiter brought him his beer along with Viola's wine and then took their food orders.

The noise level increased exponentially with the number of couples filing into the restaurant. It was Saturday, date night, and with good food, prerecorded music coming from hidden speakers and a fully stocked bar, including commercial and craft beers, Jameson's was a popular spot for locals and those from neighboring towns.

J.J. came over, sat down next to Dom and stretched an arm over the back of the booth. "I have a few minutes to catch up on what's been happening with you before I have to go back to the kitchen. It's been like a month of Sundays since you were last here. What's up?"

"Busy, J.J."

"I heard a rumor about the work on Bainbridge House. That they're turning it into a hotel."

Dom exchanged a look with Viola. A beat passed and then she give him imperceptible nod. "You heard right."

J.J. ran a finger over the noticeable bump on the bridge of his nose. "That's good. It's a shame that gorgeous piece of real estate was vacant for so long. When do you expect it to be open for business?"

"Probably not for a couple of years."

"Are you going hang around after it opens?"

Dom couldn't believe his friend was putting him on the spot in front of Viola. He had only planned to stay until the grand opening. All hotels were staffed with employees to take care of the interior and exterior of the property; it would be easy for the Williamsons to hire a workforce to do what generations of Shaws had done for years.

"Yes."

J.J. patted his shoulder. "I'm glad to hear that." He winked at Viola. "Don't be a stranger." He pushed off the booth. "By the way, what did you order, Viola?"

"The lamb burger."

"I just put that on the menu the other day. Will you let me know if you like it?"

Viola smiled up at him. "Of course."

"You know he was flirting with you," Dom said when his friend was out of earshot.

Viola gave him an incredulous look. "No, he wasn't, Dom. He was just being friendly."

He wanted to tell Viola that she was being naive. Although married, J.J. couldn't keep his eyes off Viola. And if he were honest, Dom would tell her he, too, never tired of staring at her. Whenever they were together, he was hard-pressed to keep his hands off her as well. The need to make love with Viola bordered on an obsession he'd never experienced with any other woman.

The waiter approached the table with Viola's wine and set the glass on a coaster. Dom lifted his mug of beer in a toast. "Here's to the most beautiful woman in the room." She lowered her eyes as a flush suffused her face, charming Dom with the gesture. "Did I embarrass you?"

She looked directly at him. "No. I just didn't expect you to say that."

"Men haven't told you that you are beautiful?"

Viola took a sip of wine, staring at him over the rim. "Men say a lot of things, Dom. I've learned not to believe everything I hear. It doesn't take much effort to lie, and even less effort for one to believe the lie."

"Spoken like someone with a lot of experience."

Viola wanted to tell Dom that, when she'd left home for the first time, she hadn't realized how totally unprepared she'd been for interacting with the opposite sex. If she'd attended a traditional high school, she would've been exposed to boys with a reputation for taking advantage of girls to boost their image. If she had, then she would've recognized the signals when her lover was cheating on her.

"Spoken like someone with too much experience. I don't know which I hate most—a liar or a cheater."

"Aren't they one and the same?"

"Not really. Some people lie. Some steal. And some cheat."

"That's a trifecta of deviant behavior."

Viola nodded. "And I've met folks afflicted with at least one or two traits, but rarely all three."

Dom leaned forward. "I'm far from perfect, but I will never lie, steal or cheat on you."

The seconds ticked as Viola gave him a long, penetrating stare. She didn't know why, but she believed Dom. He'd admitted having trust issues with women, which probably stemmed from someone who had lied or cheated on him. For her, it was much more simplistic. One had cheated on her while the others were liars. After a while she'd given up trying to find Mr. Right to focus on herself and her career.

"I know that," she said softly, following the pregnant pause. The admission was barely off her tongue when J.J. reappeared with her order. He set the plate on the table.

"Let me know if you like it."

Viola smiled. "If it tastes as good as the presentation, then it has to be a winner." She picked up the brioche bun holding the burger slathered with a feta yogurt sauce. She took a bite and an explosion of flavors woke up her taste buds with feta cheese and sliced red onion. She closed her eyes and sighed after swallowing a mouthful of delicious lamb. "It's perfect. The mint, lemon, juice—and substituting arugula for lettuce is genius."

J.J. smiled. "You could taste the mint?"

"Yes. It's subtle, but I know it's there."

"You're good."

"She should be," Dom said. "She's a chef."

The pub owner went completely still. "A chef, chef?"

Viola nodded, smiling. "Yes. A chef, chef," she repeated.

"Where did you go to school?"

"Tell him, babe," Dom said when she hesitated.

She narrowed her eyes at him. Viola hadn't expected him to become her publicist. "The Culinary Institute of America."

J.J. clasped his large hands. "Hot damn! It's not every day I get a bona fide chef to critique my food."

Viola wanted to tell the man she wasn't there to critique his dishes but to enjoy spending time with Dom away from Bainbridge House. Instead, she said, "I definitely give you a thumbs-up for the burger." She hadn't lied to J.J. The meat was cooked perfectly with a slightly pink center.

J.J. folded his body down next to Viola. "Where are you working?"

*Please go away and let me enjoy my burger.* Viola took another bite, hoping the man would get the hint and let her eat her dinner. But he was not to be denied. "I'm currently unemployed."

"Do you want to come and work for me?"

"I can't. I have another commitment."

J.J.'s broad shoulders slumped in resignation. "Can you tell me where?"

She knew if she didn't tell him, the news would eventually get out once the restoration was nearing completion. "I'm going to become the executive chef at Bainbridge House."

"Congratulations. Dom, you'll have to let me know to stop by once the hotel is open for business."

"Will do, buddy." Dom's order arrived, and J.J. excused himself. "I'm sorry about that, babe."

"There's no need to apologize," Viola said as she tore a piece of pita to scoop up hummus. "The restoration at the estate is hardly a secret."

"You shocked J.J. when you were able to identify the ingredients in the burger."

"It's all about developing a discerning palate. It also helps if your olfactory nerves are working."

Dom speared a cube of steak and put it on her plate. "Can you tell me what's in the steak?"

She smiled at him. "Is this a test?"

He returned her smile. "No. I want to know what's in it so one day I'll make it for us."

Viola noticed he'd said *us* and not *myself.* She popped the steak in her mouth and slowly chewed. "Garlic, onion and garlic powder, oregano and thyme. There's also some black pepper, brown sugar, cayenne pepper, chili powder and what is probably mild paprika. It's definitely Cajun."

Dom shook his head. "You're incredible. Do you think you can duplicate the recipe?"

"Probably after a few attempts. It's not the ingredients but how much of each to add."

Viola thoroughly enjoyed the lamb burger and knew it could be a delicious addition to the Mongolian beef, and sweet-and-sour mini cocktail burgers she'd planned for the bar menu.

"I am as full as a tick," Viola admitted as she fastened her seat belt.

Dom tapped the Start button. "You really didn't eat that much."

"I shouldn't have had dessert."

"I ate more than half the pie." Dom could never resist ordering Jameson's coconut custard pie. He backed out of the parking spot and turned onto Main Street.

"Do you plan to go back to Sparta tonight or stay at my place?"

"Your place."

Dom was grinning so much, his jaw ached. It was the first, and what he hoped was the beginning, of many more weekends they would spend together.

## *Chapter Thirteen*

Dom was still on a high when he walked into the château early Monday morning. There were only a few pickups and vans parked in the driveway. Viola staying with him during the weekend had given him a glimpse into what he could look forward to if they decided to live together, but he'd quickly dashed that notion. Their relationship was too new for him to entertain their cohabitating even remotely. Common sense warred with desire—he knew common sense had to hold out, at least for a while.

When Viola left Sunday afternoon to return to Sparta, he'd unloaded the fallen branches from Lollipop's bed and chopped them into firewood with an ax rather than use an electric saw. The exercise helped rid him of the sexual frustration that had been building with each encounter with Viola. He'd kissed her and she'd responded in kind, but not once had she indicated she wanted more than a kiss or an occasional caress.

Dom knew he had to go slow and not pressure her into sleeping with him or he would lose her completely and, for him, that wasn't an option. He'd told himself over and over it was infatuation or libido overload that had him lusting after a woman unwilling to take their relationship to the next level—one that included intimacy, but he deemed intimacy essential in a committed relationship.

He nodded to workers he'd come to know and recognize as he made his way to the kitchen. He stopped to peer into the smaller ballroom where faux bois specialists were restoring the walls and plaster moldings. Their work was slow and meticulous and, when completed, the ballroom would look the way it had when the château was reassembled stone by stone in 1883.

Dom stopped at the entrance to the kitchen as he spotted exposed capped wires, indicating no work had begun on updating the wiring. Turning on his heel, he went to look for Taylor. There was no way Viola would be able to prepare the food for his reception with outdated equipment.

He found Taylor with Robinson Harris. They were going over plans spread out on the table in the library. They used the library as their office now that Sonja worked from home. Taylor's head popped up when he walked in.

"Yes, Shaw?"

"I'd like to talk to you about the kitchen."

Taylor stood straight and massaged his forehead. "What about it?"

"It looks as if nothing has been done in there."

"That's because we're trying to concentrate on completing the work on the ballroom, great room and the upstairs suites," Robbie said, frowning. "Right now, the kitchen isn't a priority."

Dom wanted to tell the project foreman it may not be a priority for him, but it was for Viola. "I believe Viola would disagree with you."

Silence ensued as both men stared at him. It was apparent they did not like his response. Well, Dom was past caring what they thought. He knew how important it was for Viola to have her kitchen renovated well in advance of the wedding and didn't care if they'd believed he'd crossed the line to dictate what he thought of as a priority.

Taylor inclined his head. "Shaw's right. What I don't need is my sister getting on my case about her kitchen. And she can make life a living hell if you get on her wrong side."

Robbie glared at Taylor. "I thought you wanted to stay on schedule."

"And we will." Taylor picked up a tablet. "The sinks are due to come in on Wednesday. If you have time, Shaw, I'd like you to install them. Let me know what you need to replace the piping and Robbie will have the plumbing foreman store them in the kitchen."

"Thanks, Taylor."

"No problem." Turning on his heel, he left the library, unaware that Taylor was following him.

"Dom, please wait up."

He stopped and stared at Viola's brother. Lines of either strain or fatigue bracketed his mouth and Dom suspected the pressure of completing as much as he could before his wedding was taking its toll on Taylor.

"What's up?"

"Is Viola putting pressure on you to get the kitchen ready?"

Dom shook his head. "No. Why would you say that?"

"Because I know my sister."

"Viola has no idea that I was going to talk to you today about the kitchen."

"So, this is personal."

A hint of a smile played at the corners of Dom's mouth. "It is."

Taylor also smiled. "My sister is lucky to have someone like you advocate for her."

Dom's smile faded. "I like to think of myself as the lucky one. Viola is a phenomenal young woman."

"I agree, even though I'm somewhat biased when it comes to my brothers and sister."

"I need to confess something," Dom said in a quiet voice.

"You're in love with my sister."

Hearing Taylor say what he felt and had been feeling for a while shattered the veil of denial holding Dom captive. He knew he was falling in love with Viola, and it had stunned him because it'd happened so quickly.

"Yes, I am in love with your sister, and because of that, I've decided not to leave Bainbridge House once it opens as a hotel. I'd like to stay on and see if Viola and I can make a go of it as a couple." It was after their spending the weekend together that Dom knew he couldn't leave Viola or Bainbridge House.

"You were thinking of quitting?"

Dom crossed his arms over his chest and rocked back on his heels. "Yes. You won't need a caretaker when you'll have a staff to make repairs and maintain the entire property."

"You're right about not needing a caretaker. But what I will need is a business manager."

His arms unfolding in slow motion, Dom could not believe what Taylor was proposing. "What about Patrick?"

Taylor snorted audibly. "Patrick had no intention of leaving California to come on full-time at the hotel. And if he did, it would be as a winegrower. You say you have a degree in business so it—"

"I do," Dom interrupted.

"I was going say, before you interrupted me, that if you worked for my father, who was a hard-nosed SOB when it came to business, then I can't think of someone more qualified to run the hotel than you, Dom. I must admit that you were pretty ballsy to demand that Robbie modify his schedule to begin renovating the kitchen."

"I was no more ballsy than you were when you got in my face about Sonja. Although, if it had ended in a physical confrontation, I would've avoided hitting you in that million-dollar face, T.E. Wills."

Taylor grinned like a Cheshire cat. "So, you really thought you could take me?"

"Yes," Dom said confidently.

"Come on, brother. I have at least thirty pounds on you."

"That doesn't matter. I once knocked out a dude who had almost seventy pounds on me with an Iron Mike right hook."

"Well, shit."

Dom laughed and told Taylor about the time he'd been bullied and the steps he'd taken to end it. "I've never had to hit another human being since high school, but I have to admit it felt damn good to stand over him and see the fear in his eyes."

Taylor rested a hand on Dom's shoulder. "I think you're going to fit in quite nicely with the Williamsons."

He didn't know if Taylor was referring to him marrying Viola. If their relationship was too new to considering sleeping together, then marriage was even more remote. She was only twenty-eight and waiting two or three years to marry was within the realm of possibility for Dom. However, he would like to become a father before turning forty. Yes, he thought he had time. In fact, both he and Viola had time to plan their future and, hopefully, this time he would get it right.

"That's what I'm hoping."

"And please keep your coming on as business manager between us. I probably won't make the announcement until we're about three months ahead of the projected completion, when I'll begin hiring."

"Don't worry, Taylor. Mum's the word. I'm going to let you get back to your work. By the way, I don't plan to attend the crew meeting this morning."

"Not a problem, Shaw."

Viola felt her mind drifting as she listened to the event planner drone on and on about the logistics for Taylor and Sonja's wedding. Maybe if she hadn't stayed up well past two in the morning, even knowing she had to be out of the house by eight to meet with Sonja and the event planner at nine, she would be more alert.

Bettina Pearl, or Bette as she liked to be addressed, was a tiny, middle-aged woman with large gray eyes, dyed blue hair and boundless energy, with a prominent client list that included several celebrity weddings.

Bette had placed a seating plan on Taylor and Sonja's dining room table. "Since you're hosting a small wedding, I recommend two facing rectangular tables with the bride and groom at one end and the best man and bridesmaid at the opposite end." She set tiny plastic figures representing the wedding party on the sheet.

"Where will the parents of the bride and groom sit?" Sonja questioned.

Bette drummed her fingers on the table. "Your parents can sit on your left, while your fiancé's mother will be on his right." She placed three more figures on the sheet of paper. "I recommended you don't seat couples together but across the table from each other. I've discovered separating couples allows for more interaction between your guests."

"We've planned for a buffet dinner," Viola said, speaking for the first time. "Where do you suggest we set up the warming trays?"

Bette's eyelids fluttered. "I looked at the plans for the ballroom and I think setting up the buffet in front of the French doors is a nice touch."

Viola pointed to the table. "Then you have to change the position of the tables otherwise the bride and groom will have their backs to the French doors."

Pinpoints of color dotted the planner's pale cheeks. "You're right. Thank you for bringing that to my attention. My notes indicate you want to use Christmas-red plaid as a wedding color."

"Yes," Sonja replied. "It's to honor my fiancé's late father's Scottish ancestry and to coincide with the colors of the season. I also want the tartan plaid as the table runner."

Bette fingers flew over her laptop's keyboard as she entered her client's suggestions. "You still want red, white and green poinsettia plants positioned along two walls of the ballroom?"

"Yes," Sonja repeated.

"How about dinnerware?"

"I have more than enough for my guests. In fact, I have a set of porcelain with hand-painted mistletoe I plan to use for the cocktail hour and dinner."

Viola wanted to tell Bette that her client had cataloged thousands pieces of china, silver tableware and serving pieces and crystal. There were also hundreds of candlesticks and candelabra that needed polishing.

"The next thing on my list is the food. Do you want me to contract with a caterer?"

"That won't be necessary," Viola said. "I'm going to prepare all the food."

Bette blinked. "But aren't you the maid of honor?"

"Yes, and I'm also a chef."

"I'm impressed. What about waitstaff and servers? Do you want to hire your own?"

Viola knew she would have to contact an agency to hire the staff needed to set up, serve and clean up. "I'd like for you to handle that. Once we get a final headcount for guests, Sonja and I will let you know how much waitstaff we'll need."

Nodding and smiling, Bette said, "I was hoping you would say that. I have a very good waitstaff I use for all my weddings."

"I'm sure they are," Sonja remarked, "because you've come highly recommended."

Sonja told Viola she'd spent hours online searching for an event planner, and when Bettina Pearl's name came up with more than one hundred five-star reviews, she'd decided to contact her.

Bette powered down her laptop. "It's been a pleasure with you two ladies. The next time I come, I'd like to visit the venue to see exactly what I'm working with. I'll call you first and then we can set up a date and time that works for you."

Viola waited as Sonja walked Bette to the door and then went into the family room, flopped down on the love seat and closed her eyes. After eating dinner with Dom, she'd returned home to begin drafting menus. She'd spent an inordinate amount of time listing items on the bar menu before deleting them to start over. She'd lost track of time and when she'd finally glanced at the clock on the lower right of her laptop, she quickly saved what she'd entered, set the alarm on her cell phone and got into bed.

"You look pooped. What were you doing last night?"

Viola opened her eyes and smiled. "Working on menus."

"That doesn't sound very exciting." Sonja sat on a matching armchair and rested her feet on the footstool.

"Unexciting but necessary."

"Why the rush, Vi? You have more than a year before you even have to begin thinking about menus."

"Have you forgotten that I have to plan for not only your wedding reception, but for your guests that come in early? Tariq sent me a text that he's coming in late Wednesday or early Thursday. And that means I'll be preparing dishes all week."

"Won't that be overwhelming for you?"

Viola smiled. "Nah. I'll make up a tray of meatballs a couple of days ahead and freeze them. And trays of macaroni and potato salads can also be made in advance and refrigerated. I'll do the same with marinated meats. I've ordered six ovens for the first-floor kitchen and that's more than enough for roasting and baking."

"When I spoke to my mother a couple of days ago, she said she plans to come in midweek. And if you don't mind having someone else in your kitchen, she can make enough *arroz con gandules* in her jumbo *caldero* to feed a small army."

Viola knew the kitchen on the first floor was spacious enough for at least six people to work comfortably without tripping over one another.

"I love your mother's rice and pigeon peas."

"Is that a yes?" Sonja asked.

A rush of excitement eddied through Viola when she thought about sharing the kitchen with Sonja's mother, her mother and possibly Sonja's aunt. And she knew from experience that all three women were excellent cooks.

"It's a definite yes. Have her email the ingredients she needs to make the rice and peas and I'll include it on my shopping list."

"Now that we've had our initial meeting with the wedding planner, I think we can begin crossing items off our list."

"You're right," Viola confirmed. Sonja's parents had mailed out save the dates, and last week Viola and Sonja had sent the invitations. "When do you want to go shopping for your gown?"

"I want to wait until a month before the wedding. I'll

probably put on a few more pounds, and I don't want to have to go back too many times for an alteration."

"How much weight have you gained?"

"Four pounds."

"That's not much, Sonja."

"Right now, I'm averaging two pounds a month. Two times nine and I'll end up just under twenty pounds."

"How much weight does your doctor want you to gain?"

"At least twenty. Taylor's taking me out tonight, and he wants to know if you want to join us?"

"Thanks for asking, but I have plans for tonight."

Sonja sat straight. "Ah, Sookie, Sookie. Someone has a date," she drawled singsong.

"It's not a date, Sonja. I'm making *pastelón*." She'd promised Dom they would make the Latin-style lasagna together later that night. "And I know. Save you some."

"You're the best, Vi."

"Yeah, yeah, yeah. I know."

"I'm serious. If we weren't friends, I never would've met your brother. There are days when I believe I'm living in an alternative universe because no one should be this happy."

"Do you believe you shouldn't be happy after what you'd gone through with your crazy ass ex-husband?"

"I know I've been given a second chance, but it's going to take a while for me to get used to being so happy and crazy in love. Once I divorced Hugh, I swore I never wanted to get involved with another man, and then bam! I meet your brother and within a couple of months my entire world is turned upside down and for the good."

Viola shifted on the love seat. "I know I may sound

biased, but you're getting the best of my brothers. It's not that I don't love Tariq, Joaquin or Patrick, but for me Taylor has always been special."

"Do you think it is because of his personality or how you guys were raised?" Sonja questioned.

"It's probably a combination of both. I tend to be scattered at times, while Tariq and Taylor are calm and low key. Joaquin is happy-go-lucky and he never takes anything serious. He married a girl he'd only known for two weeks, unaware they were complete opposites. They stayed together for a couple of years then divorced. Joaquin hosted what he called an uncoupling bash for his friends to help him celebrate becoming a bachelor once again."

"Is he dating anyone now?"

"I don't know, Sonja. Whenever I talk to Joaquin, I don't ask him about who he's involved with, because the one time I did he rattled off a list of women's names that was mind-boggling. Then he laughed when I called him a serial dater. You'll have to let me know what you think when you meet Tariq."

"Why?"

"He's very quiet."

"Quieter than Dominic Shaw?"

Sonja mentioning Dom made Viola sit up straight. "Why would you ask that?"

"Because the man hardly talks."

"He does talk," Viola retorted defensively.

"Maybe to you."

"What are you trying to say, Sonja?"

"Don't get your nose out of joint because I just happen to mention something about your man. And don't deny he's your man."

Viola relaxed again on the love seat. "I'm not saying he's not."

Sonja smiled like the proverbial cat that had swallowed the canary. "I want to hear the deets."

"There are no details to tell, Miss Rios-Martin. Dom and I are dating. End of story."

"But didn't you tell me he has trust issues when it comes to women?"

"Yes. And I have trust issues when it comes to men. But we've decided not to let that affect our relationship. We're dating, not planning a future together."

Sonja pushed off the chair and came over to sit next to Viola. "Don't you want to marry and have children?"

She shrugged her shoulders. "Eventually. I have a few things on my wish list, but marriage and children aren't at the top."

"Would you marry Dom if he asked you?"

Viola gave Sonja a long, direct stare. "What's with you and Dom? Has he said anything to you about me?"

Sonja chuckled. "No. I told you the man doesn't talk much."

"He may not talk to you, but he sure enough talks to me, and love and marriage are topics we do not discuss. He admitted he was married but it ended in divorce. I don't want to know about the women in his past and I don't intend to talk about the jackasses in my past. And Dom knows I'm focused on running the hotel's kitchens, so marriage and children would definitely be on the back burners."

"I think we aid and abet jackasses when we overlook their BS. We accept it until we say enough is enough. And I'm a prime example once I decided to leave Hugh."

"Thankfully, my breakups weren't as drastic as

yours. The only one that got a little rachet was when I stopped seeing that pompous politician who refused to take rejection."

"What happened?"

Viola told Sonja about the state assemblyman who had threatened to ruin her career.

"What did he say?" Sonja asked.

"He said he was going to tell everyone that I'd served tainted seafood to his guests and some of them had to be hospitalized as a result. I'd just been hired to work at The Cellar and if word had gotten out that I was responsible for food poisoning, I would've lost my job and my reputation. I told Taylor about the threat, and he told me he would handle it."

"Did he?"

"Yes, because a week later the politician stopped by the restaurant and asked to see me. He apologized profusely and said there was no need for me to involve my brother. That was the last time I saw him. And when I asked Taylor what he'd said to him, he refused to tell me. End of story."

"Do you believe Taylor threatened him?"

"I don't know, Sonja. But the experience was enough for me to keep men at a distance because the ones I've known have been wolves in sheep's clothing. The only men I truly trust are my brothers."

Viola unfolded her legs and stood. "I have to get back home and do a few things before I make the *pastelón*." She didn't tell Sonja that she planned to go back to bed and catch up on her sleep before going to Dom's house later.

Cooking and eating together was a bonding she'd never had with anyone else except for her mother. She enjoyed doing it with Dom and knew it would continue until the hotel opened for business. Then her focus would shift from him to her guests. Viola did not want to think that far ahead, when she would no longer have the time to devote to their relationship, or wonder if it would survive if their lives were to go in different directions.

## *Chapter Fourteen*

Viola closed and locked the door to the condo and came down the steps carrying a garment and overnight bag—and stopped short when she saw Dom, wearing all black, leaning against the bumper of a low-slung, dark gray two-seater. She wasn't as shocked by the car they would take to Baltimore as she was by his appearance. He'd cut his hair.

Dom took the bags from her loose grip and leaned closer to brush a kiss over her parted lips. "There's no way Lollipop could've made it all the way to Baltimore and back without breaking down on the turnpike."

"You cut your hair." The thick, precisely cut strands hugged his head like the black glossy feathers on a raven.

"It was time."

"Why now, Dom?"

He winked at her. "Please get in the car and I'll tell you on the way."

She slipped onto the white leather seat after he'd opened the passenger's-side door. The sports car had a new-car smell. The dash was outfitted with the latest electronic components and she saw that the navigation screen was activated to display the best route to Baltimore, Maryland.

Dom stored Viola's bags in the trunk next to his luggage. He was looking forward to reconnecting with his college roommate, but that paled in comparison to spending the weekend with Viola away from Bainbridge House. She had continued to spend some nights at his house, but hadn't given him any indication that she wanted them to sleep together. He'd wanted to ask her over and over why she continued to share his roof and not his bed, but knew if he questioned her motives he would risk losing her. And that was something he swore not to do.

He closed the trunk and slipped behind the wheel. He started the engine and then snapped the buckle on his seat belt. "Your mother lives in a nice development."

Viola stared out the windshield. "It's very convenient for her."

"Do you like staying here?"

"I do. But I am looking forward to moving to Bainbridge House."

Viola had unknowingly given Dom the opening he'd needed to take their relationship to the next level. "That can happen if you come and live with me." He slowed the car to less than ten miles an hour as he approached the gatehouse.

Shifting, she turned to stare at him. "You want me to shack up with you?"

"Did I mention 'shack'?"

"Well, that's what it would be if I lived with you."

Dom nodded to the man in the gatehouse as the arm lifted. "Do you consider Taylor and Sonja shacking up?"

"No. The difference is they're engaged to marry, Dom."

"But what about before they were engaged? Are you aware they were living together before they got engaged?"

"You seemed to know a lot about my family," she snapped accusingly.

He knew it was time to end the charade. "I know that you and your brothers were adopted."

Viola stared at him wide-eyed when he gave her a quick glance before returning his gaze to the road. "How do you know that?"

"I'd overheard my father arguing with yours about something that involved his adopted kids. And Dad wasn't talking about Evan."

"Why didn't you say something before now?"

"I wanted to wait until the right time."

Viola let out a quick snort. "And you think now is the right time?"

"It's as good as any. I'm too old to play games, so I need to tell you how I feel…about you. I'm in love with you." The silence inside the car was deafening following his declaration.

Viola clapped a hand over her mouth as she struggled to compose her runaway emotions. Dom had just admitted what she'd felt and had been feeling for more than a month. She'd prided herself on being subtle as to how much she had come to love and depend on him for companionship. Their cooking together, watching movies and her sleeping over was just a ruse, when she'd prayed for him to walk down the hall from his bedroom to hers and make mad love to her.

"I could punch your lights out," she whispered between her fingers.

"For what?"

"For waiting until now to tell me that you love me. If you'd told me the last time I'd slept at your house, I would've shown you that I've fallen in love with you, too."

Throwing back his head, Dom laughed loudly, the sound bouncing off the roof of the car. "It's not too late for you to show me now. I can stop at a convenience store to buy some condoms and then we check into a motel and—"

"You're bugging," Viola said as she landed a soft punch on his shoulder.

"No, baby. I'm serious."

Viola rested her hand on his thigh. "To be continued."

"Yes. To be continued."

It was the first time in years that Viola felt everything was right in her world. The previous time was when she'd graduated from culinary school. Her relationship with Dom was so drama-free that she found herself waiting for something to come up to shatter what had become her living and breathing Hallmark movie. Yet while she knew it was inevitable that she and Dom would sleep together, Viola still wasn't ready to accept his offer to move in with him.

"Do you mind if I put on some music?" Dom asked.

"No."

"What do you want to listen to?" Tapping the steering wheel, he tuned the satellite radio to different stations.

"Anything upbeat."

"How about Club 54?" he questioned.

"Perfect."

Dom exhaled an audible breath. "You asked me about my hair. I had made a New Year's resolution not to cut it until I resolved a dilemma."

"Do you want to tell me what it was?"

He waited until he'd accelerated onto a two-lane county road to say, "I'd missed your father's memorial service because I'd gone to Arizona to ask my father for his advice about giving up my role as caretaker for Bainbridge House. I knew Conrad had gotten the approval to transfer the estate from a residence to a commercial property, but I hadn't anticipated his passing away. Then, when Elise called to tell me that her children would inherit the property and were going to be responsible for the restoration, I knew then that my days were numbered as caretaker. Taylor told me it would take a couple of years before the hotel opened for business, and that's when I decided to stay on for another two years. Then you came along, and I knew I couldn't leave."

Viola's expression stilled and grew serious. "Are you saying I resolved your dilemma?"

"It might sound trite to you, but the decision to leave the place where I was born and grew up was anything but. The day I cut my hair was like coming out of the dark and into the light. And to me, you are that light,

Viola Williamson. You live your life by your leave and there are times when I can't believe what comes out of your mouth, but I love the fact you can say what you believe without censoring yourself."

"What you see is what you get, Dom."

He smiled. "And I like it, babe."

"These declarations of love are too new and shocking for me to agree to live with you. But that's not to say it won't happen sometime in the future."

Dom placed his hand over the one on his thigh. "What did we say about time?"

"We have lots of it."

"There's no need to rush into anything like Taylor and Sonja."

Her lips parted in surprise. "You know about her?"

Dom gave her fingers a gentle squeeze. "The few times I've seen her rushing to the restroom with a napkin over her mouth, I figured she was nauseated. And that could only mean two things—a stomach virus or pregnancy. When Taylor told me he'd planned to marry this Christmas at the château because unforeseen events called for quick decisions, it was obvious Sonja was pregnant."

"It looks as if you and Taylor are rather tight for him to confide in you."

"We have to be. After all, I am involved with his sister."

Viola extricated her hand from Dom's. She stared at his distinctive profile. He had the perfect face for sculpting. There were enough angles to make it interesting. None of his features could ever be described as nondescript. "I don't want my family involved with what goes on between us."

"Neither do I, Viola. Family feuds and squabbles can get quite *ugly*."

"I agree. I like this car," she said, deftly changing the topic. "Is it a rental?"

"No. I own it. I bought it as a birthday gift to myself."

"It's gorgeous. That must be a man thing because Taylor bought his Infiniti for his thirty-fifth birthday. Where do you keep it?"

"I park it in the carriage house and take it out a couple of times a month to keep the motor running smoothly."

"Meanwhile, I thought Lollipop was your only vehicle."

"Lollipop hasn't left the estate in years."

"If I had her, I'd have her looking so sharp that collectors would be after me to sell her."

Dom smiled. "Would you sell her?"

"Hell no! If I put time and money into something I like, I'd never consider selling it."

"I'll let you drive on the way back, but only if you promise not to speed."

Violet met his eyes. "What makes you think I speed?"

"I've watched you drive the Subaru and it's obvious you have a lead foot."

"What if I set the cruise control to the speed limit?"

"What if you don't set the cruise control and try not to go over the limit?"

Reaching for his right hand, Viola brought it to her mouth and pressed a kiss on the back. "Thank you, love."

"You're welcome, babe. I'm going to stop in Philly

so we can have breakfast before getting back on the road. If you want me to stop before then, let me know."

"Philly's good."

She settled back to enjoy the passing landscape as Dom followed the signs leading to the New Jersey Turnpike.

When they reached their destination in a Baltimore suburb, Viola stared in awe at the Colonial- and Georgian-styled mansions nestled in the cul-de-sac, each set on a quarter acre of pristinely manicured lawn. Most of the front doors were adorned with large wreaths with autumnal themes.

Dom slowed down and then turned into a circular driveway in front of a three-story Colonial. The front door opened and a tall, dark-complected man wearing a baseball cap indicated Dom should park behind two other cars in the driveway.

"That's Marcus," Dom said as he shifted into Park, shut off the engine and tapped a button to open the trunk.

Without warning, the passenger's-side door opened and Viola found herself staring up at Dom's friend as he extended his hand to assist her out. She unbuckled her seat belt and then placed her hand on his as he helped her to stand.

"Welcome to Baltimore. I'm Marcus Younger, one half of your hosts for the weekend. The boss is inside putting things together for lunch."

Viola had to assume Marcus was referring to his wife. "Thank you. I'm Viola Williamson."

"And Viola's my boss."

Viola went completely still when she heard Dom's words. Was he just teasing, or did he feel because she was a co-owner of Bainbridge House and he a caretaker that he didn't view them as equals? Turning to face him, she flashed a saccharine smile. *Hardly*, she mouthed, giving him a death stare.

"Let me help you with those," Marcus said as Dom reached for the garment bags. "By the way, I like your ride. You know I had to get rid of my two-seater and trade it in for a minivan once the babies started coming."

"That will do it every time," Dom remarked, smiling and directly looking at Viola.

*I don't think so.* Viola didn't know what Dom was thinking, but having a child was not up for discussion or an option currently in her life. She thought about Sonja delaying going on birth control and the result was impending motherhood.

Viola entered an expansive entryway that opened into a great room with black-and-white vinyl flooring and a massive chandelier. "I'm going to show you to your room so you can settle in. Whenever you're ready, you can come down and eat something that will tide you over until dinner."

The wrought-iron circular staircase reminded Viola of the twin staircases at Bainbridge House, and she knew instinctually Sonja would've been able to identify the different style of furnishings in the beautifully decorated home.

"You guys are in here," Marcus said as he stopped outside a bedroom at the end of the long hallway. He gave Dom the garment bags. "There's a bathroom in the room."

Viola didn't know why, but she hadn't anticipated she and Dom would be sharing a bedroom, and wondered what he'd told his friend about their relationship. But what was done was done and she intended to be mature about it.

Dom stepped aside and she walked into the bedroom, her gaze lingering on the damask sheets, crocheted throws, lacy dust ruffle and sheer bed curtains loosely draped around a bleached-pine four-poster. The room was suggestive of a nostalgic, romantic Victorian bedchamber with pale floral rugs, a hand painted armoire and matching chests.

Dom entered the room and set the bags in front of a tapestry-covered bench at the foot of the bed. "You can use the bathroom first if you want."

"Thank you."

Viola unzipped the weekender and removed a large, quilted bag filled with personal items. She opened the door to a walk-in closet, and another one to the bathroom. The bathroom also permitted her a step back in time with a pedestal sink and a claw-foot tub with brass fittings. A stall with programmable water temperature, frosted glass and a rainfall showerhead was the only modern allowance.

She brushed her teeth, splashed water on her face, patted it dry with a guest towel and, after running a wide-tooth comb through her hair, reentered the bedroom. "It's all yours."

Dom rose from the bench. "That was quick."

Under another set of circumstances, if the Youngers weren't waiting for them, she would've taken time to unpack. "Don't forget your friends are waiting for us."

"Right. I'll be out in a few minutes, and then we can go downstairs."

While waiting for Dom to return from the bathroom,

Viola hung the garment bags in the closet and then set their bags on the floor and closed the door. Dom hadn't lingered in the bathroom and minutes later they headed downstairs.

When Marcus told him that his wife had invested in her dream house, Dom realized the home would be spectacular from the architectural design, the expansiveness and the meticulously chosen furnishings. And it definitely lived up to that promise.

"This house is magnificent," Viola whispered.

Dom nodded. "Yes, it is." Raised voices came from a room from the opposite wing of the house. "I think we've found the kitchen."

They walked into what was a chef's kitchen with a twelve-foot island, double wall ovens, microwaves, refrigerators, dishwashers and stovetops. A breakfast nook with bench seats was tucked into an alcove.

"Dom!"

He was forced to release Viola's hand when Marcus's wife literally launched herself at him. Dom had found himself drawn to the aspiring teacher the first time Marcus introduced him to Chynna as his girlfriend, a girlfriend who had become his wife and the mother of their three children. He hadn't seen her in more than a year and Dom noticed the change immediately. Her former light brown, straightened hair was now fashioned into twists that framed her rounded face.

Dom picked her up and kissed her cheek. "You look marvelous!"

Eyes the color of copper pennies shimmered in her freckled, light brown face. Chynna Younger laughed.

"Always the silver-tongued devil. You know what to say to make a woman feel wonderful."

Dom set her on her feet. "I'm not lying. You do look good."

"Stop flirting with my wife, Dom, and introduce your girlfriend."

Chynna rolled her eyes at her husband. "After eight years of marriage, three kids, and two dogs that refuse to stay out of the kitchen, Marcus accuses every man looking or talking to me as flirting."

"You know I love you, baby."

"Yeah, right!" Chynna retorted.

Viola, after witnessing the lighthearted teasing and interchange between Dom, Chynna and Marcus, straightened her spine when Dom's hand rested at the small of her back.

"Chynna, I'd like to introduce you to *my* girlfriend, Viola Williamson."

Viola extended her hand to her hostess, but was mildly surprised when Chynna enveloped her in a hug. "I'm a hugger."

"Thank you for inviting us. Your home is spectacular."

A rush of color darkened Chynna's face. "Thank you for coming," she whispered in Viola's ear. "I'll show you around once we're finished with lunch."

A tall, slender, dark-skinned woman walked into the kitchen, smiling. "Dom Shaw. We haven't seen you in a month of Sundays."

Something about the woman was familiar to Viola. She studied the delicate features in a small, round face and close-cropped natural hair. When she turned her light brown gaze on Viola, she knew where she'd seen the woman before. Not in person, but in a popular daytime soap.

"And who have you brought with you?"

Viola extended her hand to the woman. "Viola Williamson."

"Shannon Younger," she said, taking the proffered hand. She stared at Viola's left hand. "No ring?" She pantomimed.

Viola shook her head. "I hope I'm not being presumptuous, but aren't you the actress known as Shay?"

Shannon closed her eyes and expelled an audible sigh. "I was Shay in a former life. Now I'm just Shannon."

"My sister went from Shay the Actress to Shannon the Pastry Chef in three point two seconds," Marcus said, smiling.

Viola slowly blinked. "You're a pastry chef?"

Shannon gave her a steady stare. "Yes. Why?"

"I'm also a chef."

"Where did you study?" Shannon asked Viola.

"CIA."

"Wow! You're the real deal."

"Where did you study?" Viola asked Shannon.

"I graduated from Johnson and Wales."

"And she graduated at the top of her class," Marcus said proudly.

Viola smiled. "Stop playing, Shannon. Johnson and Wales is right up there with the Culinary Institute of America."

"Where are you working, Viola?"

"I'm not at the current time. And you?"

"I'm working for a tyrant who's going to get the

shock of his life when I hand in my walking papers before the end of the year."

Viola shared a glance with Dom. His eyebrows lifted and she knew they were thinking the same thing. "We need to talk. I may be able to help you, and you in turn can help me."

Shannon winked at Dom. "I like your girlfriend. She doesn't mince words."

Dom's hand slipped lower to Viola's hip. "She's definitely a straight shooter."

Viola's hand inched up Dom's back and she attempted to pinch him, but the lack of fat on his body thwarted her intent.

"I've promised Chynna I would make the desserts for the kids' and grown folks' parties," Shannon said. "Viola, would you mind giving me your opinion on what I've come up with?"

"Of course I don't mind." It would be the first time in months that she would assist in planning and cooking for someone other than Dom and her family. She glanced down at the platters filled with charcuterie, cheeses, fruits and finger sandwiches. The small triangular sandwich recalled Taylor's complaint of when he'd attended high tea.

"Where are your children?" Dom asked.

"The baby is down for her afternoon nap, and the boys went to a friend's house to play until it's time for dinner. They didn't have classes because it's professional development day for teachers. They took the dogs with them. Otherwise, I'd have to chase them out of the kitchen."

Marcus picked up two platters and walked to the breakfast nook. "Chynna only agreed to let them get a dog if they stayed out of the kitchen. We were able to train the first one, but once we got another, all hell broke loose. The little Yorkie corrupted the poodle and now they're partners in crime. Luckily, they are too small to jump up on the table."

Chynna frowned. "But that doesn't stop them from hanging out under the table. I don't know what got into me to agree to have animals in my house when I didn't grow up with them."

Marcus returned to get the other platters. "I hope you guys brought your appetites because we're going to have a fish fry out back later tonight. You know you can't come to Baltimore without sampling our incredibly delicious seafood."

"Now that I've given my brother a few cooking lessons, he believes he's ready to enter a cooking challenge."

Marcus winked at Shannon over his shoulder. "There's no way I'm going to let Dom outdo me in the kitchen. The man used to whip up the most delicious meals when we shared an apartment in college that we hardly ever ate out."

"That's probably because y'all were broke," Chynna teased.

"Come sit down, Viola. My wife's bragging because her family owned a construction company and Daddy deposited money in her account every week. Meanwhile, my folks were teachers, and you know they're underpaid, and I had to take out student loans to make up the difference for tuition."

Viola sat on the padded bench seat next to Shannon. Having to apply for student loans had never been an option for her or her brothers. Conrad had set aside money for them to attend the most expensive colleges. Chynna said her future husband and his roommate had been broke, and she wondered if Dom had had to take out loans to complete his education.

Marcus, Dom and Chynna joined her and Shannon and platters were passed around. Viola took samples of meat, cheese and fruit. The diners filled their glasses with fizzy water or lemonade.

Marcus pointed to the cheese platter. "Viola, can you recognize the different types of cheeses?"

Chynna elbowed him in his ribs. "Why are you testing the girl?"

Marcus grimaced. "Viola, this is the first time I bought cheeses other than cheddar and feta. I need to know if you like this assortment."

"I think I've created a wannabe chef," Shannon mumbled under her breath.

Viola studied the plater. "There's smoked cheddar, Greek Gouda, Parmigiano Reggiano, Robiola, Bella-Vitano and what looks like a pinot rosé. And I like them all."

Marcus smothered a curse. "You are good."

She inclined her head. "Thank you."

Viola felt as if she'd passed the test not only proving she was a professional chef but feeling as if Dom's friends had accepted her. They were friendly and unpretentious, and she knew why Dom had gotten along well enough as college roommates to have remained friends over the years.

Shannon led Viola to a room set up as a home/office. "We can talk in here," she said, closing and locking the door.

Sitting on a leather love seat, Viola told the pastry chef about the ongoing restoration at Bainbridge House and her decision to be its executive chef once the hotel opened for business. "It's going to be at least two years before we have the grand opening, but meanwhile I'll need a pastry chef for my brother's upcoming Christmas wedding."

"You want to hire me without seeing my work?"

"Girl, please. If you graduated from Johnson and Wales at the top of your class, then I don't have to test your skills."

"Have you hired any other cooks or chefs?" Shannon asked.

"No. You would be the first. But remember it will only be for one event."

Shannon clasped her hands, seemingly deep in thought. "I would love to make the desserts for your brother's wedding, but I can't afford not to work until your hotel opens."

"I realize that, Shannon."

"What if I take a few temporary positions until the hotel opens, then I'm all yours."

Viola smiled. "That will work. As a full-time employee, you will live on-site."

A grin spread over the former actress's delicate features. "It's beginning to sound even better."

"We'll discuss salary and benefits before you're hired, but I'd like you to come to New Jersey to meet with my brother and future sister-in-law to discuss what type of cake and desserts they'd want."

"I'm free every other weekend. We can exchange cell phone numbers, and I'll text you the dates and times when I'm able to drive up."

"That sounds like a plan."

"You can tell me to mind my own damn business, but how long have you and Dom been together?"

Viola could've lied and said Easter Sunday, because, although they hadn't met in person, it was the first time she'd come to the estate where he lived. "It's been a few months."

A slight frown marred Shannon's smooth forehead. "That's not long."

"It's long enough for us to think of ourselves as a couple," she said in defense of her relationship with him.

"Good for you. Dom's a real good guy. The first time I met him, he was married to a real bitch. And that's a word I hate to use when referring to a woman. Even Marcus was happy when they finally split up."

Viola had promised Dom they wouldn't talk about the people from their past, and she had no intention of asking Shannon about Dom's ex-wife. "I think we'd better get back to the others before they send out a search party for us," she said instead.

## *Chapter Fifteen*

The day that began with Viola sitting inches from Dom in a small sports car ended with them in bed, his chest pressed against her back. Both had eaten too much at the fish fry—a weekend spring, summer and fall event, which the families in the cul-de-sac alternated hosting.

"I can't believe we get to share a bed, and the only thing we'll do is sleep," Dom said as he pressed his mouth to the nape of her neck.

"Sleep and cuddle."

"I like cuddling, but I also like making love."

Viola moaned as she attempted to shift into a more comfortable position. "There's no way I'd let you do anything because I'm close to bursting. Don't forget I ate fried catfish, shrimp, clam strips, scallops with potato salad and coleslaw."

"I saw your plate, babe, and it was nothing compared to mine and some others' with mountains of food."

"It was enough."

"I have to say, Marcus has turned into quite the cook."

"That's because he has his sister tutoring him."

Dom moved closer and she felt the pressure of his erection through the cotton fabric of his pajama pants. He'd admitted bringing them in deference to her, because he normally slept nude.

"Shannon reminds me of Taylor. He went from modeling to engineering and she from an actress to becoming a chef."

"She's beautiful and talented, Dom."

"Shannon has nothing on you, babe."

Viola laughed. "You *are* a silver-tongued devil." She sobered quickly. "I asked her if she would come to Bainbridge House to meet Sonja and Taylor and talk to them about the cake and desserts they'd want for their wedding."

"You plan to hire her?" he asked.

"I do once the hotel opens. She'll be a full-time, on-site employee."

"Where will she live?"

"In what had been the servants' quarters." The live-in servants had been housed downstairs off the kitchen and storeroom.

Dom kissed her hair. "Taylor showed me the plans for that area of the château, and he wants to remove some walls to turn them into suites with en suite baths. All fireplaces will be converted to gas. They'll look nothing like they did when my grandmother lived there."

"Two years can't come soon enough, Dom. The waiting is already getting to me."

"It may come sooner than later. And a lot of things can happen during that time."

"You're right," Viola said. Those were her last two words before she fell asleep in the protective embrace of a man with whom she'd fallen in love.

On Sunday, Viola returned to New Jersey more relaxed and in love than she'd thought possible. The weekend she'd spent Dom and his friends was nothing short of Hallmark-movie perfection. She'd assisted Shannon making Halloween-themed cookies, cupcakes, a large orange pumpkin cake with alternating slices of devil's food and butter crème. Viola had carved small pumpkins and squash with mad, bad and frightening faces before lighting them with battery-operated candles.

Chynna had found a pumpkin-shaped ceramic tureen and filled it with candy for trick-or-treaters. She'd also put out platters of pastry-wrapped cocktail franks, Tater Tots and broiled chicken wings for her children and their friends.

When the children's party ended, the Younger children and their dogs had been picked up by Marcus's parents to spend the night with them. The residents of the cul-de-sac had established a 7:00 p.m. curfew for trick-or-treaters and at the stroke of nine, the adult party began in earnest. Viola felt like the moll of a mob boss, like Emma Gould, when she descended the staircase on the arm of Dom, who'd worn a suit and hat straight out of the 1920s.

Chynna and Marcus were Beyoncé and Jay-Z, while Shannon had morphed into her icon Naomi Campbell.

She'd stayed in character as she'd affected the supermodel signature runway strut. The great room had quickly filled with family and friends of Marcus and Chynna's, and Viola watched Dom reunite with the groomsmen who'd been in the couple's wedding. The DJ provided the music, a caterer the food, and a bartender was busy mixing and pouring drinks. Viola noticed Dom had nursed one drink for a long time, and when she'd questioned him about it, he'd admitted to overindulging at Marcus's wedding and the experience had been enough for him not to have more than two drinks in any given night.

"Your place or mine?" Dom asked as he drove down the street leading to the Sparta condo.

Viola looked straight ahead rather give him a direct stare. "Mine tonight. I'll come to your place tomorrow. To stay," she added after a pause. She'd shared a bed with him Friday and Saturday, and her wanting to share her body with Dom had surpassed a need to become a craving. Leaning over, she waved to the man in the gatehouse. He recognized her and raised the arm to permit Dom to drive through and park in front of the unit.

"Thank you for a very enjoyable weekend," she said as Dom removed her bags from the trunk of his car.

"I should be the one thanking you," he said, staring down at her.

Going on tiptoe, Viola kissed his mouth. "I love you."

Dom smiled. "I love you, too. I'll wait here until you get inside."

Viola wanted to tell him she was safe, that the entire development was electronically monitored, and no one could get in or out without being seen. But knowing he wanted her safe made her love for him even more real.

* * *

Dom opened the door when he heard a car's engine. Viola had come to spend the night. Inasmuch as he wanted to make love to her, he was also willing to give her an out because he wanted their coming together to be spontaneous and not something they'd planned.

When he saw her expression, he realized she was upset. "What's the matter, babe?"

"Where's Lollipop?"

Dom wanted to laugh. He couldn't believe Viola's concern for an ancient, battered pickup. "I had her towed to a garage that specializes in repairing old cars. She made some strange noises when I tried starting her this morning, so I thought it was time for a licensed mechanic to look at her. It could be the engine, transmission or even the carburetor. Whatever it is, I hope they'll be able to find the parts to make her run again."

Viola pushed out her lips. "I wanted to drive her just twice before she went to the scrap heap."

Dom reached for her weekender. "Hopefully, that will become a reality if they can repair her. Did you eat dinner?"

"Yes. What did you eat?" she asked.

"The leftover *pastelón*."

"You're still eating that?"

"What can I tell you, sweetheart."

"We made that more than a week ago."

Dom curved an arm around her waist. "I cut it into small pieces and put them in freezer storage containers. I had the last one tonight. I still can't believe it's *so* delicious." He set her bag on the first stair. "I was just getting ready to make a cappuccino. Do you want me to make one for you?"

"Yes, please."

"Your stoves came in today."

Viola let out a little shriek. "Finally! You can install the sinks once the stoves are hooked up, and I will think of that as the light at the end of the tunnel."

"We're still running gas lines. Once that's done, we'll add the stoves and sinks, and your kitchen will be close to completion."

"It's been a long time coming." Viola followed Dom into the kitchen. "That bag I brought can stay here. It has some personal products and several changes of clothes."

Dom hid a grin. Viola leaving clothes at his house was an indication that she just might change her mind and move in with him. "Do you want me to wake you when I get up, or do you plan to sleep in?"

"I'll get up with you. Taylor's birthday is today and Sonja's is tomorrow, and even though he's planning to take her out, I want to bake a little something for them."

"I can't believe their birthdays are a day apart."

"Believe it, Dom. Taylor is a year and a day older than Sonja."

"When's your birthday, babe?"

"April. And yours?"

"February. Come and relax while I make your cappuccino."

Dom felt as if he'd been holding his breath for years and only now was able to exhale. Falling in love had changed him from a frustrated, solitary man unaware of what he wanted or where he wanted to go. However, he knew if he'd remained at Bainbridge House, he would have slowly gone mad from the repetitiveness of getting up every morning to walk or ride around the estate to check for leaks, broken fence lines or missing roof tiles.

He'd become an automaton on the riding mower, driving it aimlessly over tracts of land he'd come to know like the back of his hand. Then, when he couldn't take the monotony any longer, he'd drive into town to pick up items he needed to replenish his pantry or stop at the gas station to refill the cans he needed for Lollipop, the mower, ATV and golf cart.

When he'd expressed this to his father, James had reminded him generations of Shaw men had performed the same tasks for more than a century; the remarkable difference was they'd had wives and children. Dom had not wanted to look for a woman to fill up the empty hours in his day. In the end, it wouldn't have been fair to her or himself.

Then along came Viola Williamson. Beautiful, upbeat, creative and sexy. Even their disagreements were reasonable and did not end with vitriolic threats that, once uttered, could not be retracted.

In was only weeks into his marriage that the complaints began and escalated until Dom knew he'd had to end it. It was as if Kaitlyn had known exactly what button to push to make him lose his temper. He'd tried to make a go of his marriage when his father and Marcus urged him to let her go; he was unable to give her what she wanted because she didn't know what she wanted.

He'd fallen in love with Viola, and he was willing to wait for as long as it would take for her to commit to a future together.

"Have you thought about what you want to make?" he asked as he poured coffee beans into a grinder.

"Yes. Sonja likes flan and Taylor is partial to cheesecake. So, I thought I'd make a strawberry cheese flan."

"You made tiramisu and now cheesecake. How often do you make dessert?"

"Not too often. I leave that to pastry chefs."

"Why?"

"Because I'm more of a baker."

Dom poured the coffee grounds into a well then filled the machine with water. "What's the difference between a baker and a pastry chef?"

"Bakers make cakes and pies and pastry chefs make desserts."

"Had you planned to make the desserts for Taylor's wedding?"

Viola shook her head. "No. Shannon will do that."

"That was quick."

"What are you talking about?"

"You getting Shannon to make the desserts."

"We have less than two months to pull everything together for the wedding. I had a list of pastry chefs I'd planned to interview but meeting Shannon allowed me to cross that item off my list. The wedding planner is taking care of hiring the waitstaff, DJ and ordering flowers. Sonja and I still have to look for gowns and accessories and—"

"Enough, babe!" Dom interrupted. "I know you have a laundry list of things to do, and you know I'll help out any way I can."

"I want my kitchen completed by the first week in December."

"I'll talk to Taylor and see what he can do."

Viola sat on a stool at the breakfast bar. She didn't want Dom to talk to Taylor to see what he could do, but just to do what needed to be done so she could utilize the kitchen for his wedding and the holiday party for his work crew. The last time she'd mentioned the progress, or lack thereof, about the kitchen, Taylor had practically bitten her head off. She knew he was stressed about the restoration and his upcoming wedding, and Viola promised herself not to broach the subject with him.

Dom set a cup topped off with foaming milk in front of her, the intoxicating aroma of brewing coffee wafting to her nostrils. The only smell she liked more than freshly brewed coffee was frying bacon. For Viola, they'd become an aphrodisiac.

She took a sip, moaning under her breath. Dom had made it with sweet cream. "I should hire you as a barista."

"I don't think so, babe. That would be too much togetherness."

"You're right." After several sips of the warm brew, Viola felt totally relaxed. "I don't know what it is, but drinking coffee in the morning wakes me up and drinking it at night makes me sleepy."

Dom joined her at the breakfast bar with his cup. "Why don't you go upstairs and turn in? I'll be up later after I put up several loads of laundry." He gave her a sidelong glance. "By the way, have you learned to do laundry?"

"You got jokes, Dom?"

"Well, you did tell me you didn't know how to do laundry. Not to worry, princess. I'll wash and dry your clothes."

Viola did not want to imagine his reaction when sorting her underwear. "You don't have to do that."

He leaned close, their shoulders touching. "I've seen women's panties before," he whispered.

"I bet you have," she retorted, thoroughly embarrassed. It was as if he'd read her mind. "I'm going to take your advice and turn in early."

Viola finished the cappuccino, rinsed the cup and left it in the dishwasher, feeling the heat from Dom's gaze on her, wondering what was going on behind the green orbs. Was he anticipating their sharing a bed at his house, knowing it would change them and their relationship forever, and hopefully for the best?

She blew him a kiss. "Later."

He smiled, attractive lines fanning out around his eyes. "Later, princess."

Viola picked up the weekender and walked up the staircase. She entered Dom's bedroom and set the bag on the floor in front of a closet. It was furnished with the same heavy, dark mahogany pieces that were in the bedroom where she'd slept. If her bedroom was romantic, then Dom's was dramatic with bed dressings in varying shades of grays and blues.

She brushed her teeth before stepping into the shower. Viola mentally ran down the dishes she planned for the wedding reception rather than think about making love with Dom. She wasn't a virgin—she'd slept with two men—but it had been years since her last sexual encounter. Her love for Dom, however, overrode any apprehension she felt about them sleeping together.

After towel-drying her body, she slathered on a perfumed lotion. Elise had taught her from a young girl that a woman had to make certain to take care of her skin and that meant using sunscreen and applying moisturizing cream on her face and body. Picking up the nightgown she'd laid across the foot of the four-poster,

Viola slipped it over her head, the scalloped hem ending at her knees.

Viola got into bed and turned off the three-way bulb on the bedside lamp. The only illumination came from the lamp on Dom's side. She pulled the sheet and lightweight blanket over her shoulders, closed her eyes and fell asleep.

Dom walked into the dimly lit bedroom and as he approached the bed, he realized Viola had fallen asleep waiting for him. He got into bed and turned off his bedside lamp, plunging the room into darkness. He inhaled the familiar scent of her perfume and smothered a groan. Sharing a bed and not making love to Viola had become a test, a test that threatened to shatter his self-control, but he had to remind himself that she was worth the wait. He went completely still when he felt Viola move closer and rest her leg over his.

"Did I wake you, babe?"

"No. I was just napping while waiting for you."

Dom splayed one hand over her breasts under the cotton fabric. "Your heart is racing."

"I'm okay, Dom."

Her admitting she was okay was the signal he needed to demonstrate wordlessly how much he wanted and loved her. Dom reached over and opened the drawer in the bedside table and removed a condom. Inasmuch as he wanted to father children with Viola, he knew that was far from becoming a reality. And he knew she would be an affectionate, gentle mother when he'd watched her cradle Marcus's nine-month-old daughter to her chest while singing nursery rhymes, which had delighted the baby as she'd laughed hysterically.

He forced himself to go slow when he tenderly kissed Viola. Her arms went around his neck as he increased the pressure on her mouth until her lips parted. Everything in his past dissipated like a drop of water on a heated surface when he relieved her of the nightgown, paused to slip on protection, and made slow, tender love to the woman in whose arms he wanted to breathe his last breath.

Viola felt as if she were drowning in a tidal wave of pleasure from which there was no escape. Long-forgotten orgasms came rushing back, sweeping her up in a maelstrom of ecstasy, holding her captive before finally releasing her in a shattering climax, hurtling her higher than she'd ever been before. She was shaking and crying at the same time from the aftermath. She pressed her mouth against the column of Dom's neck as he groaned into the pillow under her head. She'd confessed to Dom that she loved him. Now, she'd shown him how much she did.

"I love you," Dom whispered over and over.

"I love you more," she said.

As the next few weeks passed, Viola finally understood what Sonja had been talking about when she'd said she was living in an alternate universe of unabashed happiness. Viola, too, had been so afflicted when she'd found herself more in love with Dom than she could've ever imagined.

Since making love with him, one week had blended into the next as if in a time warp. All the kitchen appliances were now installed, the wall of windows facing what had been a vegetable garden replaced, and she'd spent time examining and polishing the copper cookware. The pieces that needed to be relined she'd put aside to be sent to a company specializing in repairing copper utensils.

Shannon had driven up from Maryland to meet with Taylor and Sonja. In keeping with the wedding colors of red, green and white, Shannon had baked samples of red velvet, pistachio, and white cakes. She also had made Christmas-red plaid ribbons that would encircle each layer of the white-chocolate three-tier cake. When Sonja asked Shannon if she could design eatable poinsettia leaves as the cake topper, Shannon stated she was willing to give the bride whatever she wanted.

Shannon had asked Viola if she could come to Bainbridge House three days before the reception to bake the cake rather than transport it from Baltimore, and Viola had quickly given her consent.

Elise had returned from her cruise, tanned and several pounds heavier than when she'd left. Viola drove her mother to the shop where she and Sonja had selected their gowns. Elise decided on a green floor-length, long-sleeved gown that flattered her curvy body.

Viola thanked her mother for not taking an inordinate amount of time to find her gown, unlike Sonja, who'd tried on nearly a dozen before settling on a silver-hued empire-waist gown of beaded silk crepe and silk georgette. It lent itself to the Regency period and deemphasized her expanding waistline. They had agreed in advance that Viola would wear red, and she'd found a cherry-red gown needing only a minor alteration.

For Viola, however, gearing up for the wedding meant spending less time with Dom. He would come to the kitchen whenever she was alone to kiss her and confess how he missed having her spend the night at his house. They had decided it would be best for her to sleep in Sparta once Elise had returned to the States. When she'd told him she did not want to hide their affair from her mother, Dom had insisted he wanted to wait until after Taylor and Sonja were married to make their relationship public. She'd then realized the focus should be on her brother and his bride and not her and Dom, and agreed. Their day would come soon enough.

## *Chapter Sixteen*

Cradling her face in his hands, Taylor kissed Viola's forehead. "You outdid yourself, kid. When you asked me if you could host a gathering for the work crew, I wanted to refuse because you had enough to do cooking for my wedding reception."

Her hands circled his wrists, pulling his hands away from her face. "Brother love. How little faith you have in me," she teased.

"Not anymore, baby sis. When I told them to come by tonight and bring their significant others, I don't think any of them suspected they were going to be wined and dined."

"They deserve it, Taylor. They've put in long hours to get the ballrooms, kitchen and the upstairs suites ready in time for your wedding."

Taylor nodded. "They're the best crew I've ever

worked with, and I'm looking forward to the time when the entire estate is restored and we can throw a party to end all parties before the grand opening."

"I hope to be fully staffed by then. Now, I'm going home to get some sleep." She'd been up more than sixteen hours prepping and cooking for the party.

"Are you going back to Mom's or Dom's place?"

Viola froze, her gaze meeting and locking with Taylor's. "Who told you?" She and Dom hadn't flaunted their affair, and she'd hoped he hadn't let it slip that he was seeing Taylor's sister. Not when both had agreed to wait until after the New Year to go public.

"Don't get your cute nose out of joint, baby sis. Dom didn't say anything. But only someone visually impaired wouldn't be able to see how he looks at you. And I shouldn't have to remind you that the entire property is electronically monitored, and I get a report from the security company a couple of times a month. When I recognized Mom's Subaru parked at Dom's house overnight, it was obvious you were spending time with him."

Viola couldn't stop the heat sweeping over her face and chest. "Do you have cameras inside his house?"

Taylor frowned. "There's no need to get defensive, Viola. You're a grown woman and what you do with a man is none of my business. I'm glad it's Dom you're involved with because he's a welcome change from those other losers you dated."

"You approve?"

"It's not up to me to approve who you…" His words trailed off.

"Fall in love with," Viola said.

"You're in love with him?"

She almost laughed at his seemingly shocked expression. "Yes, Taylor. I am in love with Dominic Shaw."

Taylor ran a hand over his face. "I never saw that coming. I just thought you two were, like…"

"Like what, Taylor? Just fooling around with each other?" Viola shook her head. "What we have goes beyond fooling around."

"When's the big day?"

"Are you talking about marriage?"

"Yes."

"Even if Dom and I decide we want to marry, that's not going to happen for a while."

Taylor angled his head. "How far off is 'a while'?"

"I want to wait until the hotel opens for business even before I can consider marriage."

"Do you think the man is going to wait that long for you?"

"If he loves me as much as he claims he does, then he'll wait."

A beat passed. "I hope you're right, Viola. Thank you again for all you've done. Now go home and get some rest."

*Do you think the man is going to wait that long for you?* Taylor's question nagged at Viola as Bainbridge House became a bevy of activity as preparations for wedding were finalized. The scaffolding around the château had been taken down, and flameless candles in the windows of every room made the structure appear magical when seen from a distance. The protective floor coverings had been removed and the marble floors polished. Even when dimmed, the light from the great room's massive chandelier shimmered on the highly polished flooring like stars.

Joaquin, along with Patrick and his fiancée, Andrea, had flown in from California. Tariq, who didn't like flying, had opted to drive up from Alabama. Elise was beside herself having all her children together again.

Viola discovered why Elise didn't like Patrick's fiancée when she demanded they change suites because she didn't like the one she and Patrick had been assigned. The stalemate ended when Patrick had told her that he had no intention of moving into another room after unpacking because he was dealing with jet lag. Viola knew her brother well enough to know he was stressed whenever he combed his fingers through that wealth of reddish hair before massaging the back of his neck. She wanted to warn Andrea that it was in her best interest not to push Patrick or he would send her back to California—alone.

Joaquin took one look at Shannon and followed her around like a lost puppy looking for a home. Viola had to threaten him to stay out of the kitchen or she'd have him barred permanently. She noticed that Shannon appeared to enjoy his company, and Viola wanted to warn the pastry chef her brother was an incurable flirt and to ignore his advances.

Dom felt as if he'd been waiting years rather than weeks to reconnect with Viola. He'd waited until she was alone in the kitchen before approaching her. She sat on a stool, cradling a cup of hot liquid in both hands.

"Hey, babe."

She smiled at him over the rim. "Hey, yourself." She set the cup on the table behind her.

He closed the distance between them, leaned over and pressed a kiss to her forehead. He'd noticed a slight puffiness under her eyes, indicating she wasn't getting enough sleep. "How are you holding up?"

She smiled. "Well enough. Everything is prepped and, once the waitstaff gets here, I'll begin putting dishes in the oven. Shannon has offered to supervise the kitchen, so I don't have to do double duty as chef and maid of honor. One more day, and I'll be able to sleep for as long as I want."

Dom ran his forefinger under one eye. "What you need is a vacation. After the wedding, what do you say we go away for a few days? We'll be back in time for you to celebrate Christmas with your family."

"I like the sound of that."

"I asked Sonja the color of your gown and when she said red, I thought this would go nicely with it." Reaching in the pocket of his jeans, he removed a ruby-and-emerald bracelet. He fastened it around her wrist. "This bracelet has been in my family for a long time. My father gave it to my mother as a wedding gift, and I'd be honored if you wear it tomorrow."

Viola's jaw dropped. "I can't."

"You can if you love me."

"You know I love you, Dom."

He pressed a kiss to her mouth. "Then, will you wear it?"

"Yes. I'll give it back after the wedding."

He shook his head. "You don't have to do that. Think of it as a pre-Christmas gift."

* * *

Viola had seen the photos Sonja had taken of the jewelry she'd cataloged, and the bracelet like the estate pieces was appraised at thousands of dollars. "It's too much."

"It's not enough, babe. England's crown jewels wouldn't be enough."

She covered her mouth with her hand to stop the giggles from escaping. "What am I going to do with you?"

"Marry me."

The two words rendered her mute. "I… I…"

"You don't have to give me an answer now. Remember, we have time."

Viola hadn't realized her hands were shaking when she pressed her fingertips to his mouth. The love she felt for Dom was indescribable. "I will wait only because I love you so much."

"Am I missing something?"

When Dom turned and Viola saw that her mother had entered the kitchen, she wondered how long she'd been standing there. "Momma, I didn't know you were there."

Elise's blue eyes darkened. "That's because you were too busy making out with the hired help."

"Momma!"

"Wait a minute!"

Viola and Dom had spoken at the same time.

"Momma, how could you even bring yourself to say something like that?"

"Well, he is the hired help."

Dom took a step. "I think it's time I leave before I say something I might later regret."

"Don't move, Dom!" Viola shouted. "Please stay,"

she pleaded in a softer tone. "You need to hear what I have to say to my mother."

He shook his head. "No, I don't. As much as I love you, I will not come between you and your family." He nodded to Elise. "Good night, Mrs. Williamson."

Viola wanted to scream and stomp her foot as she'd done as a child when things didn't go her way. But she wasn't a child; she was an adult capable of seeing whomever she wanted without asking anyone's permission. She watched the only man she'd ever loved walk out of the kitchen and probably out of her life.

"How could you, Momma?"

"I can, Viola, because I don't want to see you hurt."

"Hurt how?"

Elise moved closer and reached for her hands, but Viola thwarted her when she put them behind her back. "Have you thought that maybe he's after your money?"

"What money? I'm certain this bracelet Dom gave me is worth more than I have in my savings account."

"I'm not talking about now, Viola. Have you forgotten you own one-fifth of this estate, and once the hotel opens for business, you'll become a very wealthy woman."

Viola slipped off the stool. "You're wrong if you think Dom is after any money I may or may not have. He was seriously thinking about leaving Bainbridge House, but changed his mind when we fell in love."

"He could've told you that as a ruse."

Viola threw up both hands. "When did you get so suspicious? You don't like Patrick's fiancée and you don't like Dom. What's the matter, Mom? You don't want to see your kids happy, or maybe you can't let them go?"

Elise's eyes filled with tears. "That's a cruel thing to say. You should know I want the best for my children. I was happy for you when you were seeing that politician."

"That pig was nothing more than a user. He used me to cater his fundraisers. Then, when I refused to cater for his friend who was a little short on cash, he called me names I'll never repeat and threatened to ruin my career. When I told Taylor, he reassured me he would take care of him. I don't know what he said or did to him, but after that, I wanted nothing to do with a man."

"I'm sorry, Viola. I didn't know."

"Then you're going to have to let your children make their own decisions as to whom they love and want to marry. I'm surprised you haven't tried to talk Taylor out of marrying Sonja. Oh, I forgot. She's carrying your grandchild."

Viola knew her words had hurt her mother when the natural color drained from her face. "That's another cruel thing to say."

"And you weren't cruel when you called Dom hired help? The next time he asks me to marry him, I'm going to say yes because I don't want to lose him. Good night, *Mother*. I need my sleep before tomorrow."

Viola held back her tears as she walked up the staircase to her suite of rooms. The joy of becoming a bridesmaid and catering the reception had vanished with her mother's accusation that Dom was using her. It was only when she closed the door that she broke down and cried herself to sleep.

Dom accepted the plaid boutonniere from the usher and pinned it to his lapel. His first impulse had been not to attend the wedding, but he'd changed his mind—Taylor had nothing to do with his mother's spiteful reproach that he wasn't good enough for Viola. But he had elected to sit with Sonja's friends and family rather than Taylor's. He shared a smile and a handshake with one of the carpenters. The entire construction crew had been invited to the wedding and the reception dinner to follow.

Still, Dom couldn't take his eyes off Viola. The red dress shimmered against her exposed skin as did the rubies in the bracelet adorning her slender wrist. She had worn his gift. His gaze lingered on the black curls pinned atop her head and festooned with jeweled pins and tiny rosebuds. She was beyond perfection.

Taylor, wearing a dark suit with a plaid tie, stood next to Robbie, also sporting a plaid tie, and the minister waiting to perform the ceremony. Prerecorded music flowed from speakers set up around the great room. Everyone came to their feet when the music changed with the familiar chords of the "Wedding March." Sonja came down the staircase on her father's arm, the veil pinned to the back of her head trailing on the stairs. Dom knew Sonja was repeating a tradition of countless brides who had come down the staircase at Bainbridge House.

Dom was too much of a realist to attempt to imagine Viola and him standing where Taylor and Sonja were, pledging their love before family and friends before they became husband and wife. He loved her, would always love her, yet he refused to come between her and her family.

With the exchange of vows and rings, Taylor and Sonja were now married.

Members of the waitstaff filed into the room, some rearranging chairs while others circulated with flutes of wine or trays from which wafted mouthwatering aromas. Dom reached for a glass of champagne and took a small plate and napkin from a young woman offering him bite-sized sticky ribs, cocktail franks and meatballs and miniature sesame prawn toasts.

He recalled Viola going over the menu for the cocktail hour, adding and crossing out items. She'd done the same with the reception buffet, claiming she didn't want the ubiquitous prime rib, chicken cordon bleu or fish plate. Dom had teased her about going to restaurants and spending hundreds of dollars for a portion measuring about three inches in diameter. She'd laughed and promised the food at her brother's reception would be a departure from what was usually offered at wedding receptions.

The music changed, becoming more upbeat as more trays were circulated. Dom ate sparingly because he wanted to save room for the buffet, but each time someone came around with the Mongolian and sweet-and-sour meatballs, he speared them with a toothpick.

The hour passed quickly, and everyone was directed into the small ballroom. Soft gasps sounded as the guests saw the banquet table set with fragile porcelain, silver and delicate crystal. Red-jacketed waiters stood behind long tables with warming trays.

Dom smiled when noting table seating was positioned to view the tiny lights entwined in the branches of trees outside the French doors. It had taken him two days to string the lights because of rapidly dropping temperatures.

He wasn't aware there would be place cards at each

seat. As he pulled out his chair at the far end of the table, Dom saw that he was sitting on Viola's left. It was apparent the seating arrangement had been planned, and he didn't want to be rude to ask someone to exchange seats.

The wedding party entered the ballroom to thunderous applause. Dom met Viola's eyes. She'd attempted to conceal the puffiness under her eyes with makeup. His heart turned over, and he knew she'd been crying on a day that should've been nothing short of happiness because her best friend had married her brother.

He sucked in his breath when she sat next to him after Robbie had seated her. Dom averted his eyes when the project manager rested a proprietary arm over the back of Viola's chair as he leaned close to whisper in her ear.

Jealousy roiled in Dom like a coiled snake ready to strike to cause serious injury; he wanted to get up and walk out, and return home where he wouldn't have to see the woman he loved become an object of affection from another man.

Instead, he turned his attention to a woman who introduced herself as Sonja's aunt, Yolanda Rios. There was a sprinkling of gray in the neat braids pinned in a twist on her nape. Her flawless nut-brown face was wrinkle-free.

The event planner directed the wedding party to the buffet table to be served first. Then, in quick precision, others were ushered toward the buffet until everyone had been served. True to her word, Viola had prepared an eclectic cuisine with dishes from Korea, Mexico, Italy, the Caribbean, the American South, China and the Middle East.

"This is an incredible buffet," said the girlfriend of one of the electricians. "It's too bad I didn't wear my stretchy pants, but I intend to sample every dish until I can't eat any more."

There were murmurs in agreement as Dom asked the waiter for some Jamaican-style oxtail. He accepted a spoonful of rice and peas to add to the Korean fried chicken, crispy shredded beef, and linguine with clam sauce. He wanted to agree with the woman about stretchy pants.

The bartender was doing a brisk business pouring and mixing drinks, and by the time the clock had made one revolution, the decibel level had increased exponentially. The DJ had also increased the music's volume, and Dom found himself singing along with others to a classic popular song. The vivacity was infectious because Taylor had given the contractors a two-week paid vacation through the New Year, while Taylor had surprised Sonja with a ten-day vacation in Bora Bora.

The tempo slowed as Taylor and Sonja shared their first dance as husband and wife. He then danced with Elise while Sonja danced with her father. Dom glared at Robbie when he held Viola too close, as evidenced by her pushing against his shoulder. He waited until she'd returned to the table to grasp her hand.

"May I please have this dance?"

Viola wanted to refuse because he'd ignored her all night, yet the need to be in his arms overrode her annoyance. "Yes."

She tried to keep her expression impassive as he led her to the dance floor, but she suppressed a moan of satisfaction when he pulled her into a close embrace. It hadn't been twenty-four hours since the altercation in the kitchen with her mother, and since that time she and Elise hadn't exchanged more than ten words. She could not understand why the woman who had taught her children to be respectful of others despite their position in life had belittled Dom because of what she'd deemed his station.

"We need to talk," she said softly.

"No, we don't, Viola. If anyone is going to do any talking, it is me and Elise. Until that time, I think it best if we do not see each other. Your mother insulted me once, and I can assure you, I will not put myself in a position to be insulted again."

She lowered her eyes. "I'm sorry about that, Dom."

"Don't apologize. It's Elise who should do the apologizing."

"Will you forgive her if she does?"

"I'll think about it. What I want is for her not to interfere. There's nothing worse than a meddling mother-in-law."

Viola's head popped up. "You still want to marry me?"

He smiled. "I'll always want to marry you. However, that will never happen if there's enmity between our families."

She felt a sudden surge of confidence. "I'm not going to tell mother to apologize. That's something she's going to have to do on her own."

"And if she doesn't, Viola?"

"Then I will never marry."

"Don't say that. One of these days you'll meet someone your mother will approve of and what we have will become a distant memory."

"That's where you're wrong, Dominic Shaw. If I don't marry you, then you'll become the last man in my life. Now, please let me go."

"I'll walk you back to the table."

"Don't bother." Viola pulled away and walked out of the ballroom.

Dom was still standing in the same spot where Viola had left him when Taylor approached him. "What's going on with Viola?"

"It's just a little misunderstanding." He wanted to tell Taylor that the misunderstanding was his mother, but he didn't want to ruin his friend's special day. That said, he walked out of the ballroom and into the near-freezing night.

Dom looked up at the three-quarter moon that lit a sky littered with millions of stars, reminding him of diamond dust on black velvet. He caught movement out of the corner of his eye and then a flash of red. He realized Viola had also come outside. He noticed she was rubbing her bare arms.

He took off his jacket, walked over to her and draped it around her shoulders. "You shouldn't be out here without a coat."

"I could say the same thing about you."

Dom wanted to remind Viola that he was wearing a long-sleeved shirt and he also was used to being outdoors in cold weather. "Don't stay out too long."

"Where are you going?"

"Home."

"What about your jacket?"

"Keep it."

* * *

Viola refused to cry any more.

When she'd woken that morning, her eyes were so swollen, she'd been forced to apply ice to her face to bring some of it down. An extra layer of concealer when putting on her makeup had done the trick. She was still wearing Dom's suit jacket when she'd returned to the ballroom to ask Sonja if she could stay in her condo once she and Taylor left for their honeymoon. Her new sister-in-law had given her consent, unaware that Viola needed to put some distance between herself and her mother.

## *Chapter Seventeen*

"What the hell is going on between you and Mom?" Taylor asked when he opened the door.

"Ask her," Viola retorted angrily.

"Look, Viola. I'm leaving tomorrow morning for my honeymoon, and I don't want spend that time wondering why my mother and sister are at each other's throats. Ask her what?"

Viola brushed past him and headed for the staircase. "Why she is acting like a snob."

"You know Mom is anything but a snob."

"Yeah, right."

"The only thing I'm going to say is you better work out your problems before I get back. I'll be damned if I'm going to begin a new year with my family in turmoil."

Viola wanted to tell Taylor that if Elise didn't apologize to Dom, then she was going to lose her only daughter. She was aware that her mother was overly protective when it came to her, but to reject and insult the man she had chosen to love was unforgiveable.

Dom walked into his house after spending a week in Tucson. Work had halted on the restoration until after the new year, and he'd increased the security company monitoring since the estate would be left unattended until his return.

It had felt good to get away from Bainbridge House and focus on something else rather than what had gone on in the kitchen the night before Taylor and Sonja's wedding. He knew he'd shocked James and Hallie when he'd told them he'd needed a change from the cold weather and wanted to fly down and celebrate Christmas with them.

This visit had been different from the year before. Dom had not felt the need to unload on his father about his life. At thirty-five, he knew it was time to try and sort out his own problems without running to James. They had simply enjoyed each other's company.

He dropped his bags and headed for the downstairs bathroom where he stripped naked and walked into the shower stall. Dom, with a towel wrapped around his waist, went upstairs to dress when he heard an approaching engine. He quickly pulled on a pair of briefs, sweatpants and a tee, and then went downstairs.

When he flung open the front door, he saw the Subaru, but when the driver's door opened, he froze. The driver wasn't Viola. It was Elise. His first thought was, how had she gotten through the gates? Then he remembered that Viola had attached the remote device to the visor of her mother's vehicle.

Missing was the professionally coiffed woman. Her hair appeared as if it hadn't been combed, and lines of tension ringed her nose and mouth. His former anger vanished when her eyes filled with unshed tears.

He reached for her hand. She was shaking uncontrollably. "Please come in." Dom escorted her into the living room and seated her on the love seat. "Can I get you something to drink?"

Elise rested a hand along the side of her face. "Yes. I rarely drink, but I could use something strong right about now."

Dom wasn't certain he'd heard right. "You want something alcoholic."

Elise trained her dark blue eyes on his like a heat-seeking laser. "That's exactly what I said."

"Yes, ma'am."

Dom went into the kitchen and took down a glass from an overhead cabinet, then opened the bottle of scotch Taylor had left earlier that summer. He filled the glass with an ounce of liquor and handed it to her.

She stared at him. "Are you going to have some, too?"

"Of course." He would say anything to humor her and keep her from crying.

He repeated the action and sat down across from Viola's mother, watching as she took furtive sips of the premium liquor, he following suit.

"You must be curious as to why I've come to your home."

Dom nodded. "I am."

"Well, I'm here to apologize," Elise said before taking another swallow. “I had no right to say what I did to you.”

“You’re apologizing for what you said, but not what you meant. You called me ‘hired help’ and I’m anything but.” When she did not respond, he went on. “I don’t know what Conrad told you, but he didn’t hire me, and he couldn’t fire me. My status as this estate’s caretaker was established more than one hundred years ago in order to absolve your husband’s ancestor of his guilt for seducing a teenage girl and getting her pregnant. He was an older, married man with children, yet he couldn’t stay away from a girl the same age as one of his daughters. Today he would’ve had to register as a sex offender and spend time in prison. What he didn’t count on was Melanie Shaw blackmailing him so she could secure the future of her illegitimate son and every male Shaw for generations to come.

“Conrad asked me to work for him when Patrick left the company because, not only did we share DNA, but he knew he could trust me. I wonder what he would say if he’d known you’d called his relative the hired help. I don’t need your money, and I don’t need Viola’s money. The bracelet I gave Viola is one of a dozen pieces Conrad gave Melanie that have been passed down to Shaw women over the past four generations. They’ve been appraised at seven figures and if sold will bring a tidy sum.”

Elise lowered her eyes. “Conrad never discussed his business with me, and I had no idea he’d hired you for the investment firm. I’m sorry, Dominic. I misjudged you.”

“Why, because you thought I wasn’t good enough

for your daughter, or that I didn't have enough money to keep her in the lifestyle she was used to?"

Elise pinched the bridge of her nose with her free hand. "It was both. I've been very protective of Viola, and sometimes that has made us bump heads. She's independent and impulsive, but much too trusting. She's been known to attract men who see her as someone they could use and manipulate."

"That's not the Viola I know."

"Then you must have changed her."

Dom shook his head. "I had nothing to do with that. The only thing I want from Viola is her love. Nothing more, nothing less. And she can expect the same from me."

Elise extended her glass. "That was good. May I have some more?"

He gave her a skeptical look. "Are you sure?"

"Yes, I'm sure."

"Look, Mrs. Williamson—"

"It's Elise. If you're going to marry my daughter, then there's no need to be so formal. Now, can you please refill my glass? And don't forget to fill yours, too. I hate drinking alone."

"Yes, ma'am."

Dom knew if Elise continued to drink, it wouldn't be safe for her to get behind the wheel of her car. He poured several ounces in both glasses and then, with the excuse he had to get something upstairs, he removed his cell phone from one of his bags and took the stairs two at a time. He tapped Viola's number. It rang three times before he heard her voice.

"Hello."

"Hello, Viola. Your mother's at my home, and she's been drinking your father's scotch."

"What! What are you talking about? My mother doesn't drink scotch."

"Well, she is tonight."

"What have you done to her?"

Dom heard the panic in Viola's voice. "She's on her second glass and I don't trust her to drive—"

"I'm on my way."

The line went dead and Dom knew she'd hung up on him. He palmed the phone, went downstairs and left it on the table in the entryway.

"I was waiting for you to come back before I drank some more."

Dom was just beginning to feel the effects of jet lag, and drinking alcohol was exacerbating it. He decided talking could delay him finishing the second glass, so he asked Elise to tell him about raising and homeschooling five children.

She quickly warmed to his suggestion and launched into telling how she'd first become a foster mother for Taylor. She'd just finished his story when Viola walked through the door.

With wide eyes, Viola stared at Elise on the love seat, holding an empty glass. "What have you done to her?"

"He didn't do anything to me." Elise slurred the words. "Dom's a very nice boy."

Viola leaned over, prying the glass from Elise's hand. "Why were you drinking, Momma?"

Elise closed her eyes. "I thought it would help me forget that my only daughter moved out and refuses to talk to me."

"No, you didn't," Dom said under his breath.

Viola glared at him over her shoulder. "Stay out of this."

"It's too late, babe. Your mother came here to apologize, and I've accepted it."

Elise affected a lopsided grin. "If you want my blessing to marry, then you have it."

"Thank you, Elise."

"So, now it's Elise?" Viola asked Dom.

Dom winked at her. "That's what she wants me to call her."

Elise tried getting up, but flopped back on the love seat. "I think I need to lie down."

Dom moved quickly, scooping her up in his arms. "I'm going to take you upstairs so you can relax."

*Relax!* Viola thought. It was apparent her mother was under the influence, and Viola blamed Dom for plying her mother with alcohol. She still was trying to reconcile that what she'd believed was her wonderful life had been upended because Elise did not approve of her daughter's choice for a life partner. First, it was Patrick's fiancée, and now Dom. There was no doubt Andrea was spoiled and Patrick indulged her, yet Elise did not view her as hired help as she had Dom. She walked to the fireplace and stared at a photo of a teenage Dom with his parents and younger brother.

"I think she'll be all right after she sleeps it off."

Viola turned around. It had been ten days since she'd last seen Dom and the absence had done little to quench her love and lust for him. She'd lost track of the number of times when she'd wanted to call him and let him know she would marry him that day because she loved him just that much.

"My mother never drinks hard liquor."

"I quickly discovered that. Your mother and I had a long talk and, as crazy as it may sound, I understand where she's coming from."

"You do?"

"Yes, I do. She probably won't admit it, but Elise Williamson is an elitist. She believes her children should marry within their own social class."

"You're wrong about my mother. Why would she adopt five kids from different racial backgrounds if she is, as you say, an elitist?"

Dom walked over to Viola and wrapped his arms around her waist. "There are poor, middle and upper income, and extremely wealthy people, in every race. It is that social class—the money—that makes all the difference to some people. I met a guy in college who had a family mandate that he only marry a college graduate. I don't know enough about your mother's family, but she probably was told the same thing. Conrad never told her that I'd worked for him at the firm or that I had graduated college."

Viola rested her head on Dom's shoulder. "I told you before that my father never talked about his work at home, and neither did Patrick once he went to work for him."

"I suppose that could be a good thing, because that shouldn't be the topic of conversation at the family's dinner table."

Leaning back, she studied the face of the enigmatic man with whom she'd fallen in love. "What's going to happen to us, Dom?"

"Not much until you make up with your mother. Once she wakes up, you need to have a heart-to-heart talk with her. I don't want another generation of hostility between the Bainbridges and the Shaws."

Viola's lids fluttered. "Momma isn't a Bainbridge."

"She married one, Viola, so that makes her a Bainbridge, and so are her children because they're legal heirs to this estate."

Viola suddenly realized she hadn't thought of herself as a Bainbridge. "Okay."

Dom dipped his head and kissed her; she tasted the scotch on his mouth. "How much did you drink?"

"Not as much as Elise," he said before deepening the kiss. "You have no idea how much I love you."

She smiled. "I think I do. Once we sort out this misunderstanding, I think we should start planning our future."

"Are you proposing to me, Miss Williamson?"

"I think I am, Mr. Shaw."

Dom picked her up and swung her around and around. "Long or short engagement?"

Viola wrapped her arms around his neck and pressed her mouth to his ear. "We'll figure that out later."

# *Epilogue*

*Valentine's Day*

Dom paced the floor like a large, caged cat. Viola had reconciled with her mother and moved back into the Sparta condo until Elise set off on another cruise. This was to be the first night she would come back to his home and stay for the next two months. Her living with him would give them a glimpse into what they would experience as a married couple. Although they'd talked about marriage, they'd yet to set a date. He knew Viola wanted to wait until the restoration was completed, and he was willing to wait if it meant giving her what she wanted. And for him, it was all about giving the woman he loved what she wanted to make her happy. Marcus had reminded him that happy wife meant happy life.

He stopped pacing and opened the door when he heard the car come to a stop. He walked out of the house to find Viola with her hand over her mouth. He'd sought to surprise her, and apparently he had.

"Lollipop!"

Reaching into his pocket, he took out a delicate gold bracelet with a charm of a red pickup truck. "Happy Valentine's Day. She's all yours." He put the bracelet around her wrist and closed the clasp.

"She's beautiful," Viola whispered. "I can't believe you had her restored."

"It took a long time for the mechanic to find parts for her before I took her to a body shop to make her look like new."

"Thank you, Dom. I love your surprise."

"That's only your first." He reached into the other pocket and took out a ring that his father had given to his mother for their engagement. Dom held Viola's left hand and slipped the cushion-cut emerald with a halo of diamonds on her finger. "Miss Viola Williamson, will you do me the honor of becoming my wife?"

Viola cried and laughed at the same time. "Yes, yes, and yes, Mr. Dominic Shaw, I will marry you."

Dom knew he'd been given a second chance at love, but he never would've expected it would be with Conrad's daughter. "Do you want to marry at the château?"

Viola looped her arms under his shoulders. "Yes. We'll marry at the château and raise our children in this house where generations have lived and loved."

Dom buried his face in Viola's curls and exhaled a sigh of contentment. With Viola beside him, he was more than sure of himself and his rightful place in the universe, and together there was nothing they couldn't do. She would become the executive chef at Bainbridge House and he the business manager. He was just waiting for the time when he would be able to disclose that to her.

* * * * *

*For more heartwarming holiday romances, try these other great stories:*

Moonlight, Menorahs and Mistletoe
*By Wendy Warren*

Their Texas Christmas Gift
*By Cathy Gillen Thacker*

Sleigh Ride with the Rancher
*By Stella Bagwell*

*Available now wherever Harlequin Special Edition books and ebooks are sold!*

COMING NEXT MONTH FROM

HARLEQUIN

# SPECIAL EDITION

### #2881 THEIR NEW YEAR'S BEGINNING

*The Fortunes of Texas: The Wedding Gift* • by Michelle Major

Brian Fortune doesn't think he will ever find the woman he kissed at his brother's New Year's wedding. So when the search for the provenance of a mysterious gift leads him into a local antique store a few days later, he's stunned to find Emmaline Lewis, proprietor—and mystery kisser! Brian has never been the type to commit, but suddenly he knows he'll do anything to stay at Emmaline's side—for good.

### #2882 HER HOMETOWN MAN

*Sutton's Place* • by Shannon Stacey

Summoned home by her mother and sisters, novelist Gwen Sutton has made it clear—she's not staying. She's returning to her quiet life as soon as the family brewery is up and running. But when Case Danforth offers his help, it's clear there's more than just beer brewing! Time is short for Case to convince Gwen that a home with him is where her heart is.

### #2883 THE RANCHER'S BABY SURPRISE

*Texas Cowboys & K-9s* • by Sasha Summers

Former soldier John Mitchell has come home after being discharged and asks to stay with his best friend, Natalie. They're both in for a shock when a precious baby girl is left on Natalie's doorstep—and John is the father! Now John needs Natalie's help more than ever. But Natalie has been in love with John forever. How can she help him find his way to being a family man if she's not part of that family?

### #2884 THE CHARMING CHECKLIST

*Charming, Texas* • by Heatherly Bell

Max Del Toro persuaded his friend Ava Long to play matchmaker in exchange for posing as her boyfriend for one night. He even gave her a list of must-haves for his future wife. Except now he can't stop thinking about Ava—who doesn't check a single item on his list!

### #2885 HIS LOST AND FOUND FAMILY

*Sierra's Web* • by Tara Taylor Quinn

Learning he's guardian to his orphaned niece sends architect Michael O'Connell's life into a tailspin. He's floored by the responsibility, so when Mariah Anderson agrees to pitch in at home, Michael thinks she's heaven-sent. He's shocked at the depth of his own connection to Mariah and opens his heart to her in ways he never imagined. But can an instant family turn into a forever one?

### #2886 A CHEF'S KISS

*Small Town Secrets* • by Nina Crespo

Small-town chef Philippa Gayle's onetime rival-turned-lover Dominic Crawford upended her life. But when she's forced together with the celebrity cook on a project that could change her life, there's no denying that the flames that were lit years ago were only banked, not extinguished. Can Philippa trust Dominic enough to let him in...or are they just cooking up another heartbreak?

---

*Brian Fortune doesn't think he will ever find the woman he kissed at his brother's New Year's wedding. So when the search for the provenance of a mysterious gift leads him into a local antique store a few days later, he's stunned to find Emmaline Lewis, proprietor—and mystery kisser! Brian has never been the type to commit—but suddenly he knows he'll do anything to stay at Emmaline's side—for good...*

*Read on for a sneak peek of the first book in the The Fortunes of Texas: The Wedding Gift continuity,* Their New Year's Beginning, *by* USA TODAY *bestselling author Michelle Major!*

"I'd like to take you out on a proper date then."

"Okay." Color bloomed in her cheeks. "That would be nice." He leaned in, but she held up a finger. "You should know that since Kirby and the gang outed my pregnancy at the coffee shop, I'm not going to hide it anymore." She pressed a hand to her belly. "I'm wearing a baggy shirt tonight because it seemed easier than fielding questions from the boys, but if we go out, there will be questions. And comments."

"I don't care about what anyone else thinks," he assured her and then kissed her gently. "This is about you and me."

Those must have been the right words, because Emmaline wound her arms around his neck and drew closer. “I’m glad,” she said, but before he could kiss her again, she yawned once more.

“I’ll walk you to your car.”

She mock pouted but didn’t argue. “I’m definitely not as fun as I used to be,” she told him as he picked up the bags with the leftover supplies to carry for her. “Actually I’m not sure I was ever that fun.”

“As far as I’m concerned, you’re the best.”

After another lingering kiss, Emmaline climbed into her car and drove away. Brian watched her taillights until they disappeared around a bend. The night sky overhead was once again filled with stars, and he breathed in the fresh Texas air. He needed to stay in the moment and remember his reason for being in town and how long he planned to stay. He knew better than to examine the feeling of contentment coursing through him.

One thing he knew for certain was that it couldn’t last.





HSEEXP1221

*Learning he's the secret heir to a business mogul, Kenan Rhodes has a lot to prove. His best friend, lingerie designer Eve Burke, agrees to work with him... if he'll help her sharpen her dating skills. Soon, fake dates lead to sexy nights...*

*Read on for a sneak peek of* The Perfect Fake Date, *by* USA TODAY *bestselling author Naima Simone.*

The corridor ended, and he stood in front of another set of towering doors. Kenan briefly hesitated, then grasped the handle, opened the doors and slipped through to the balcony beyond. The cool April night air washed over him. The calendar proclaimed spring had arrived, but winter hadn't yet released its grasp over Boston, especially at night. But he welcomed the chilled breeze over his face, let it seep beneath the confines of his tuxedo to the hot skin below. Hoped it could cool the embers of his temper…the still-burning coals of his hurt.

"For someone who is known as the playboy of Boston society, you sure will ditch a party in a hot second." Slim arms slid around him, and he closed his eyes in pain and pleasure as the petite, softly curved body pressed to his back. "All I had to do was follow the trail of longing glances from the women in the hall to figure out where you'd gone."

He snorted. "Do you lie to your mama with that mouth? There was hardly anyone out there."

"Fine," Eve huffed. "So I didn't go with the others and watched all of that go down with your parents and brother. I waited until you left the ballroom and went after you."

"Why?" he rasped.

He felt rather than witnessed her shrug. The same with the small kiss she pressed to the middle of his shoulder blades. He locked his muscles, forcing his head not to fall back. Ordering his throat to imprison the moan scrabbling up from his chest. Commanding his dick to stand down.

"Because you needed me," she said.

So simple. So goddamn true.

He did need her. Her friendship. Her body.

Her heart.

But since he could only have one of those, he'd take it. With a woman like her—generous, sweet, beautiful of body and spirit—even part of her was preferable to none of her. And if he dared to profess his true feelings, that was exactly what he would be left with. None of her. Their friendship would be ruined, and she was too important to him to risk losing her.

Carefully, he turned and wrapped her in his embrace, shielding her from the night air. Convincing himself if this was all he could have of her—even if it meant Gavin would have all of her—then he would be okay, he murmured, "You're really going to have to remove 'rescue best friend' off your résumé. For one, it's beginning to get too time-consuming. And two, the cape clashes with your gown."

She chuckled against his chest, tipping her head back to smile up at him. He curled his fingers against her spine, but that didn't prevent the ache to trace that sensual bottom curve.

"Where would be the fun in that? You're stuck with me, Kenan. And I'm stuck with you. Friends forever."

Friends.

The sweet sting of that knife buried between his ribs.

"Always, sweetheart."

*Don't miss what happens next in*
The Perfect Fake Date *by Naima Simone,*
*the next book in the Billionaires of Boston series!*





HDEXP1221